"Oh, no," [illegible]

Kane and the [illegible] cause of Brigid's agitation, but she telegraphed it to them by her tense posture.

Berrier's image dissolved into a glittering swarm of pixels which leaped across the room and resolved into Tara. In a clear voice, she announced, "Implementing maximum defense measure Z for Zulu, D for Doomstar. Activation code zero-zero-doomstar-zero."

Tara extended her arms outward from her body, keeping her palms flat and perpendicular with the floor, forming a *T*. She arched her back, thrust out her firm breasts, and a diamond-shaped slit opened between them. A swirling splash of multicolored light spilled out.

Calmly she said, "Doomstar program now on-line."

Other titles in this series:

Exile to Hell
Destiny Run
Savage Sun
Omega Path
Parallax Red

JAMES AXLER

OUTLANDERS™

DOOMSTAR RELIC

A GOLD EAGLE BOOK FROM
WORLDWIDE®

TORONTO • NEW YORK • LONDON
AMSTERDAM • PARIS • SYDNEY • HAMBURG
STOCKHOLM • ATHENS • TOKYO • MILAN
MADRID • WARSAW • BUDAPEST • AUCKLAND

First edition September 1998
ISBN 0-373-63819-1

DOOMSTAR RELIC

Special thanks to Mark Ellis for his contribution to the Outlanders concept, developed for Gold Eagle Books.

The moist star upon whose influence
Neptune's empire stands was
sick almost to doomsday with eclipse.
—Act I, *Hamlet*
William Shakespeare

The Road to Outlands—
From Secret Government Files to the Future

Almost two hundred years after the global holocaust, Kane, a former Magistrate of Cobaltville, often thought the world had been lucky to survive at all after a nuclear device detonated in the Russian embassy in Washington, D.C. The aftermath—forever known as skydark—reshaped continents and turned civilization into ashes.

Nearly depopulated, America became the Deathlands—poisoned by radiation, home to chaos and mutated life forms. Feudal rule reappeared in the form of baronies, while remote outposts clung to a brutish existence.

What eventually helped shape this wasteland were the redoubts, the secret preholocaust military installations with stores of weapons, and the home of gateways, the locational matter-transfer facilities. Some of the redoubts hid clues that had once fed wild theories of government cover-ups and alien visitations.

Rearmed from redoubt stockpiles, the barons consolidated their power and reclaimed technology for the villes. Their power, supported by some invisible authority, extended beyond their fortified walls to what was now called the Outlands. It was here that the rootstock of humanity survived, living with hellzones and chemical storms, hounded by Magistrates.

In the villes, rigid laws were enforced—to atone for the sins of the past and prepare the way for a better future. That was the barons' public credo and their right-to-rule.

Kane, along with friend and fellow Magistrate Grant, had upheld that claim until a fateful Outlands expedition. A displaced piece of technology...a question to a keeper of the archives...a vague clue about alien masters—and their world shifted radically. Suddenly, Brigid Baptiste, the archivist, faced summary execution, and

Grant a quick termination. For Kane there was forgiveness if he pledged his unquestioning allegiance to Baron Cobalt and his unknown masters and abandoned his friends.

But that allegiance would make him support a mysterious and alien power and deny loyalty and friends. Then what else was there?

Kane had been brought up solely to serve the ville. Brigid's only link with her family was her mother's red-gold hair, green eyes and supple form. Grant's clues to his lineage were his ebony skin and powerful physique. But Domi, she of the white hair, was an Outlander pressed into sexual servitude in Cobaltville. She at least knew her roots and was a reminder to the exiles that the outcasts belonged in the human family.

Parents, friends, community—the very rootedness of humanity was denied. With no continuity, there was no forward momentum to the future. And that was the crux—when Kane began to wonder if there *was* a future.

For Kane, it wouldn't do. So the only way was out—way, way out.

After their escape, they found shelter at the forgotten Cerberus redoubt headed by Lakesh, a scientist, Cobaltville's head archivist, and secret opponent of the barons.

With their past turned into a lie, their future threatened, only one thing was left to give meaning to the outcasts. The hunger for freedom, the will to resist the hostile influences. And perhaps, by opposing, end them.

Chapter 1

South central Alaska

The lights of the aurora borealis surged in the northern sky. The glitter of the first stars of the evening was swallowed by the great iridescent bands of green and blue and purple. The ethereal colors shimmered on the blanket of white that draped the land near the top of the world. The atmospheric display of pyrotechnics, breathtaking in magnitude, held no interest for the twin figures making their way steadily across the frozen landscape.

Both of their bodies were concealed by heavily padded, quilted thermal coveralls. Thick woolen scarves wound around their faces, and their eyes were protected by frost-rimed goggles.

Barch clenched his teeth to keep them from chattering and for the hundredth time in the past six hours regretted he'd ever allowed himself to seduce Berrier. He'd read of other men and what they had done to obtain fortune and glory, to achieve their dreams of possessing pieces of raw, naked power. In ancient legend, such power was always harnessed and contained in such fragile vessels as chalices, boxes, amulets and even crude wooden and stone spears.

Barch knew most of the stories were indeed only that—fictions dreamed up when mankind still possessed the spirit to dream and the leisure time to put such fantastic stories down on paper. He wasn't a believer in magic or the mystical, but he had been a player in the Intel loop long enough to know that things were never as they appeared to be.

Barch liked being one of those lucky ones allowed access behind the stage dressing. It delighted him to have the keys to the back door and to know all the locks to the hidden doors of influence of Ragnarville. But even his knowledge and position as the Magistrate Division administrator went only so far.

Even a Magistrate, a high-ranking member of the Ragnarville Trust, could freeze to death in forty-below-zero temperatures. Ultimately the subzero Alaskan air would take its toll, the predark tech and weapons caches of Redoubt Zulu be damned. There were still some places on Earth where the nuclear winter, the skydark of two centuries ago, had never relinquished its icy grip. Alaska was one of them.

Under the protective helmet and woolen cap, Barch's skull was clean shaved, without so much as a tuft of hair to act as additional insulation against the cold. His dark, sharp-boned face possessed only a single obsidian black eye, his left one. The right was covered by a leather patch. But his one eye was capable of boring a hole of fear through even the most fearless of people, as Berrier had reason to know.

The woman stopped at the lip of a ledge and from a case hanging from her shoulder, she removed a compact set of binoculars. Lifting her goggles, she raised them to her eyes. For a few long, silent seconds, she peered into them, making adjustments now and then. Barch waited, not giving in to the impulse to stamp his booted feet. A stiff breeze stirred up loose snow, setting into a motion a brief flurry around them. He saw nothing in the snow-swept valley below but black spruce thickets protruding above the snow line. Here and there, in the low country, snow had blown away from the round knobs of small outcroppings. Barch had never seen such a vista of desolation, not even in hellzones.

"There," Berrier said hoarsely, extending a gloved finger to point to the snow waste. Her voice was muffled by the layers of wool. "We're far enough away from the redoubt now to get a full view. If you give your eyes time to focus when using the binoculars, you can spot the tops of the antenna array."

She held out the binoculars. Barch took them, raising his goggles, blinking at the exquisite sting of the dry, cold air against the moisture of his eye. He peered into the eyepiece, across the snowscape to the coordinates Berrier had indicated. The vision enhancers were of predark manufacture, possessing ultra-low-dispersion elements in the lenses to allow stable, distortion-free long-distance viewing even in low light.

Squinting, Barch held back his impatience and gave his eye time to adjust, as the archivist had instructed. After a few seconds, the dark metal frameworks of the antennae came into sharp relief against the white blanket of snow, sticking up like skeletal, long-dead trees. He silently approximated the distance, realizing the diameter of the half-buried rims of the transmission dishes had to be immense in order to be seen at all from a mile away.

"You see them?" Berrier asked, interrupting Barch's thoughts.

"I see them," answered Barch. "How the hell could you have spotted that array out there? You told me your eyes were bad." He felt the saliva in his mouth dry up from the brittle cold, even in the short time his mouth was open to speak.

"My vision *is* pretty piss poor," Berrier admitted. "I'm just well-informed."

"Knowing where to look, that's the secret isn't it, Berrier?"

"You know damn good and well it is, Barch."

"Since you're so well-informed, explain to me why anyone in their right minds would build a military installation up in this part of the world."

"Privacy, for one," she said, adopting a detached, lecturing tone. "And don't forget, when this installation was constructed, the weather here was much different. This part of Alaska wasn't frozen over. The air was cold, yes, but there was little snowfall and it wasn't in a permanent deep freeze. Weather patterns went all screwy during the skydark. Besides, if this is the spot I think it is, the builders could have designed their own weather systems and kept their own climate as snug and warm as a tropical island within a five-mile radius had they chosen to do so."

"Yet another application of the system?"

Berrier nodded. "Weather control would have been just the beginning."

Barch waited for her to say more, refusing to ask "Like what?" for elaboration, even though the cold had penetrated the fleece lining of his boots and made his toes ache. He had to maintain his dominance over the archivist, and that couldn't be done if he allowed himself to be tested like a child.

At length, Berrier said, "There were rumors of mind-control technologies, of using accurately timed, artificially excited electromagnetic strokes to induce a pattern of oscillations over certain regions of the Earth. The brain performance of large populations could be impaired and channeled to adhere to certain behaviors."

Barch shifted his feet in the crusty snow, looking first at the nearly buried antenna array, then back to Berrier. "Sounds like more predark techno-bullshit."

The archivist stiffened and replied sharply, "Before the nukecaust, before the skydark, humanity had added a substantial amount of electromagnetic energy to Earth's environment. There wasn't one spot on the planet that didn't have some form of electromagnetism zapping it, from radio waves to microwaves.''

''So?''

''So, the first attempt to coordinate all that radiation was made here, the first attempt to convince six billion human beings to be obedient, unquestioning slaves.''

Berrier gestured to the vista of white all around them. ''That was the ultimate aim of the High-frequency Active Auroral Research Program. There were other HAARP installations on the planet, but this one was the nexus point, the hub of the wheel.''

She turned her head to stare at Barch, and even through her goggles, he felt the heat of her stare. ''Now do you understand why this redoubt is so important, why I chose this one out of all the others?''

Barch didn't respond. He visualized the staggering population of Earth before the nuclear megacull of 2001. Whole nations of people ran out of control, demanding rights, rioting and warring to grab their piece of fast-vanishing natural resources. A program, a device like HAARP would have solved an inestimable number of global problems without a single mushroom cloud or a speck of fallout.

His teeth began to chatter, but he managed to grin nevertheless. He couldn't repress a shiver, but it wasn't due to the cold. It was anticipation. He wheeled around. ''Let's get back inside.''

The entrance to Redoubt Zulu was recessed into

the side of a mountain. An ice-encrusted and rutted, crumbling blacktop road led up from the mouth of the shallow valley. Barch and Berrier trudged up it, heads bowed against the strong gusts of wind so cold they felt as if it blew from the gulfs of deep space. Berrier panted and struggled, feet seeking purchase on the frozen asphalt, but she didn't complain. Barch couldn't help but feel a twinge of admiration for the woman. An academic she was, a key tapper and paper pusher who had never left Ragnarville, but she was tough of spirit.

Barch remembered how confident Berrier had seemed when the historian approached him over a month ago regarding some information she had found in the archives computer database. Barch had planted the seed in Berrier's brain nearly a year before, during an investigation of certain members of Ragnarville's Historical Division. The archivists were plentiful—intelligent men and women chosen for their memory skills, their innate abilities with a computer keyboard and, best of all, their ability to process information and comprehend. However, no matter how bright members of the Historical Division might be, they were only human, and as such, were vulnerable to frailties, like loneliness.

Barch did his research on the existing pool of mid-level archivists in an attempt to seek out the right man or woman, and had settled on Roberta J. Berrier, who fit the profile that he had assembled. Berrier was young, under the age of thirty. Single, apparently celibate, with some old family connections stretching downward into the Tartarus Pits, the lowest levels of ville society. She was very intelligent, with a tested IQ and Rothman ratings that were both at the top of their respective scales. Yet her psychological profile—a profile Barch had access to as administrator of the Magistrate Division—also damned the young woman as being too trusting, with a strong streak of romanticism.

Not that Berrier was a doormat. She was also quite arrogant and self-confident to the point of being reckless.

Barch didn't mind. He believed in using arrogant people, bending them to his will, since they were usually too proud to create problems and too embarrassed to risk exposure of their own foibles. Berrier had plenty of them.

The investigation of the Historical Division was fairly routine, a standard feint to ferret out potential seditionists and Preservationist sympathizers. According to ville dogma, the Preservationists were archivists scattered throughout the nine-ville network. They were devoted to secretly preserving past knowledge, to piecing together the unrevised history of not only the predark, but also the postholocaust world.

Therefore, Barch arranged to have Berrier accused of being a Preservationist sympathizer. The terrified young woman was dragged away from her workstation in the middle of her shift, stripped naked and thrown into the cell blocks.

In most instances, 99.9 percent of them, in fact, any type of accusation made by a Magistrate resulted in a termination warrant. Berrier knew this, and Barch let her think it over for twenty-four hours, naked and shivering in the bare, six-by-five cell.

At the end of those twenty-four hours, Barch personally released her, apologized profusely for the grievous error made by one of his overzealous subordinates and promised she was now under his protection. Berrier was so grateful, so weak with relief and hunger, all she could do was hug his knees and sob.

Thus began their relationship, and Barch was careful to keep it platonic at first. The physical aspects of it would come later, after he discovered how devoted she was to him. One afternoon, during a routine tour of the Historical Division, he said to her casually, "If you happen to uncover anything about the redoubts, I'd be very grateful."

Berrier managed to keep most of the shock she felt from showing on her face, but not all of it. Barch repressed a self-congratulatory grin. Over the course of postskydark generations, strange stories, rumors, legends had circulated about bizarre places buried deep in what was formerly known as the Deathlands. The tales had these subterranean enclaves stuffed with breathtaking scientific marvels, fabulous technological treasure troves.

The enigmas of the redoubts, especially those connected to the Totality Concept, were one of the most ruthlessly guarded secrets of the baronies. During the Program of Unification, some eighty-five years before, the locations of the redoubts within the territories of the villes were sought out and secured. Anyone who spoke of having knowledge of them, even based on hearsay, was hunted down and exterminated. Tales of the redoubts were suppressed to such an extent that they became baseless folktales, dismissed as sheer legend.

Only a member of the Trust like Barch, or an arrogantly curious archivist like Berrier, would know otherwise.

"I thought the Magistrate Division had their own drones to do this sort of covert information dig," Berrier had retorted, but kept her arrogance in check due to her gratitude toward the Mag.

"Can't trust my own, Berrier. I trust you as I hope you trust me."

He lowered his head to close to Berrier's left ear, so close he could see the fine pores in the historian's smooth skin. "I'm looking for something to help both of us. So we can always be together. A Mag and an archivist can't be legally matched, you know. To be together, we need to find a place for ourselves, far from the power of the baron."

That whispered suggestion of living without the heel of a baron on her neck was all the motivation Berrier needed. However, searching the Historical Division's database required time, patience and stealth. The files containing direct references to the redoubts were restricted to archivists holding Xeno clearances. Berrier had no choice but to sneak in through digital back doors. If she hadn't been so confident in her abilities to manipulate the computer system, she wouldn't have made even the first attempt. But she found very little following such a slow, painstaking procedure. Only her wellspring of arrogance and the romantic dream Barch had implanted in her imagination kept her going.

When her motivation flagged, diluted by doubts and fear of discovery, Barch decided it was time to move their relationship into the physical realm. One night, he made love to Berrier—actually, he fucked her, but he did his utmost to convince her that he was making love to her. He was only a little surprised to learn she was a virgin. After that night, any doubts she might have harbored evaporated. Still, the data search was excruciatingly time-consuming.

Then, a month ago, after a council of the nine barons, the path to the secrets in the database was cleared. All of the baronies in the ville network united in a cooperative mission—to recce the redoubts and their individual territories for any recent signs of use or entrance. The mission was, of course, covert and the reasons behind it murky.

Even as a division administrator and a member of the Ragnarville Trust, Barch still wasn't certain of the purpose of the effort. According to fragments of Intel, just over six months ago a couple of Magistrates in Cobaltville had gone renegade and disappeared. And more recently, they had returned to the ville and kidnapped a high-ranking archivist, allegedly right under the nose of Baron Cobalt.

Another, current piece bit of Intel, this one originating in Sharpeville, indicated that one of the turncoat Mags had been sighted in Redoubt Papa and seriously injured Baron Sharpe, perhaps even chilled him. A report on whether the baron had survived the encounter was still pending. The man, Kane by name, sounded like Barch's kind of Magistrate.

At any rate, it was patently obvious the fused-out Mags knew about the mat-trans gateways in the redoubts and used them to elude apprehension.

None of that particularly interested Barch. All that the project meant to him was the opening of hitherto locked doors of information and opportunity. He inveighed heavily upon Ragnarville's senior archivist to upgrade Berrier's clearance to Xeno in order to adequately fulfill the lord baron's command. Shortly thereafter, she found the specs and data regarding Redoubt Zulu.

Barch's treaded boot soles slipped on a patch of ice and he nearly fell, jerking his thoughts back to the present. Berrier was in the lead, so she didn't notice. He swore under his breath as he regained his balance. Before they came here to Alaska, to Redoubt Zulu, the woman would have dogged his heels, never daring to walk in front of him.

The massive sec door had been left up, and snow had drifted over the threshold. Once beyond it, in the corridor, Berrier punched in the code on a green liquid-crystal display pad. With a hissing, squeaking rumble of buried hydraulics, the multiton door slid down, seamlessly joining with the floor with a dull thud. The knife-edged wind ceased to slash at them.

Sighing in relief, Berrier removed her head coverings, letting the goggles dangle around her neck by the elastic strap. She was not very tall, barely five foot five. Her hair was pale yellow and as fine as a newborn's, cropped so close to the scalp it should have been a severe, military-style bristle cut, but due to its softness the hair had a feathered look. Her hair was the only thing soft about Berrier. Intelligence showed in the high arch of her brows. Her lips were dark and full. The potential for coldness, even cruelty, was evident in her aquamarine blue eyes.

Barch liked that potential. It was the only thing he found truly attractive about the woman. Tugging down his scarf, he scratched at the flakes of frost in his goatee. He rested his goggles on his forehead and asked, "So, what have we stumbled onto here, Berrier?"

Berrier smiled bleakly. "The legacy of Nikola Tesla. What was built here stretches all the way back to him."

"Who is Nikola Tesla?"

"A predark genius, a theoretician, an engineer. His work goes back into the early 1900s by the old calendar." Berrier's smile stretched into a grin. "He was the archetype of the mad scientist...mysterious, misunderstood and exploited by those who followed him. Guys like Edison and Steinmetz were one thing, but Tesla...he was a true visionary.''

Barch only vaguely recognized the name of Edison, and Steinmetz meant nothing at all to him. ''You sound impressed.''

The historian shrugged. ''I am. The man was truly ahead of his time. In fact, some of his ideas were so advanced, they were looked upon as black magic, or sorcery mixed with science. Mankind was only beginning to catch up with him by the late twentieth century, but of course, the human race took a giant step backward and such things as the discoveries of a long-dead scientist and inventor took a low priority to daily survival.''

''Spare me the history lesson, Berrier. What's Tesla got to do with HAARP?''

Berrier's eyes narrowed in irritation. ''Simple. He invented the goddamn thing. At least, he invented the core of the idea. See, back in his time, his more advanced theories were viewed as strictly speculative. For example, the notorious Tesla Death Ray might have really been a particle-beam idea that Tesla tried to sell the old-style U.S. military as an antiaircraft weapon.''

Barch sighed impatiently. ''There's got to be an op center for the redoubt for HAARP somewhere in here.''

Berrier pursed her lips and slid a hand inside a pouch pocket of her thermal garment. She withdrew a folded map and opened it up. Since their arrival in the installation via the mat-trans gateway six hours earlier, the two people had made an attempt to explore the layout of the immense, multilayered installation. According to Berrier, Redoubt Zulu was possibly the largest complex of its kind in the Totality Concept network, housing at one time a thousand people and the last one constructed before the end of the twentieth century. It was virtually a small city buried within a mountain.

During the Program of Unification, Redoubt Zulu had been ceded to the territory of Baron Ragnar. It made sense only because Ragnarville was the northernmost ville in what once was the continental United States.

Poring over the map, Berrier murmured, "When Zulu was secured, a tremendous storehouse of predark relics were found. They were removed to the Historical Division."

"What about personnel?"

Distractedly, finger tracing a line on the map, she answered, "According to the records I found, there was evidence squatters had occupied the place a time or two in the past. But we're the first people to enter Redoubt Zulu in over eighty years. We won't bump into anybody, so don't worry."

"I won't," Barch retorted dryly. "Not as long as this place is all you've claimed it is. If it isn't, you're the one who'll be worrying."

Berrier didn't react to the undertone of menace in

his voice. She tapped the map triumphantly. "There. A sealed-off section near the bottom of the redoubt. It has no reference key or ID number."

She moved down the broad corridor excitedly. Barch glared after her, then fell into step behind her, discreetly unzipping the seal on the right wrist of his coverall so, if need be, his Sin Eater could spring smoothly into his hand.

Berrier turned to the left down a side passageway. After a dozen yards, it ended at the landing of a spiral staircase. The stairs went up and down. Without pause, Berrier stepped out onto the metal risers, walking down the first turning. Barch hesitated, moving only when she said urgently, "Come on."

The stairs wound around and down, but not as deeply as Barch initially figured. At the base of the staircase was a foyerlike room with blank, featureless walls. Only a double set of heavy steel doors interrupted the smoothness. Berrier touched the square lock mechanism tentatively, then removed the glove from her left hand. Pressing her fingertips against the portal, she cast Barch a wide-eyed, surprised glance. "Cold."

"So the fuck what?" he snapped. "Its a goddamn deep freeze for hundreds of square miles. Maybe the doors lead to the outside."

Berrier shook her head, pointing to the dark passageway on the far side of the staircase. "A secondary exit is down there, clearly marked on the layout. No, these doors lead to something else."

Barch eyed the twin slabs of steel doubtfully. "Take a dozen high-ex grens to blow those. Maybe even a couple of kilos of C-4."

Smiling wryly, a little patronizingly, Berrier dipped a hand inside of her coverall. She produced a small oval of molded black plastic. "Not necessary, not when you have a key."

She trained the device on the doors, thumbed a stud on its surface and two electronic *queeps* sounded from the lock. Solenoids snapped loudly, and with a prolonged pneumatic hiss, the double doors slowly swung inward.

Barch squinted suspiciously at the sonic key in her hand. "Where'd you get that?"

She shrugged negligently. "Where else? The archives. It was part of the Zulu collection of artifacts."

Barch watched the ponderous doors inch open, resisting the impulse to unleather his Sin Eater. There was nothing to shoot at except billows of foglike mist. A wave of overwhelmingly frigid air surged out between the doors, so bone-numbingly cold both of them recoiled. As the warmer air of the foyer met it, a shroud of vapor formed.

It wasn't the kind of cold they had experienced outside the redoubt. This was different, a cold so unfathomably deep it could freeze the air in their lungs, turn all the moisture in their bodies to ice.

Berrier made a move to step forward, but Barch

restrained her with a firm grip on her shoulder.
"Wait," he cautioned.

Barely visible through the fog, lights began to
glow. The opening of the doors activated a lighting
system. In a swift, one-by-one progression, overhead
light strips flickered to life and cast a steady yellow
illumination.

The thicker clouds of mist dissipated, and Barch
stepped closer to the doors. A long, hexagonal shaft
yawned away before him, the sharply angled walls
glassy and gray. It was so long, the nether end was
lost in the fog-clouded distance. A low hum seemed
to fill the passageway, a subsonic tone that vibrated
gently against his eardrums.

Fanning away the vapor, Berrier shouldered past
Barch, over the threshold. Inlaid in the walls behind
glass panels stretched maddeningly intricate ribbons
and patterns of circuitry. Tiny lights flashed and
blinked intermittently, but synchronously.

Barch fought against a sense of unreality, of a sudden panicky suspicion that he was hallucinating. He
shut his eye, then opened it, and the hexagonal tunnel
was still there.

"The nerve center of the redoubt," Berrier stated,
voice quivering with barely leashed excitement.
"And probably the HAARP array, too."

She entered the passageway, taking long-legged,
purposeful strides. Barch followed, but he didn't try
to catch up to her as she disappeared into the mist.
This time, he was glad she took the point. Due to the

influx of warmer air, little droplets of condensation were already forming on the transparent panels covering the integrated circuit boards. The glass panes threw back his distorted reflection, transforming his sharp-featured face into a dark, elongated smear.

Somewhere up ahead, he heard Berrier's voice rise in a short, wordless cry of wonder. He increased his pace, inhaling a deep breath and wincing as the cold air sliced his sinuses like razors. He found Berrier standing at the edge of a perfectly circular area. It was ringed by a continuous lap-level console, studded with regular rows of alternating white and red buttons. Small readout-display screens flickered in tandem.

In the center of the circle, inset in the floor, rose a low square dais of gleaming chrome. The dais supported a couch, with curved sides. On the couch, wrapped tightly in a muslinlike fabric, lay a woman.

She lay unmoving on her back, eyes closed. She was dead and had been for a very, very long time, though her body had not decomposed. The deep-freezing air had maintained a fair state of preservation, but her pale blue flesh was stretched drum tight over her facial bones, her lips were peeled back from her teeth and her eyes were sunk down into their sockets. Metal glinted on her face, delicate inlays of circuitry following the contours of cheek and brow.

There was no way to tell the color of her hair or even if she had any. Her skull was concealed by a metal crown inscribed with microcircuitry. Thread-like filaments stretched from the crown like Medusan hair to a multitude of sockets on the console directly behind her head. On the forepart of the crown gleamed a small round convex lens crafted of dark crystal.

Barch looked closer at the headpiece and with a jolt of nausea realized the crown was actually her skull casing, the scalp peeled away and the naked bone sheathed in alloy and electronics.

Only the woman's emaciated right arm was visible, crooked slightly at the elbow and propped up by a plastic sling-type contrivance bolted to the side of the couch. Tiny fiber-optic filaments extended from the tips of four of her stiff fingers to four buttons on a console.

Berrier's wide eyes shone with awe as she stared at the recumbent figure. Barch struggled to understand, to comprehend even a scrap of the sight. In a hushed voice, he asked, "You ever seen anything like this?"

In an equally hushed tone, touched with fear, Berrier answered, "I've never even *heard* of anything like this."

Her bright eyes darted back and forth over the console, to the four buttons connected to the woman's fingertips. They were red, white, red and white.

Stepping into the circle, Berrier reached for the console.

Barch half shouted, "What the fuck are you doing?'' He was ashamed by the quavery, high note of fear in his voice.

Berrier affected not to have heard him. She tapped the buttons in a rapid sequence. Barch's stomach muscles clenched in an instant of blind, irrational terror that the frozen corpse would suddenly sit up, revived by nothing more than the pressing of a few buttons.

The instant passed and nothing of the sort happened, but Barch didn't relax. Berrier stepped away from the console, face full of disappointment. A chime suddenly bonged softly, and her expression changed to surprise.

The warm, liquid female voice came from everywhere and nowhere. The timbre was a flat alto, but it held an odd, harsh echo, as if metal struck metal at the back of her throat.

"You have accessed the Thermonic Autogenic Robotic Assistance data network out-feed. How may you be assisted?"

Berrier swiftly skipped away from the couch, her eyes and Barch's fixing on the waxy features of the dead woman. Her tightly stretched lips hadn't moved.

"What the hell?" Barch snarled, only distantly aware of the Sin Eater slapping into his palm.

The voice spoke again. "Non sequitur. You have accessed the Thermonic Autogenic Robotic Assistance data network out-feed. How may you be assisted?"

Barch looked all around, to the left and right, up and down and behind him, but saw nothing but wisps of mist, gray alloy and circuitry. "Where are you?" he demanded.

"Non sequitur. Please restate your inquiry."

Berrier said softly, "Barch, it's a machine. A computer program of some kind. We're inside of it, so it's everywhere."

Raising her voice, she announced, "Assist us in learning the primary operational functions of this installation."

"Complying."

Both Barch and Berrier heard the low, ever present hum change slightly in pitch, dropping in register. All the console readouts flashed brightly. Circuitry clicked. From the lens on the dead woman's skull, a tiny bead of light sprang up, like a star somehow captured and miniaturized.

It hovered over the woman's head, then swiftly expanded, from a diamond-shaped spark to an eruption of dazzling light. It seemed to fan up and out in a soundless explosion.

Barch shielded his left eye with his hand, fighting to see between his fingers. The hum climbed in volume, undulating in a one-two-three rhythm. Bright patterns danced and flashed as his vision adjusted to the glare.

The shimmering radiance blended with the mist and twisted into a figure floating above the supine corpse on the couch. A woman formed, bit by glow-

ing bit, pixel by pixel. Her outlines were of glowing
fog, but Barch could see the slender, nude body with
taut, tip-tilted breasts and long legs and the beautiful
face above the lovely throat line. She was totally
hairless, the only exception being the suggestion of
aristocratically arched eyebrows and lashes. Her eyes
were big, but seemed to have no true color. The naked woman was incredibly beautiful by any man's
standards, a silent feast of sensuality even if her near
translucent skin exuded a faint, strobing glow, like
quicksilver sliding to and fro beneath a strong light.

The woman's lips parted. ''I am the holographic
interactive program of the Thermonic Autogenic Robotic Assistance data network out-feed. Please be
specific in the manner in which I may assist you in
learning the primary operational functions of this installation. I am here to serve.''

Chapter 2

Kane crouched in the sheltering shadows of the cypress tree and listened to the steps of the swampies who hunted him.

He knew he was being followed almost as soon as he left the no-name saloon in the pesthole settlement of Boontown. The humid, sweltering night breeze carried the drunken laughter of the patrons and the pungent fumes of the cauldron-brewed pop-skull. Still, he could hear the slapping of bare feet on moist ground.

Boontown didn't sleep despite the lateness of the hour. Outland settlements never slumbered, for they existed outside the direct laws of the villes and catered to a never-ending stream of wanderers, farers, roamers and outlaws—like him.

Populated by a number of scrawny dogs, only a couple fewer children and a horde of men and women, Boontown was built around a stone building. Stucco walled with a roof of woven reeds, the structure was of prenuke origin and served as the settle-

ment's saloon and community center. He had no idea
what it had been, but Lakesh had told him the entire
region had once been a state park, a wildlife refuge.

Boontown was tucked away in a steamy, swampy
pocket of what was once Louisiana, a couple of hundred miles from Norleans. The town, if it could be
called that, was little more than a comparatively high
and dry spot in the soggy bayou. Now it was the
only flyspeck of freedom on the Gulf Coast, where
the basest human impulses could be indulged without
fear of intervention from the cushioned tyranny of
the villes.

Technically, Boontown fell under the jurisdiction
of Baron Samarium, but the settlement was so difficult to find, much less reach, its citizens were left to
their own devices. There were secret trails through
the tangled morass, paths known only to the offspring of the original colonists who had spent their
lives here.

Kane quietly loosened his fourteen-inch combat
knife in its boot sheath, glancing over at the stagnant
black waters of the canal behind him. The still surface reflected the flickering torches that served as
Boontown's streetlights. He strained his ears for the
sound of stealthy footfalls. He heard nothing.

The dark men and slatternly women in the saloon
had paid no attention to him, and that in itself made
his pointman's sixth sense come to full alert. Despite
his shabby garments, he was obviously not one of
them. At six feet one inch of hard muscle, he towered

over the tallest man in Boontown. He was dirty enough, yes, but the grime wasn't the accumulated detritus of years spent scavenging in the bayous.

Only Kane's gray-blue eyes, startlingly bright and cold in his mud-encrusted, high-planed face, revealed a trait the Boomtowners could recognize and relate to. His eyes were those of a man who had killed many times and had little compunction about doing so again. Therefore he knew the swampies' apparent lack of interest in him was a pose.

Now several people were paying attention to him, just as he had hoped, stalking him with all the cunning of a snow wolf. The thought of snow made him wish he had traded assignments with Grant and Baptiste. He dabbed at the film of sweat on his forehead with the loosely woven sleeve of his tunic.

Kane wondered briefly if Samariumville's Magistrate Division had planted a spy here just in case he or Grant and Baptiste turned up, but he discarded that possibility. Mag spies would not live long in Boontown, but local informers were different altogether.

He pressed his back to the tree trunk and made a careful visual recce of the area. At one time, buildings had stood around the canal. Now they were empty, roofless ruins. Time and neglect had worn away and blurred whatever features they might have possessed. He gazed at the shells, considering hiding himself among them.

As soon as the notion registered, he heard the footsteps again. They quickened, slowed indecisively, then quickened again. Kane counted the sound of three pairs of feet. His fingers touched the nylex handle of his knife. He didn't want to chill all of them. He needed one alive to carry the tale of his appearance through the bayou and eventually to Baron Samarium himself.

Three figures shifted in the shadows, drew abreast of him, passed and Kane moved in a catlike spring. He didn't draw his weapons, neither the knife nor the Sin Eater holstered to his right forearm beneath the loose sleeve of his tunic.

Reaching the nearest figure, he slid his left arm around a squat neck and jerked backward. The small, wiry body writhed in his grip, mewling with fright. The other two figures whirled, and even in the dim light, Kane saw they were grimy men dressed in a mismatched conglomeration of rags.

The body in Kane's arms thrashed, and he tightened his grip, using his right arm to secure a hammerlock. As he did so, he felt not the smooth flatness of a man's chest but the budding breasts of a young woman.

The men stared at him unblinkingly. Kane stared back, noting the small, crude crossbows strapped to their forearms. They wore long kaiser knives, also known as sling blades, at their hips.

The stench of the female in his arms clogged Kane's nostrils, and he breathed shallowly through his mouth. It was anybody's guess if swampies were true muties or simply inbred holdovers who had inherited a variety of genetic quirks from isolated Cajun ancestors.

Dark-skinned, stocky and solid of build, under medium height, they possessed negroid features although hair and eye color varied widely. Other than exuding an odor that reminded Kane of an open cesspool ripening in the summer sun, they exhibited no outstanding mutie characteristics. None of the swampies had fingernails, but that lack could be attributed to their genotype rather than mutation. A network of scar tissue surrounded the men's eyes, and Kane guessed they were caste marks.

"Who yo' be?" demanded one of the men, glaring ferociously from beneath a mop of curly peppercorn hair falling over his broad forehead. He spoke in a singsong cadence, his tone overlaid with the lilting accents of Boomtown's own peculiar dialect. His English sounded unpracticed.

"I think you have a pretty good idea of who I be," Kane replied coldly. "That's why you're sniffing along my track."

Both men blinked at him, not responding to his statement. The other swampie, one wearing a ragged red-and-yellow bandanna over his head, pointed with his crossbow to the girl.

"What yo' do?" he demanded. "Yo' gon' chill Hoggette?"

"Nice name," Kane muttered.

"Yah," the female whispered. "It be French. Yo' gon' chill me?"

"Not unless you force me. I want some information."

Peppercorn's eyes narrowed to suspicious slits. "'Bout what?"

"How often do Baron Samarium's sec men come this way?"

Bandanna snorted out a scornful laugh. "Rast, man—dey never come to Boontown. Dey no find us."

"Then you meet them somewhere."

The two men glowered, not answering. The girl twisted uncomfortably in his arms. Tremulously, she said, "Dey come to edge of bayou. Las' night of ever' full moon. Las' couple o' times dey ast about strangers in Boontown. Dey never ast before."

"Hush yo' hole, slut," Peppercorn hissed.

Kane chuckled quietly. "And they asked about three strangers in particular, didn't they?"

Hoggette tried to nod, but could only incline her head a fraction of an inch due to Kane's elbow crooked at her throat. "Give us pix. Say dere blood warrant, say give us lots o' jack, we tell 'em we see t'ree strangers."

"Who has the pix?"

"Me do," Hoggette replied.

"Let's see the pix," said Kane. "Move nice and slow, sweetheart."

Moving her hand with exaggerated care, Hoggette fished around inside her rags and brought out a large square of paper, folded in half and frayed on the corners. She unfolded it and held it up so Kane could see.

Three grainy photographs were arranged side by side, all head-and-shoulders shots, reproduced from ID pix taken in Cobaltville at least three years ago. He looked at his own face, clean shaved with short, crisp, neatly combed hair. It was hard to understand how the swampies had recognized him from the black-and-white photo. His hair was longer, not combed, and his face bore three days of beard stubble.

The next pix was of Grant, and if he had strolled into Boontown, there would have been no question that his appearance matched the picture. He was heavy and wide about the shoulders, his dark face square jawed and weatherbeaten, his shadowed eyes shrewd and watchful. Though he now wore a downsweeping mustache, the new addition wouldn't have disguised his face much.

The third photo was of Brigid Baptiste, and of the three of them she had changed the least. Though there was no way to tell that her big, slanted eyes were jade green, or that the color of her thick mounds of hair was the golden red of a sunset, the dusting of freckles over the bridge of her nose and smoothly rounded cheeks was discernible. Despite the feminine softness in her features, there was a hint of iron resolve in them, too. Looking at the poor reproduction awakened a strange pang within Kane, and he realized with shamed surprise that he missed her, even though less than ten hours had passed since he had last seen her.

No copy complemented the photographs, and Kane wasn't surprised. By and large, all outlanders were illiterate, and more than likely, the residents of Boontown were proud of it.

"Did the Mags—the sec men—give you the names of the strangers?" Kane asked.

Bandanna nodded, answering promptly, "Yo' be Kane. T'other black man be Grant. Slut be Baptiste."

"And why are they looking for us?" Kane had the feeling he was coaching a group of not very bright children in reasoning out a simple math problem.

As if by rote, Peppercorn announced, "Yo' t'ree be traitors to unity. Yo' be big-time criminals. Barons wan' yo' brought to justice. Sec men pay well iffen we he'p dem do it."

Kane nodded. "Very good."

Bandanna shifted his feet slowly, and Kane knew he was edging to get into position for a clear shot with his crossbow. "Yo' make us deal?" he demanded. "Yo' give us mo' jack not to turn yo' in to sec men?"

Kane grinned, a humorless baring of his teeth. "By no means. I want you to tell the sec men all about me. Tell them you saw me, tell them that me and my friends will make the bayou our home. We like it here."

The pair of swampies goggled at him in disbelief. "Yo' wan' live here?" asked Peppercorn.

"Why not?"

"Sec men hunt for yo', find yo', chill yo'."

"Let 'em try," Kane replied disdainfully.

Hoggette said sourly, "Iffen dey know yo' here, dey wan' know why we don' chill yo', turn in yo' bodies."

"Tell them the truth. Tell them I got away from you."

"Truth?" Bandanna echoed scornfully. "Truth be yo' no get away from us. Truth be we *do* chill yo', bring yo' body to rendezvous, get our jack. *Dat* be truth!"

Swiftly, Bandanna raised his right arm, clenched his fist and triggered the little crossbow. The quarrel itself was less than six inches long, but Kane glimpsed a brown, tarry substance on the sharp point. He instantly knew the stuff was poison, and probably so virulent that even a scratch could bring death.

Instinctively, he ducked and the small shaft buzzed past his left ear, close enough so the fletching lightly whipped his hair. Even as he crouched down behind Hoggette, he reflexively tensed his wrist. A tiny electric motor whirred, activated by sensitive actuators on his tendons, and the big-bored Sin Eater slid into his right hand, the butt unfolding and slapping firmly against his waiting palm.

The Sin Eater had no trigger guard, so he kept his index finger extended in order to keep the blaster from firing automatically. Hoggette squealed when the arrow zipped over her head, and the squeal became an aspirated, hate-filled shriek when she saw the Sin Eater fill Kane's hand.

"He be fuckin' sec man hisself!" she shrilled. "Dis be trick o' Mags!"

The little swampie woman seemed to explode in Kane's grasp, savagely struggling to free herself from his loathsome touch. Muscles coiled and bunched beneath her dusky skin like steel cables. Kane tried to hold her, realized he couldn't, then flung her away, propelling her forward with a knee thrust hard against her broad backside.

Hoggette's short, squat stature kept her from falling, but she stumbled, slap-footing loudly against the marshy ground. Peppercorn sidestepped quickly out of her way, aligning his crossbow with Kane's chest.

Kane crooked his finger around the trigger, and the Sin Eater thundered, flame blooming from the muzzle. His aim was hasty, and the 9 mm round only tore a gouge in the swampie's curly mass of hair.

Peppercorn squalled in pain and rage. The string of his crossbow twanged, and the quarrel drove over Kane's head. He heard it strike the trunk of the cypress tree behind him.

Bandanna and Peppercorn fumbled to slap new arrows into their weapons, pulling back on the bowstrings. Swinging the barrel of the Sin Eater in short half arcs to cover both of them, Kane bellowed, "Freeze, slaggers!"

He used his Mag voice, a sharp, commanding tone at a volume that in the past intimidated malefactors and broke violent momentum. But the swampies weren't slaggers. They were outlanders, fueled by a generational hatred of sec men and the barons. They continued loading their crossbows with single-minded purpose, their discolored teeth bared.

Kane brought Bandanna's torso into target acquisition and squeezed the trigger. The 248-grain round struck the man with a devastating punch high in the chest, bowling him off his feet, arms flailing. He hit the ground with a squashing sound, and Kane swung his blaster toward Peppercorn. He fired a single shot. The swampie catapulted backward, limbs thrashing.

Training the bore of the Sin Eater on Hoggette, Kane listened with dismay to the echoes of the shots rolling through the night sky. The echoes were replaced by voices raised in questioning shouts from the vicinity of Boontown.

Hoggette's lips writhed back over her teeth in a vicious grin. In a husky whisper, she said, "Oh, dey catch yo' now, sec man. Dey peel yo' skin offen yo'. I make 'bacco pouch outten yo' dick. Yo' so big-time dead."

Kane sidled around her, toward the shadows of the bayou, blaster aimed at her head. "If they come after me, they'll end up like your friends here."

Bandanna's and Peppercorn's bodies suddenly twitched. They dragged air into their lungs with raspy rattles. Kane felt his nape hairs tingle and lift, and cold fingers of disbelief, then terror caressed the base of his spine.

The two swampies stirred, groaning, and pushed themselves into sitting positions. Then they staggered to their feet, swaying. For a mad instant, Kane thought he might have missed with his shots and that the swampies had only pretended to be hit. Then, in the next instant, he wondered if his bullets had missed vital organs. But he saw moonlight glistening wetly on the patterns of blood soaked up by their ragged clothing.

In a strained half gasp, Bandanna said, "Yo' got to do better dan dat, sec man."

The voices from Boontown climbed in volume, and Kane glimpsed figures silhouetted by the guttering torchlight. Knife blades glinted. Hoggette cupped her hands around her mouth and screeched an unintelligible torrent of words.

Her screech was immediately answered, so Kane put his head back, lifted his legs and ran. An uproar of outraged howls erupted behind him. As soon as he reached the tree line, it was as if he went blind. Although moonlight shone brightly upon the top of the jungle mat, little of it penetrated to the treacherous morass of foul water, tangled cypress roots and creepers that formed the bayou floor. Vines dangled snakelike from tree limbs, entwining with the thick gray Spanish moss to make an almost impenetrable barrier.

Groping around inside his tunic, he found and withdrew his dark-vision glasses. The treated lenses allowed him to see clearly in deep shadow as long as there was some kind of ambient light source. Once he had them on, his sight improved somewhat, but not as much as he had hoped.

Kane sought the trail he had followed from the underground installation. It had taken him well over an hour to negotiate it when there was still a late-afternoon sun to light his way, and that was by walking cautiously and pausing every so often to get his bearings. He had taken his precautions. But sprinting through the bayou at an hour past midnight with a horde of unkillable swampies on his heels didn't permit precautions.

Cypress, pine and mangrove trees reared their pillared trunks all around him. Huge ferns, their glossy fronds gleaming metallically, curved over the trail. Insects chirped and buzzed from the deep shadows. He didn't worry overmuch about sucker flies or brain ticks. He couldn't afford the luxury.

Kane slogged through a patch of mud, the stench of marsh gas filling his nostrils and turning his stomach. Still, the sulfurous stink wasn't much more nauseating than the effluvium exuded by the swampies.

Reaching higher ground, he stopped to catch his breath and listen. Owls hooted eerily in the upper branches of the trees. He heard the bawling of the pursuing swampies, undercut by gleeful laughter. He wet his lips, realizing he was providing the citizenry of Boontown with sport, a welcome diversion from their monotonous, rudimentary lives.

Kane started running again, wishing he could be

stealthy but knowing he couldn't without sacrificing speed. He sucked in great gulps of the humid air as he struggled across roiling, muddy creeks, sinking almost to his knees in some places. He began to curse Lakesh, then remembered this was one mission he couldn't blame on the old man. It was all of his own devising. If he could have freed one of his feet from the insistent tug of the bog, he would have kicked his own ass.

With the search for Kane, Grant, Baptiste and Lakesh extended to encompass the nine villes and their territories, diverting attention from the Cerberus redoubt was of tantamount urgency. Although the mountain pass to the installation in Montana's Bitterroot Range had been blocked in a fairly recent defensive move, eventually it would be investigated, simply as part of the process of elimination. All possible bolt-holes for the fugitives and their alleged captive would be searched.

Kane had concocted a plan to confuse and deceive the barons by planting false trails and evidence of their presence in widely separated territories. During his many years as a Magistrate in Cobaltville, he had read intelligence reports from Samariumville in which Boontown had figured prominently. Criminals from Baron Samarium's territory inevitably struck out for the bayous. The main source of Boomtown's revenue derived from information provided to Samariumville's Magistrate Division.

Kane figured that if he made himself visible in the

Boontown vicinity, the focus of the search would concentrate on the tangled green hell of the swamps. Simultaneously, Grant, Domi and Baptiste were on the other side of the country, in a redoubt in Minnesota, which fell under Ragnarville's jurisdiction, to spread out sign and spoor that it had been recently occupied.

The small installation he made for was codenamed Redoubt Delta, part of the Totality Concept's bioengineering researches, a subdivision of Overproject Excalibur known as the Genesis Project. The Totality Concept was the umbrella designation for American military supersecret researches into many different arcane and eldritch sciences, which included matter transfer, time travel and a new form of genetics. The Totality Concept had been instituted at the close of World War II and continued until that end-of-the-world year of 2001. The primary legacy of the Totality Concept's many subdivisions was the network of underground redoubts that housed the mat-trans gateway units.

Suddenly, the hooting of the owls ceased. In the moment of heavy silence, Kane heard the faint thrumming of a bowstring. The small bolt buried itself in the ground near his left boot.

Spinning around, leading with his Sin Eater, he raked the darkness behind him with a full-auto burst. The staccato hammering reverberated through the bayou, chopping splinters from cypress trees, tearing bark from pine. The muzzle-flash momentarily limned the shapes of two swampies beneath a canopy of undergrowth. He adjusted his aim, and the stream of 9 mm rounds shredded leaves, stems and branches, violently shaking the foliage like a gale-force wind. Over the drumming roar of the blaster, he heard bleats of anger and fear.

Relaxing his finger on the trigger, Kane pivoted and started running again, not expending any time or effort on gauging the accuracy of his shots. A mocking voice floated behind him. "Done tol' you', sec man—yo' gots to do better dan dat!"

Chapter 3

Kane muttered, "Sons of bitches."

Out of the many things in his life he hated, being pursued, forced into the role of prey topped the list. It didn't come naturally to him. As the swampie's taunt echoed through the bayou, Kane decided he'd had his fill of it. He left the trail, pushing his way through a tangle of overgrowth.

On his way to Boontown, he had crossed a rickety bridge spanning a stream and he made his way for that. As the mud under his feet became softer, he slid the Sin Eater back into its holster and reached down to the nylex handle of the combat knife in its boot scabbard. Pressing the positive-release button, he drew the long, double-edged, blued blade. He used it to push aside and chop a path through the heavier thickets of foliage in his way.

Kane picked his way over the upthrusting cypress roots, tasting the salt of his sweat flowing down his face. He couldn't imagine Magistrates believing that he would seek sanctuary in the bayou, with its constant oppressive heat, humidity and the vile, strontium-tainted marshlands. No hellzone could be worse than this.

The stream wasn't much more than a shallow channel where brown, brackish water flowed sluggishly between mangrove-lined mudflats. About twenty yards to his right, he saw the bridge. A number of the timbers had broken loose from the rope bindings, and he remembered how it had shaken dangerously when he crossed it.

As he waded out toward the bridge in the hip-deep water, he conjured up images of carnivorous bullfrogs the size of dogs, of dragonlike alligators with jaws so huge they could devour a man in a single gulp. Mosquitoes began to attack him. He didn't slap at them, fearing the noise, so he silently endured their sharp bites.

When Kane reached the rotting cross braces, he heard a faint mumble. He quickly squatted down, lowering himself into the tepid water so only his nose was above the surface. He had figured the swampies would send out a pointman while the others scoured the trail for him.

He edged beneath the sheltering shadows provided by the sagging timbers, peering up through the wide spaces between them. Fisting his knife tightly, Kane focused all his senses on the source of that faint, mumbling voice. Something small burrowed its way out of the mud beneath his boots, sliding over his ankles. He ignored it.

A man Kane recognized as Bandanna appeared out of the tangle of vegetation on the bank and paused before stepping out on the bridge. He looked this way and that, mumbling to himself. Blood glistened on his chest. He gripped his sling blade in his left hand, the crossbow in his right.

The swampie moved onto the bridge, placing his feet with care, obviously aware of which timbers were safe and which ones were not. Kane waited until Bandanna was directly over him, in midstride, before he surged upward. Using his shoulder as a lever, he shoved up against a timber and it ripped loose with the wet, mushy sound of rotted wood.

In the same motion, he made a sweeping slash with the combat knife, aiming at the back of Bandanna's left knee. He felt and heard the razored steel sink deep into flesh, muscle and tendons.

Bandanna's leg buckled instantly, and his scream of surprised pain rose to a gargle before he splashed into the water like a fallen tree. His arms thrashed the water to froth, but Kane didn't give him the opportunity to lift his head out of the water and voice a warning cry.

Without hesitation, he clapped a hand over the swampie's mouth, pressed a knee into the small of his back, then sliced the blade's edge across the man's squat neck.

Bandanna thrashed the water, rolling, clutching at his throat, gurgling horribly as he tried to force a scream through a severed larynx and windpipe. Blood spewed through his fingers, forming a darker stain in the dark water around him. Slowly, it seeped away downstream.

Bandanna's body turned onto its back, his face breaking the surface, eyes rolled up. Reddened water poured from his silently screaming mouth. Kane watched as the swampie twitched and quivered as his life pumped out through a severed carotid artery.

Gripping a handful of his rags, Kane hauled Bandanna to the opposite bank and dropped him on his back in the mud. His lips formed a grimacing rictus, and the red-rimmed slash across his throat mimicked it.

Kane bent over, hands resting on his knees, and breathed deeply. Gazing at Bandanna, it occurred to him that the flow of blood from the wound seemed to be slowing. As the notion registered, Bandanna's legs jerked. For an instant, Kane assumed the movement was nothing more than a postmortem spasm.

Then the swampie jackknifed up at the waist, ghastly, liquid burbles issuing from his open, dripping mouth. Little blood bubbles formed on his lips. He clawed out for Kane's face.

Clamping his lips tight on the cry of horror climbing up his throat, Kane grasped Bandanna's left wrist and yanked him sharply forward. The swampie's head was snapped back by the quick jerk, and Kane thrust the knife at an upward angle through the underside of his jaw.

He heard the point grate along the vertebrae as fourteen inches of titanium-jacketed tungsten steel drove through the roof of Bandanna's mouth and into his brain stem. Kane held the knife tightly in position, pressing the hilt against his chin as the swampie writhed and kicked feebly. He almost snarled in satisfaction when the shivers and trembling ceased. The swampie's body settled and he yanked his knife free, a ribbon of crimson trailing from the point. He wiped the blade clean with one of Bandanna's rags.

Kane had encountered a variety of genetic perversions over the past few months, and the swampies were yet another example, disgorged either by the deliberate biological tinkering of Genesis Project or as an accidental result of radiation. Either way, the question of whether swampies were indeed muties had been answered.

He guessed they had developed—or been given— a dual circulatory system, with two sets of hearts and double arteries. His bullet had perforated only one of Bandanna's hearts, and likewise he had cut through only one of two carotid arteries. However, Kane was sure the swampie didn't have twin brains.

Kane went up the bank and into the foliage paralleling the trail. The root-clotted mudflats gave way to more solid ground, and he increased his pace, running on the balls of his feet. He kept alert for any sound behind, particularly an angry uproar when Bandanna's body was discovered.

A vine snared his ankle, and he fell to the soft earth, sprawling awkwardly as he tried to keep from falling on his knife. He kicked free of the vine and started to push himself erect. The vine, as thick as his wrist, suddenly wrapped itself around his lower leg.

Another vine whipped out of the shadows beneath the undergrowth and fastened itself around his left wrist. It was tipped with a cruelly curved thorn, like a cat's claw. The point of the hook pricked the back of his hand, and almost immediately a cold numbness crept up his wrist and down into his fingertips. More vines began lashing out of the foliage, darting like snakes.

Kane struggled as they began to pull at him, looking in the direction he was being tugged. The vines ended some twenty feet away in a thick, enormous flowering growth in the shape of a shallow, open bowl at least six feet in diameter. The rim had long furlike hairs lining its outer edge and an inner lining of a rich bloodred. It gleamed stickily in the dim light. The bowl opened and closed like a hungry mouth, making obscene slobbering sounds. About the base of the plant he saw a scattering of old bones, dull white in the dim light. They were discolored, and a closer look showed him that the bones had been eaten way, as if by acid, dissolving the hard surfaces to expose the spongy marrow within.

With a mounting fear, Kane understood the moisture gleaming within the bowl of the plant was a corrosive secretion, a digestive fluid by which it consumed its food. A nerve toxin in the hooked thorns numbed its prey. Multiple stings doubtlessly resulted in complete paralysis.

The vines locked Kane in a viselike grip, dragging him toward the wet, gaping maw. He clawed at the ground, dug in his heels. All of his life, he had heard tales of the diversity of mutated flora and fauna spawned by the nukecaust. Radiation and vast ecological changes had transformed many harmless species into nightmarish, deadly parodies of their original forms. He could only guess at what the predark progenitor of the flesh-eating plant might have been. He realized its vines were like sensitive antennae, reacting to ground vibrations. It hadn't stirred until he began to run.

The concept of giant bullfrogs seemed almost quaint as he grappled with the darting, slithering tentacles.

The vines tightened like steel cables around Kane's arms and legs. He didn't draw his Sin Eater. Bullets would be of no value, since a plant had no vital organs and the shots would only pinpoint his position to the pursuing swampies.

But even if a plant had no vital organs, it had no bones or muscles in its tentacle vines. He still had one leg and one arm free, but his half-numbed knife hand was caught at the wrist and inexorably being stretched out in the direction of the moist, gaping maw. He reached out with his free hand, avoiding a hooked vine that darted for it, and grabbed his knife by the blade, nicking one finger on the sharply honed point.

He closed his hand around the nylex handle and

slashed at the vine around his right wrist. The fiber was tough, and he had to saw at it to sever it. Responding to the stimuli, other tendrils snaked across the bayou floor to recapture his arm. Twisting over, half sitting up, he lowered his head between his shoulders as one of the hook-tipped green tentacles sought to encircle his throat. He cut through the vine wrapped around his ankle and stood up, even as two more tendrils lashed at him, one securing a grip around his waist, another across his chest, the curved thorns fouling in his clothes.

Rather than resist the tug, he used all his strength to rush toward the yawning red mouth of the carnivorous plant. The vines had evolved to prevent the escape of a victim, moving away from the bowl-shaped maw, and they had little strength to resist forward direction. They doubled up, looping at his feet, and Kane slashed them loose from his body.

The plant responded violently, sending other tentacles to recapture him. A huge tree loomed up on his left, rearing from a slightly humped hillock of earth. Kane lunged for it, bounding over a snarl of vines, reaching the higher ground in one leap. He put the trunk between him and the plant and forced himself to stand motionless.

The vines quested for him, touching the deeply rutted bark, but encountering nothing that moved or exuded body heat. After a minute, they slowly withdrew, slithering back into the undergrowth.

Kane managed to soften his harsh respiration, hugging the bole of the tree. His heart thudded in his chest, he trembled a little, but he told himself the reaction was due to adrenaline, not fear.

He heard a faint mutter of voices and the rustle of foliage. He pressed against the tree trunk and waited. Within a moment, a quartet of swampies quietly pushed its way through the brush, gazing around alertly, first at the ground, then at the undergrowth. Peppercorn led the way, and he swept his loaded crossbow back and forth in tandem with his scarringed eyes.

With a surprising delicacy of tread for such ungainly builds, the swampies moved forward, one step at a time. They obviously knew of the grimmer plant and how its vines responded to vibration.

When the four swampies had passed him by, Kane shifted stealthily away from the tree, avoiding all loose twigs and dry leaves. Then he began to run furiously in place, boots thumping a fast, violent tattoo on the ground.

Although the swampies spun around within half a heartbeat of the first drumming footfalls, the vines were faster. A dozen of them snaked out of the brush, whiplashing over the ground toward Kane's legs.

A sideways lunge put him against the tree again as the vines flicked like serpents in search of living prey. They found it on the swampies. The tendrils snapped around the ankles and lower legs of the four men, who squalled in fright, kicking and stamping.

Their efforts to free themselves only attracted

more vines, as they lashed up and out from all sides, coiling around arms and waists, the hooked thorns securing grips in rags and the skin beneath. A slender cluster of tentacles surrounded Peppercorn's head. As he opened his mouth to shriek, a hooked tip entered it and the shriek became a strangulated sob.

Kane watched with a cold sense of detached horror, imagining the vine slithering down the man's esophagus, into his stomach, squirming about, hooking into his intestinal wall, withdrawing and dragging his guts up his throat and into the waiting maw of the plant.

The swampies' screams were answered from deeper in the bayou. Kane couldn't afford to stay and see how the plant consumed its food. He moved away from the tree, swiftly dodging a pair of vines that darted toward him.

He continued through the gloom, cutting back after a hundred yards to the trail again. Behind him he heard a cacophony of voices lifted in angry shock as the swampies discovered the predicament of their comrades.

Kane kept to the path after that, hoping the swampies would either stop to rescue their companions before they were devoured or be so discouraged by their fate they would postpone the hunt for the sec man for another night.

He wolf-trotted for the next several minutes, alternating a swift walk with a long-legged lope. He swatted irritably at the mosquitoes that made strafing dives at his head. Every so often he heard splashes in the bog on either side of the trail as if creatures jumped for cover at his approach. Sensation began to return to his thorn-pricked hand.

Reaching inside his tunic, he unzipped the waterproof pouch attached to the waistband of his trousers and withdrew his trans-comm. The palm-sized radiophone had a clear range of only a mile, but he estimated he was well within those limits now. With a thumb, he flipped open the protective cover and keyed in Rouch's frequency.

She responded almost instantly, her filtered voice accurately conveying her anxiety. "Is that you, Kane?"

"It is," he replied, holding it near his mouth. "I'm on my way back to you."

In a tone full of blended relief and reproach, Rouch said, "You've been gone so long, I got really scared. This place is—"

He cut her off. "Did you spread around the evidence?"

"I did just what you told me to do," she replied defensively. "Empty ration packs, messed up the beds, tracked mud around. It looks like people have been living here, all right."

"Good. I'll be back in a few minutes. Be ready to jump. I don't want to spend any more time here than I have to. I've already overstayed my welcome."

In a slightly puzzled tone, she asked, "What do you mean?"

"Just stand by." He closed the frequency and returned the trans-comm to his pouch.

The overgrown trail intersected with the crumbling remains of a narrow, two-lane blacktop road. He followed it for a hundred yards, climbing over a heap of scrap metal that had been a security gate. The cyclone fence and the porcelain current conductors that had electrified it were overgrown with vegetation.

Creepers and leafy kudzu twined all around the flat-roofed, single-storied concrete building, making it one with the jungle floor. Unlike most of the redoubts he had visited, this one had a single, normal-sized door. Beth-Li Rouch stood at the threshold, eyes bright and watchful. The slender young woman's lovely Asian features were tight with worry, but they relaxed when he spoke her name.

She reached for him, then paused, stepping back. Her delicate nostrils flared, dark almond-shaped eyes narrowing. Almost involuntarily, she brought a hand to her nose. "You smell like—"

Kane pushed past her, saying harshly, "I know, Rouch. Get used to a little stinking reality when you make these field trips. You're the one who volunteered, you know."

She glanced at him a little reproachfully, but said nothing, casting her eyes down. Rouch was the newest arrival among the exiles in Cerberus, only a couple of months out of Sharpeville. Her mouth was wide and sensuous, her ears and nose tiny and delicate. Shiny, raven's-wing black hair fell nearly to her waist.

Lakesh had arranged for her exile to fulfill a specific function among the men in Cerberus, but he had made it quite clear that Kane was the primary focus of his—and Rouch's—project to expand the little colony.

Her function had yet to be fulfilled, and Kane couldn't help but suspect that Rouch's eagerness to accompany him to Redoubt Delta wasn't to participate in the mission, but to be alone with him, far from the Cerberus personnel in general and Brigid Baptiste in particular. Regardless, judging by the way she recoiled from him, even if he suddenly decided to cooperate with Lakesh's project, she would run, gagging, into the bayou.

Her body tensed, eyes fixing on the gleam of blood on the knife blade in Kane's hand. In a quavery whisper, she asked, "Is that—?"

Rouch had told him the sight of blood made her queasy, so he swiftly resheathed the weapon in his boot.

"Did you chill someone?"

He hesitated a moment before answering. But if Rouch wanted to be part of an away team's mission, she had to accept death as an inevitable. "Yes. I had no choice."

Rouch's reaction surprised and disturbed him. Instead of looking stricken or uncomfortable, her eyes widened, her mouth parted and her tongue touched her lower lip. "How did you do it?"

Kane felt his eyebrows knitting. "What do you mean?"

"Did you stab somebody or cut a throat?" She seemed thrilled by either notion.

Kane gazed at her silently for a second, then grunted, "It's not important. Let's go."

The small door opened onto a broad stretch of corridor nearly a hundred feet long. It ended at a double set of sec doors. The vanadium-alloy portals were open, spanning a doorway forty feet wide. On the right-hand wall, near the frame, the word Goodbye had been neatly stenciled, at least two hundred years before.

The sec doors opened and closed at the prompting of an interrupted photoelectric beam, unlike those in other redoubts which responded only to a certain numerical code punched into a keypad. As they passed through the doorway, the huge metal slabs slid ponderously together, joining in the center with only the faintest of visible seams.

The corridors were a pale cream in color, curving slightly to the left, lit by dim light strips in the ceiling. Every so often, they strode beneath deactivated vid spy-eyes bolted in the angle of the wall and the roof.

The corridor kept curving in an ever narrowing spiral fashion. Rouch trailed a few paces behind Kane, saying nothing, but he was sure she would have rather been upwind of him. Glancing behind him, he saw his boots were making appropriately muddy tracks on the floor.

The passageway led to another open sec door. On the other side of it, Kane pushed the green lever set in the frame, and the massive portal slid shut with a faint hiss of hydraulics.

The control room for the mat-trans system was filled with cheeping, blinking banks of computers and electronic consoles. Powered by the nearly eternal energy of nuclear generators, the control systems still worked in most of the redoubts. The mat-trans units required a maddeningly intricate number of electronic procedures, so the actual conversion process of matter to energy was automated, overseen and sequenced by computers.

Strangely, Redoubt Delta didn't have a small antechamber to serve as a ready or recovery room. The control center opened directly onto the smoked blue armaglass walls of the gateway. However, it did have the customary sign above the keypad control box beside the door. It read Entry Absolutely Forbidden To All But B12 Cleared Personnel. Mat-Trans.

The only other place Kane had seen that notice was on the jump chamber at Cerberus, and not for the first time he wondered what had become of personnel who held B11 or below clearances.

He tapped in the Cerberus destination code, adding the two-digit encrypted ID number. Rouch did her best to hide her nervousness when she followed Kane into the jump chamber. By the metal handle affixed to the armaglass, he sealed the door. The lock clicked, circuitry engaged and the automatic transit process began.

As the hexagonal disks above and below them exuded a silvery glow, Kane wondered briefly if the stink of the swamp would make the quantum jump with him. Again he wished he had exchanged destinations with Grant and Brigid. Though he couldn't be certain, he seriously doubted they would return from their mission in Minnesota smelling and feeling like an outhouse.

The energy forms resembling white, early-morning mist began wafting from the emitter array above and below. Kane closed his eyes, waiting to be swept up in the nanosecond of comfortable nonexistence.

Instead, he felt a sickening, wrenching moment of dislocation.

Chapter 4

Centered atop a high, cold hill, the imposing mass of man-made structures that carried Baron Ragnar's name rose monolithically above the packed powder of dirty snow and ice. Each of the ville's walls stood high in a defiant thrust of chiseled stone and forged steel. Sheer fifty-foot walls offered flat buttresses of impregnable protection, and were regularly raked at night by the beams of powerful spotlights mounted both on top and at the bottom of the imposing edifices.

Frowning down from each corner of the outer shell that kept the inner maze of Ragnarville secure could be found manned Vulcan-Phalanx gun towers, the heavy-caliber weapons ready and waiting to fend off any sort of attack. One of the reasons for fortifying the villes was a fear of an invasion from foreign, nuke-blasted nations. Another reason was protection from clans of mutants, like the vicious stickies. After nearly a century, neither fear proved to have any foundation.

Within the impregnable walls were the Enclaves, the four multileveled towers of the elite, and all of these towers in turn were connected by a series of walkways and outcroppings to the massive cylinder of white stone looming three hundred feet into the air over all other structures, the Administrative Monolith.

The bottom level of the monolith, Epsilon, served as a manufacturing facility. In turn, Delta Level was home to the necessary and vital service of food growth, preservation and distribution.

Above that, C Level was where the laws of Ragnarville were duly housed and enforced via the Magistrate Division—black-armored men of unyielding morality and justice, men with the reputations of being totally ruthless in the stone-cold performance of their duties as judges, juries and executioners. However, even the Mags were answerable to their own, and the lawgivers were policed by administrators, men who had earned those positions by being the most ruthless in a caste system where ruthlessness was rewarded.

In layout and design, Ragnarville was identical in form and function to the other eight baronies consolidated by the Program of Unification, but the frontier ville also had enough differences to stake out its own pocket of individuality.

Ragnarville was the only spot of true civilization to be found on North America's side of the Arctic Circle—although the mass of towers and walls and buildings that made up Ragnarville was far from being a center for anything which passed as culture.

The chem storms and geological catastrophes that

had rocked the central United States and the western and eastern seaboards had transformed those sections of the country into a patchwork of hellzones. The upper reaches of the continent suffered, too, but the number of nukes that fell was smaller, and the ecological damage less.

In the treasure trove of archives of each of the nine baronies, stacks of crudely printed posters were filed away, unadorned by decoration or frame. A grateful populace had made up these posters during the time when civilization was reclaimed, and the posters now kept like all artifacts as reminders, bits of yesterday to be cataloged and filed by the archivists in case of future need.

Although each of the nine villes shared superficial similarities in appearance and government, they were very different from each other, depending upon the whims of the individual ruling baron. The one link they all shared were the Unity Through Action posters stored away like holy texts within the records of all villes. The illustrations were very simple—line drawings of two hands clasping each other, joined at the wrist by a chain.

Over eighty years before, "Unity Through Action" was the rallying cry that had spread across the Deathlands by word of mouth and proof of deed. The long-forgotten trust in any form of government had been reawakened, generations after the survivors of the nuclear war had lived through the deadly legacy of politics and the suicidal decisions made by elected officials.

The leaders of these powerful baronies, the hidden ones, offered a solution to the constant state of worry and fear—join the unification program and never worry or fear or think again. Humanity was responsible for the arrival of Judgment Day, and it must accept that responsibility before a truly utopian age could be ushered in.

All humankind had to do to earn this utopia was to follow the rules, be obedient and be fed and clothed. And accept the new order without question.

For most of the men and women who lived in the villes and the surrounding territories, this was enough, more than enough. Long-sought-after dreams of peace and safety had at least been transformed into reality. Of course, fleeting dreams of personal freedom were lost in the exchange, but such abstract aspirations were nothing but childish illusions.

At least that was the dogma put forth by the barons, and no one knew what the barons dreamed of, or even if they slept.

The barons did indeed sleep and dream, but not as humans understood the concept. The isolated lords of the villes slept because they needed a certain amount of dreaming not just to maintain a psychological balance, but to review and sift through the data stored in the conscious mind and discard that which was not necessary to the performance of their duties. The tissue of their hybridized brains was of the same visceral matter as the human brain, but the fifteen million neurons that formed the basic wiring operated a bit differently in the processing of information. The sleep of the barons was more like a state of meditation, and the narrative structure of their dreams very linear. Therefore, they rarely confused their dreams with reality.

When Baron Ragnar saw the nude woman standing at the foot of his bed in his private quarters, he experienced not even a moment of confusion regarding her reality—even if her near-translucent skin shed a shimmering glow in the darkness.

Still, Baron Ragnar's double-lidded, slanted eyes widened at the beautiful form facing him.

"Who are you?" he demanded in the musical voice all of his kind possessed.

"I have been designated as Tara," the woman replied in a flat alto.

He sat up straight. "How did you get in here?" His question came out as a whispered hiss. He didn't raise his voice. He knew that within the center complex of Alpha Level he was safe, and that one of the elite Baronial Guards stood just outside his ivory-and-gold-inlaid door. He did not reach for the array of alarm buttons or the weapon next to his bed.

The woman didn't respond to his question. She stared at him calmly, contemplatively. He stared back, running his gaze along her sleek, long-limbed body, over the firm, hard-nippled breasts. He found her lack of body hair extremely arousing, though he couldn't quite seem to focus on the juncture of her smoothly molded thighs.

Baron Ragar sat up straighter, leaning against the headboard. "I said, how did you get into my chambers? Don't you know who I am?" The question was so ludicrous, and the answer so obvious, that the baron felt a flush of anger heating his face at having to ask the second of his two questions. The first enquiry was the true mystery. Without his knowledge no one, absolutely no one, was allowed access into the top spire of the Administrative Monolith.

"You are Baron Ragnar," she replied. The first question remained unaddressed. Oddly, her lips didn't seem to be in synch with any of her words, like the timing was off on an unspooling reel of projected film, but the baron didn't comment on it.

"Yes, yes," the baron replied, rapidly growing impatient with the game.

"Then you have been preselected for us."

Baron Ragnar cocked his high-domed head at the sight of the naked woman, and slowly a smile creased his lipless mouth. Unlike most of his hybrid brethren, Ragnar had developed a near insatiable lust for human females. He wasn't quite sure why, but when he allowed himself to think about it all, he speculated that his human genes must have derived from exceptionally highly sexed individuals.

As far as he had been able to determine, he was an anomaly among the baronial olgiarchy. Since the barons didn't reproduce, their sexual organs were vestigial, tiny reminders of the human biological material that composed perhaps a tenth of their metabolisms.

Baron Ragnar hadn't allowed his physical shortcomings to deter him from glutting his desire for the physical sex act. His personal staff had provided him with prosthetic enhancements, archived artifacts from coitally fixated predark days. With the aid of his trusted inner circle, the baron had indulged his carnal lusts with some of the most succulent women Ragnarville and the surrounding Outlands had to offer.

Sex with the baron was an experience none of the selected women had been allowed to report after the fact, even the ones who had not gone slightly mad from the meshing of physical and mental intercourse. There would be no bragging of "fucking the baron." Besides, his true form was the most closely guarded of secrets, and as such no one outside of a precious few was allowed access to his hidden quarters.

"I usually do the preselection," Ragnar said, each word falling from his slit of a mouth like notes of music.

"So we have been informed," Tara said, and a ghost of smile crossed her exquisite features.

"By whom?"

The faintest hint of a frown drew her delicately arched eyebrows toward the bridge of her nose. "That data is classified."

Baron Ragnar decided his female visitor was

slightly deranged, but the hot lust building within him melted his suspicion. He was certain the woman had been brought to him by one of his staff, chosen because of her exotic looks. Such gifts were not unheard-of, nor unwelcome.

"Come and join me," the baron said smoothly, patting the side of the bed. He smiled at her invitingly.

"No. We cannot." Tara's expression became slightly troubled.

"Then why are you here?" demanded Baron Ragnar. "You said you were preselected for me."

"That is true. You are our preselected target."

"Target?" echoed the baron, confusion driving away desire. "Meaning what?"

"Your termination." The woman's facial expression didn't change, nor had the inflection in her voice; the declaration was made all the more chilling by the lack of emotion.

Baron Ragnar continued to wear his open and inviting smile, but he was no longer even remotely aroused by the woman, who had just delivered a capital crime threat against his life. "You are here to assassinate me?"

Tara inclined her hairless head in a nod. "We will accept that as alternate reference to my mission."

The baron narrowed his eyes, compressing his mouth so it looked like the edges of a raw wound. "I command you to tell me who sent you here."

"Your command cannot countermand our preselection. We have confirmed your identity and must proceed.''

Ragnar snarled, his right hand darting to the bedside table. It gripped a blaster that was at least two times too large for his delicate fingers and hand. The gun was a modified Spectre automatic, similar to the big-bored autoblasters known as Sin Eaters carried by all Magistrates as standard-issue side arms, but minus the customized features. The gun had been the baron's weapon of choice for over a decade, and he always used it when he engaged in the pastime of target shooting—another practice that revealed his differences from his eight hybrid brothers.

Ragnar thumbed the firing-rate selector to full auto and squeezed the trigger. Six 9 mm hollowpoint rounds tore into the woman's face, neck and upper torso. The baron experienced a millisecond of regret over the mutilation of her splendid breasts. Other matters were far more pressing, including discovering which spoke of the wheel of his incredibly stupid trusted inner circle had sent this madwoman to him. His thoughts were already jumping ahead to an emergency meeting of the Trust.

All thoughts of terrorizing his staff vanished when Baron Ragnar realized the woman had not staggered, fallen or shed so much as a drop of blood. The thunderous echoes of the shots still reverberated when he saw how each of the six bullets had impacted haphazardly at full velocity against the wall behind her.

The baron gaped in surprise, then shock, at Tara's beautiful, uninjured body still standing before him.

His mind wheeled with wild conjecture. He heard himself whisper, "I do not miss."

"You did not," she replied.

Tara extended her arms outward from her body, keeping her palms flat and parallel to the carpeted floor, forming a T-shape. She arched her back, thrusting out her taut breasts. Baron Ragnar continued to gape, and his mouth fell open when a diamond-shaped slit appeared to open between her breasts. A swirling splash of multicolored light spilled out.

A heavy fist pounded on the other side of the door. Baron Ragnar opened his mouth wider and began to shriek, but the woman allowed him no time to put words in his scream. She glided to the bedside, and swung her arms and hands around, slapping them together, catching the baron's head between them.

Baron Ragnar's eardrums thundered deafeningly, and he convulsed as a knife of ice seemed to thrust its way through his body from his brain to his toes. His arms and legs instantly numbed, nervous system refusing to respond. His sight was dimmed by a frost that seemed to rim his eyes. Then he felt a vast wave of heat suffusing him, like invisible flame scorching through his body, bringing explosions of burning agony to his muscles.

With the scream dying on his lips, Baron Ragnar's head became a mass of flickering blue flames, jetting up from the pores of his skin. His narrow features peeled, blackened and disintegrated, and his thin blond hair smoldered, turning to gray ash. The blood in his veins sizzled, the moisture in his mouth boiled away and evaporated, issuing between his lips in a small puff of steam. His big dark eyes melted like tallow candles within their deep sockets. Blisters popped out on his fingertips and burst with fine sprays of flame, immediately igniting the pillow and the quilted headboard. Acrid smoke plumed up in corkscrew swirls. The stench of burned flesh flooded the bedchamber.

Tara released the baron's head and stepped away from him, turning as the door swung open violently, shouldered aside by a Baronial Guardsman. His white uniform jacket and tight red trousers accentuated his Herculean physique.

Without a microinstant of hesitation, he lunged for the nude, hairless woman standing at his baron's bedside. He towered a head and a half over her, the enormous breadth of his shoulders making her appear frail in comparison. His blue eyes caught glints of red from the firelight.

His conditioning to protect the baron stemmed from a deeper source than physiological conditioning—it was encoded in his genes, an instinct, not a learned behavior. He and his brother guardsmen were bred to perform only one function, and cerebration had little to do with his actions.

Tara didn't try to evade his lunge or the hands sweeping to clutch her sleek, slim form. Eyes drawn to it, the fingers of the guardsman's right hand plunged into the diamond-shaped aperture between her breasts, as if he were seeking to tear out her heart.

He froze, his muscles seizing, joints locking, body twisting in spasms. Tara calmly laid both hands against his flat, hard-muscled belly. A gray haze shimmered around them. With a ripping of cloth, a wet rending of flesh and muscle, his belly stretched toward her hands like metal leaping toward a magnet. It swelled and burst open.

The guardsman shot away from her. In a screaming, thrashing half spin, the man soared the length of the room. His intestines trailed out like a blue-sheened banner from the cavity splitting his torso from pelvis to sternum. The guardsman landed on his face and sprawled with his arms flung wide, his entrails strung out to Tara's hands.

She dropped them and stepped over them as she walked to the door. The guardsman jerked once and died.

Chapter 5

The trans-comm on Royce's desk shrilled with a rising and falling warble. Snorting awake from the half doze, he blinked at the black comm box and stabbed a clumsy finger to the Receive button. A harsh, babbling voice burst out of the speaker grid, but he recognized it as Hoffman's.

"Commander Royce? Do you copy? Oh, for fuck's sake, sir—"

"What the hell is going on?" Royce demanded.

Hoffman continued to yammer about triple-red alerts and section security breaches, calling out over and over for the watch commander.

Royce, the watch commander, repeated his question in a half shout. "What the hell's going on?"

Then he realized he hadn't thumbed the Transmit button on the intercom and angrily mashed his thumb down on the tiny key. "Dammit, Hoffman, what the hell is going on?"

"Sec breach, upper level, Alpha." Hoffman's voice sounded less frantic now that he was speaking to his superior officer.

"*Alpha?*" Royce's voice hit a high note of incredulity. Ragnarville security problems almost always occurred in the Pits and very rarely on the residential Enclaves. In his recollection, there wasn't even a rumor of a sec breach ever happening in the Administrative Monolith, much less on Alpha Level.

"Yes, sir," Hoffman responded. "The spire. The baron's quarters, sir."

"The baron...!" Royce felt his facial muscles twist into a mask of shocked disbelief. Sweat sprang from his receding hairline and almost immediately trickled down his bulldog-jowled cheeks. "What about the guardsmen?"

"I don't know. The alert came from Walsh, one of the baron's staff." Hoffman's voice trembled, as if he were on the verge of panic.

"Current status?"

"Dixon is responding and should be on scene now."

"Good, get him a backup squad in full armor. I'll be up, stat."

Royce lunged up from his desk, making sure his Sin Eater was snugly strapped to his forearm and his portable trans-comm clipped to his belt. He didn't bother snatching his black Kevlar-weave coat from a wall hook before running out into the corridor. Dixon and the backup squad would be in full armor, as per official division policy. Every duty shift had to have at least three hard-contact Mags in readiness, though three of his best were on a recce assignment in the hinterlands. Royce's high-collared, pearl gray uniform would have to suffice to get him through the sec checkpoints to Alpha Level.

As he sprinted for the lift, he couldn't help but curse Barch beneath his breath. The man had appointed him division commander less than a month ago, right before he embarked on his mission for the baron. A sec breach of this magnitude had never happened before, and he cursed both Barch and fate that it was happening on his watch.

THE NAKED WOMAN seemed serenely oblivious to the stares directed at her as she strode down the corridor. Men in bodysuits pressed their backs against the wall as she passed by, eyes and faces registering wonder and fear.

"Freeze, you slaggin' bitch," a commanding voice roared from behind her.

Tara paused, appearing to spin on the ball of her left foot, and turned enough to see and identify who had shouted the order. A man, encased in black body armor, stood approximately fifteen feet away, inside an open stairwell door. He trained the hollow bore of a Sin Eater at her head.

"Face the wall, hands and legs spread. *Now!*"

Tara continued to stand there, having frozen as directed. Brilliant light from the aperture on her chest cast shifting prismatic reflections on the Magistrate's polycarbonate armor.

The Magistrate advanced on her, his eyes protected by the red-tinted visor attached to his helmet.

The only visible part of the man's face was a tiny lower section of mouth and chin. A tiny pin microphone extended out from the helmet's jaw guard near his right cheek.

"Central, this is Dixon. I have the intruder on Alpha at Magenta Level Two."

"Copy that, Dixon. Backup is on the way," Hoffman said. "What's the story?"

"I think she was in the baron's chambers," Dixon replied. "I'll investigate when backup gets here."

"Stand by. Royce is on his way up, too. What's the bitch look like?"

Dixon half smirked. "Great, if you like 'em as bald and as naked as a newborn."

"Naked and bald?"

"Totally. Looks like the baron has fused out another one."

The woman continued to gaze at him steadily, unblinkingly, and he felt a quiver of dread in the pit of his stomach. Whether it was a trick of the muted lighting, he realized he couldn't make out the color of her eyes, but he felt her level stare.

Lowering his voice, Dixon said into the pin mike, "There's something triple strange about her. Recommend you advise Barch if he has turned up."

"He hasn't," Hoffman replied. "Royce is still filling in for him."

A new voice filtered into his helmet's comm-link. "Dixon, this is Royce. I'm on the way with your backup."

"Copy that, sir. I recommend sending a member of the team to the baron's quarters. I've gotten conflicting reports about a fire, gunshots and a dead guardsman."

The woman shifted position, and Dixon bellowed, "Bitch, I told you to face the wall and spread 'em. Do it!"

Tara turned toward the opposite wall and took a long step.

"Not that one," shouted Dixon. "The other one."

Tara ignored him, continuing to stride forward.

"Fuck this," Dixon muttered. He decided he wasn't going to waste any more time yelling orders at one of the baron's stray, fused-out pieces of ass.

The Sin Eater in his hands spit flame once as he touched the crooked index finger of his right hand to the trigger, and the sound of the gunshot rebounded from the walls of the corridor. Not being a total idiot, nor wanting to have to explain why he had blown away one of the baron's whores, he aimed his shot high for one of her shapely shoulders.

Tara continued walking, apparently untouched by the heavy-caliber round. It struck the wall behind her in an explosion of plaster dust. Dixon felt hot blood rush to his face in prickles of shame. As a veteran Magistrate, he took quiet pride in his ability to aim, fire and shoot with a more than average success rate.

He squeezed the trigger a second time, and this shot went low, aiming for an equally shapely upper thigh. His second shot dug a fist-sized crater in the wall, and the woman kept walking.

Spitting a curse, Dixon bounded toward her, Sin Eater held high to deliver a clubbing blow to her round, perfectly shaped skull. As he brought the barrel of the blaster down against the crown of her head, Royce and a pair of armored Magistrates pounded around the corner.

The metal of the blaster touched the woman's head, and a popping, pinpoint white flash at the contact point sent Dixon flying across the corridor, arms and legs flailing. He crashed loudly into the wall, a network of fine cracks crisscrossing the plaster. He fell face-first to the floor, limbs flopping bonelessly.

The Magistrates rocked to unsteady, stumbling halts. They watched the iridescent woman step into the opposite wall. It seemed to absorb her, like a pebble dropped into the still surface of a pond, except there were no ripples, no sound of a splash. One instant she was there, and in the next she wasn't.

All three of them continued to stare at the blank wall, none of them truly believing what they had just witnessed or willing to admit, even to themselves, that it had even happened.

Royce shook himself, as if coming out of a dream. He glanced from the wall to Dixon slumped on the floor and back to the wall again. "What's on the other side of that?"

Neither of the Mags answered him, nor had he actually expected them to. The layout of the baron's quarters was a total unknown, except to the baron himself and a handful of trusted advisers. Rumors described it as a labyrinth, a maze of secret passageways and hidden chambers.

Striding to Dixon, Royce kneeled beside him and wrestled him onto his back. The man uttered no sound or moved at all, not even when Royce pushed up his visor. Dixon's eyes were open, staring fixedly at the ceiling. Bloody froth flecked his lips. He still lived, but he didn't respond when Royce spoke his name or slapped his cheeks.

His belt comm chirped, and Royce unclipped it, opening the channel. Gage's voice filtered out of it, quavering and faltering. "Sir, I'm in the baron's bedroom...." He trailed his words off helplessly.

"Speak up, Gage," snapped Royce.

The comm transmitted an unsteady exhalation of breath. "He's dead, burned to death looks like."

The corridor seemed to stagger and tilt around Royce. He planted a palm flat against the floor to keep from keeling over. He nearly dropped the comm. Gage continued, "He tried to defend himself—there are bullet holes in the wall. One of his guardsmen is here, too...with his guts hanging out."

Behind Gage's voice, Royce heard hysterical shrieks and cries. "A couple of the baron's staff are in here, sir. Fused-out big-time."

Royce slowly climbed to his feet, fighting to free his mind from its horrified paralysis. "Send the least fused-out of them to me, Gage. Stay there, don't let anybody else in.''

Royce returned the comm to his belt and surveyed the half-hidden faces of his Magistrates, standing there uncertainly, wielding blasters with nothing to shoot at. He realized bitterly he had no idea of what to do next, where his authority began and ended. Under any other circumstances, in any other place, he would have ordered an airtight lockdown. But Alpha Level was like a separate sovereign state within the monolith, within Ragnarville.

As the Mag Division administrator, Barch would most certainly know what steps to take, whom to order around. But a mere commander like himself could only stand dumbly like a dray animal waiting to pull a plow.

A man in a finely tailored, pale orange bodysuit appeared at the far end of the corridor. His graying hair was in disarray, his steps reeling, face wet with tears and mucus. He shied away from Dixon's body as he approached.

Royce snapped, "Who are you?"

Voice thickly blurred by barely repressed sobs, he replied, "I'm Walsh. I made the call."

Walsh was in a very obvious state of shock, and Royce wryly noted that if Gage had chosen him as the least fused of the staff, the others had to be curled up in puddles of their own urine.

Royce jerked a thumb toward the wall. "What's on the other side of that?"

Walsh gaped at him in teary-eyed bewilderment. "What? What's that got to do with anything? Baron Ragnar is dead, murdered in his bed—"

Grabbing a handful of the man's bodysuit, Royce shook him and snarled, "I know that, stupe. His killer went through that wall."

Walsh blinked repeatedly, trying to comprehend the Magistrate's words. "Went *through* the wall?" he snuffled. "How did she go through the wall?"

Royce bared his teeth. "How the fuck do I know how she did it? Is there a room or stairs or a lift back there?"

Walsh shook his head. "I can't tell you that. It's classified information."

Royce released the man, growling wordlessly in disgust. He had half expected Walsh's response. "Whatever is behind that wall, that's where we'll find the baron's assassin."

Dabbing at his wet nose with a sleeve, Walsh said nothing for a long moment. Royce studied the play of conflicting emotions in the man's eyes. At length, he husked out, "We'll check it out. Only you are permitted to come with me."

Turning to the pair of Mags, Royce said, "Get a medic up here for Dixon. Contact Intel section and have them recall the recce squad out in the field. Update them on the situation. I want the division back up to full muster as soon as possible."

He fell into step beside Walsh, accompanying him down the corridor. The man mumbled, "Nothing like this has ever—I mean, I can't believe it happened. It's unthinkable.''

Royce didn't respond to Walsh's litany of denial. He experienced a great deal of difficulty acknowledging a baron's mortality himself. The concept had never occurred to him before. He was forty-two years old, and Baron Ragnar had ruled the ville his entire life, and that of his father's father, as well.

Baron Ragnar was like the sun, always there, immutable, unchanging and, as far as he knew, immortal.

Walsh clutched at the tear-and-mucus dampened front of his bodysuit, squeezing the fabric tightly. He keened, ''What will we do now? What will the Directorate do now?''

Royce swung his head toward him. ''The what?''

Walsh's lips clamped shut, he shook his head furiously, a flood of sudden fear washing away the shocked grief in his eyes. Faintly, he said, ''You didn't hear that. I didn't say the name.''

''You definitely said something,'' Royce grated. ''You said, 'what will the?'''

Walsh cried out beseechingly, desperately, ''I didn't say the name! It's so very important that *I didn't say the name!*''

Royce recognized the symptoms of hysteria. Walsh tottered on the brink of it, and if he fell over, he would be of no further use to him. ''All right, all right,'' he told the man quietly. ''I didn't hear anything. You didn't say the name.''

Walsh whispered gratefully, "Thank you."

They entered a dimly lit branching passageway. It ended abruptly after twenty paces at a flat expanse of wall. Royce saw only a blank wall, then his eyes picked out a tiny keypad, the LED on it glowing green.

Walsh's trembling fingers hovered over the buttons. "You're not authorized to even know about this place, much less enter it."

"Neither was the bitch who chilled Baron Ragnar," Royce retorted angrily. "And she's maybe in there, and we're standing out here on our dicks."

Walsh still hesitated. "Only Barch knows about this."

"He left me in command." Hefting his Sin Eater threateningly, Royce said, "Key us in, or I'll blow it open. Do it."

A shudder racked Walsh's shoulders, and he punched in a three-digit code. An electronic chime rang, and a hairline crack appeared in the wall. It quickly became a seam, running vertically from a point just below the ceiling to the floor. The wall split in half, turning into a double set of doors.

Beyond them, Royce saw a small room, filled with chattering computer consoles and purposefully flickering light panels. On the far side of it was another room, smaller and sparsely furnished with only a table.

Beyond that, atop a raised platform, Royce saw a six-sided chamber made of upstanding slabs of smoked, steel gray armaglass. He stepped into the room full of electronics, sweeping the barrel of his blaster back and forth. Walsh followed uncertainly as he went through the small anteroom and then faced the armaglass chamber. He saw a wedge-shaped handle and another keypad on the door.

"What's in there?" he demanded.

Walsh said, "Nothing."

"Open it."

Swallowing very hard, as if trying to dredge up a shred of resolve from his shocked spirit, Walsh said, "If the woman went in there, she is long gone."

Royce whirled on him, barely able to keep himself from barrel-stroking the man's face. "What do you mean?"

A low whine suddenly sprang from the platform beneath the armaglass chamber. In the electronics room, indicator lights on the consoles flashed, and circuit switching stations clicked. The whine climbed in pitch, swelled in volume to a hurricane howl. Flares of light burst on the other side of the arma-glass portal.

Walsh took a stumbling backward step, crying out, "The gateway is cycling, transmitting someone through!"

Royce wasn't quite sure what the man meant, but the screechy, terrified timbre of his voice motivated him to assume a combat stance, holding his Sin Eater in a two-fisted grip, aiming at the armaglass. He had heard the legends of the gateways, of course. Anyone who had served long in the Magistrate Division was bound to hear some scrap of rumor about the esoteric predark researches involving matter transfer through a device known as a gateway. He had always dismissed the stories as folklore.

The wailing wind noise faded to a whine again, which slowly dwindled. The flashes of light on the other side of the armaglass disappeared. After a moment, the door handle moved.

The slab of armaglass slowly, silently swung outward, pushed from within by a tall figure that definitely wasn't female in form. On second glance, Royce wasn't even certain it was human.

Clad in a thickly padded coverall, the face concealed by scarves and goggles, the figure responded instantly to Royce's bellowed ''Freeze, slagger!''

A familiar, muffled voice demanded, ''What the fuck are you doing in here? Walsh—are you a jolt-brain or what?''

Royce almost gasped in relief at the sound of the voice, but he kept his blaster up and trained. He didn't relax enough to lower it until the figure in the chamber raised its goggles and pulled away the scarves. Barch's single eye was piercing and his dark face etched in lines of anger.

Royce's shoulders sagged, and he allowed his Sin Eater to dangle from the end of one arm. His words came out in an aspirated rush. ''Oh, fucking fireblast, sir. Sorry. You're back. Thank you for being back.''

Barch stepped down from the platform, glancing

from Walsh to Royce. "Yes, I know I'm back. Walsh, you stupe bastard, did you bring him in here?"

Walsh ducked his head. "I had to."

"Had to?" echoed Barch dangerously.

Walsh's tone held far more relief than apprehension. "Circumstances arose, and since Royce here was next in the chain of command—"

Barch interrupted. "Circumstances which forced you to violate our protocols?"

Royce had no idea of the protocols to which his superior referred, and at the moment, he wasn't interested in learning about them. Flatly, he declared, "Sir, Baron Ragnar has been murdered. By a woman."

Both Royce and Walsh waited for Barch's reaction of stunned, helpless disbelief. But his face remained as immobile as a teak carving. His one visible eyebrow raised slightly.

Musingly, he murmured, "Murdered by a woman. It appears I returned from the baron's mission a little too late. But I'm here now."

Royce was no less shaken by Barch's phlegmatic restraint than by the initial report of the baron's murder. All he could think of to say was a hushed "Yes, sir. You're here now."

Chapter 6

There was nothing so disorienting as enduring a matter-transfer jump. During her days of research as a historian in Cobaltville, Brigid Baptiste had read the accounts written by Dr. Mildred Wyeth, who described the symptoms of jump sickness, the pain and nightmares she and her comrades had suffered while traversing the Deathlands via the mat-trans conduits.

Wyeth and the others who had followed the legendary Ryan Cawdor had been forced to jump blind, without the knowledge of how to program specific destination points. As a result, they were subjected to physical and mental tortures that would have tormented the damned.

Even now, with all of the hyperdimensional pathways routed and the destination codes preprogrammed, jumping was still a hell of a way to travel.

Brigid opened her eyes, struggling against a spasm of nausea and vision-clouding vertigo. She blinked, and saw the silvery shimmer fading from the hexagonal metal disks on the floor.

She pushed herself up, leaning against the wall, seeing her companions stirring dazedly on either side of her. Grant groaned, and Domi made a dry-heave retching sound, but she didn't throw up. A few strings of bile dangled from her lips.

She covered her mouth with her hand and said in a faraway whisper, "Feel sick. Big-time sick."

Grant achieved a half-sitting position and glowered at the girl. "Thought you knew better than to eat right before climbing into one of these things."

The white-haired, white-skinned girl wiped away the spittle and reached down to use her pant leg to clean her hand. "Didn't eat," she replied defensively. "Still kind of weak, I guess. Sorry."

Grant said nothing more. He levered himself to his feet, swaying on unsteady legs before straightening up to his full six feet four inches. He was broad shouldered and deep chested, and his high forehead was topped by short gray-sprinkled hair. A down-sweeping mustache showed black against the dark brown of his face.

He reached down with a gloved hand to help Domi to her feet. She took it and stood beside him, smiling up abashedly into his scowl. The two people were a study in complete contrasts, not just physically but emotionally.

Domi barely topped five feet in height, and she couldn't have weighed more than a hundred pounds. Her slender build was insolently curved, with generous hips, long slim legs and perky breasts.

A mop of ragged, close-cropped bone white hair framed her pearly, hollow-cheeked face. Despite her albinism and burning red eyes, she was very pretty.

Raised in the Outlands, she displayed the free style and outspoken, rough manner acquired in the scramble for existence far from the cushioned serfdom of the villes.

Domi held her right arm at a stiff, unnatural angle. A little less than a month before, she had suffered a gunshot wound to the shoulder. DeFore, the Cerberus redoubt's resident medic, had performed major reconstructive surgery, fitting her with an artificial ball-and-socket joint. Only two days before, DeFore had allowed her to shed the sling.

Brigid lithely arose, tossing her loose tumbles of thick, wavy, red-gold hair out of her face. Her big, slightly slanted emerald eyes looked around the chamber. The armaglass walls were tinted a dull red, not the rich brown earth tones of the chamber in Cerberus. In many ways, the color of the armaglass matched that of Domi's eyes. Grant scanned the LCD readout of the motion detector strapped to his left wrist.

"Clear," he announced in his deep, rumbling tones.

Stepping to the door, he heaved up on the handle and pushed it open on its counterbalanced hinges. Beyond lay the antechamber, a combination of ready and recovery room. Beyond it, through the open door, they saw the control room.

Chill air flooded into the gateway unit. Grant buttoned his long, Kevlar-weave black coat. "Cold," he said simply.

Brigid nodded, picking up the canvas sack from the floor. "Northern Minnesota has that reputation, especially at this time of year. During the skydark, it was a deep freeze covering a hundred thousand square miles."

As an ingrained precaution, she checked the small rad counter on the lapel of her coat. The needle wavered at midrange green.

Warily entering the antechamber, Grant asked, "What do you know about this place?"

Brigid assumed he addressed her. Not only was she a former archivist, but she was also the possessor of an eidetic, or "photographic" memory. She instantly and totally recalled in detail everything she had ever seen or read. Given a twenty-digit number, she could repeat it in exact sequence days later. Due to her years as a historian, her mental stockpile of predark knowledge was profound.

In her precise, clipped tone, she answered, "It's about thirty miles southwest of where Duluth used to be, where Ragnarville is now. According to the database, Tango was a medical redoubt where research and experiments in cryonics were conducted. Its main significance is primarily historical."

"How so?"

"This is where Dr. Mildred Wyeth was found in cryogenic stasis and revived by Ryan Cawdor."

Grant nodded distractedly, crossing the antechamber to the doorway. He held Mildred Wyeth in no special regard or esteem. To him, she was just another name from the dark past. Brigid Baptiste viewed her differently. In many ways, for good or for ill, the doctor's memoirs were responsible for Brigid's exile from Cobaltville.

Some thirty years before, a junior archivist in Ragnarville had found an old computer disk containing the journal of Mildred Winona Wyeth, a specialist in cryogenics. She had entered a hospital in late 2000 for minor surgery, but an idiosyncratic reaction to the anesthetic left her in a coma, with her vital signs sinking fast. To save her life, the predark whitecoats had cryonically frozen her.

After her revival nearly a century later, she joined Cawdor and his band of warriors. At one point during her wanderings, she found a working computer and recorded her thoughts, observations and speculations regarding the postnukecaust world, the redoubts and the wonders they contained.

Although the *Wyeth Codex*—as it came to be called—contained recollections of adventures and wanderings, it dealt in the main with her observations, speculations and theories about the environmental conditions of postnukecaust America.

She also delved deeply into the Totality Concept and its many different yet interconnected subdivisions. The many spin-off experiments were applied to an eclectic combination of disciplines, most of them theoretical—artificial intelligence, hyperdimensional physics, genetics and new energy sources. In her journal, Wyeth maintained that the technology simply didn't exist to have created all of the Totality Concept's many wonders—unless it had originated from somewhere and someone else.

Despite her exceptional intelligence and education, Wyeth had no inkling of the true nature of the redoubts, the Totality Concept or even of the involvement of the Archon Directorate, but a number of her extrapolations came very close to the truth.

In the decades following its discovery, the *Wyeth Codex* had been downloaded, copied and disseminated like a virus through the Historical Divisions of the entire ville network.

That particular virus had infected Brigid one morning nearly two years ago, when she found a disk containing the *Codex* at her workstation in the archives. After reading and committing it to memory, she had never been the same woman again. She still wasn't sure if that was a blessing or a curse.

Domi and Brigid followed Grant into the control room. He surveyed the banks and consoles of electronics and computers for a moment, then strode over to an instrument panel bearing the blank screens of a closed-circuit vid system. He thumbed a row of toggle switches, and pale black-and-white images appeared, most of them displaying interior views of the redoubt. They showed nothing but empty, dimly lit corridors. One screen lit up with an exterior view, a wooded, snow-covered landscape silvered by the moon. It looked quiet and almost hauntingly peaceful.

At the sec door, Brigid punched 3-5-2 into the electronic keypad. The slab of vanadium alloy rumbled aside, and she looked down the main corridor. Light strips on the ceiling provided a weak, wavery illumination. The temperature was even colder in the corridor, and she drew her fleece-lined jacket close around her, adjusting the .32-caliber Mauser in its slide-draw holster at the small of her back.

The three people walked into the hallway, checking the rooms on either side of it. They saw pretty much what they expected to see—laboratories, bunks and wardrooms and bathing facilities. A large chamber held cylindrical cryonic-stasis canisters. They were obviously empty, but Brigid had to resist the impulse to see if one of them might have Mildred Wyeth's name on it.

In one of the bunk rooms, Grant and Domi crumpled up sheets, moved furniture around and generally put it in a state of disarray. From her sack, Brigid took dried particles of mud and tossed them liberally over the floor.

In a wardroom, they scraped chairs back and forth repeatedly, making sure they scored the linoleum. They scattered wadded-up self-heat ration packs, paper plates encrusted with old food, turned on the faucets and splashed water over the countertops.

Grant wore his habitual scowl, but he hummed as he worked, obviously taking a certain pride, if not pleasure, in littering. Brigid's neat, almost compulsively tidy nature prevented her from performing an exemplary job of pigging up the place, but Domi and Grant more than made up for her deficiencies.

Grant and Domi went into a bathroom, where they repeatedly flushed three of the toilets in tandem until the pipes couldn't take the load and began overflowing. Brigid heard Domi giggling in a wickedly mischievous manner, and she hoped the half-feral girl didn't decide to urinate in one of the toilets for that extra fillip of evidence that Redoubt Tango had been recently occupied.

Brigid called out, "We want the barons to believe that criminals hid out here, not a fugitive herd of pigs."

Chuckling, Grant called back, "If you put in the years of regimentation I did, you'd find it refreshing to be a slob."

Brigid suppressed an exasperated sigh. "We can show a little restraint."

"A little," called Domi between giggles. "Only a little."

Meeting back out in the corridor, Grant gestured to the passageway. It led to a flight of stairs. "Should the fugitive pigs see what kind of mess they can make topside?"

Brigid shrugged. "I suppose it wouldn't hurt."

Redoubt Tango appeared to be in remarkably good condition, but inasmuch as its primary purpose had been medical, it only made sense. It had little tactical importance, and so was spared even a close nuclear strike. Brigid thought back to the shambles of Redoubt Papa, on the outskirts of Washington, D.C.—or, as it had been called for the past two centuries, Washington Hole. Situated at ground zero, it was a wonder it had remained even marginally intact.

Grant took the point, consulting the motion detector every few yards. The stairs led up to another broad corridor, interchangeable with the one below. They didn't bother to do more than glance into the rooms. Most of the doors were ajar and revealed nothing but emptiness.

Brigid recalled all of the medical equipment at the subterranean installation in Dulce and wondered briefly if much of it had been salvaged from Redoubt Tango.

After several turns, the corridor stretched straight ahead for a hundred feet, terminating at the main entrance sec doors. Grant nodded to them. "Want to take a look-see outside?"

"Let's do," spoke up Domi. "Want some fresh air."

"That fresh air is liable to be below freezing," Brigid commented wryly.

"Don't care. Like to see new places."

They approached the massive, multiton vanadium-steel portals. When they were within two yards of them, a clanking rumble filled the corridor. All three of them rocked to abrupt, simultaneous halts. Hydraulics squealed, pneumatics hissed, gears and cables groaned. The sec door shivered and ponderously rose, like a foot-thick curtain. Dim moonlight spilled in, outlining three pairs of legs on the other side.

Instantly, Grant saw and recognized the standard-issue thick-treaded boots and black polycarbonate shin guards. The Sin Eater blurred into his hand. *"Shit!"* he hissed in a whisper. "Back to the gateway."

They wheeled around and retraced their route in a sprint. Grant brought up the rear, not only so he could have a free field of fire, but also so his Kevlar-sheathed back might provide a modicum of protection for Brigid and Domi. He cast backward glances as he ran, desperately hoping they could reach the first bend in the corridor before the sec door fully rose.

The women reached the turn in the wall. Before Grant followed them, he looked over his shoulder. He saw three armored figures silhouetted at the threshold. One of them stabbed an arm out toward him, voicing a shout of alarm. Between clenched teeth, Grant muttered, "Fucking fireblast."

He assumed the Mags were dispatched from Ragnarville on a recce tour. Sheer rotten timing intersected their respective visits. Dourly, he thought that at least there would be no question about Redoubt Tango's recent occupation.

Brigid, Domi and Grant pelted down the stairs, taking three steps at a time. Domi, as graceful as an albino gazelle, reached the foot of the stairwell first and paused long enough to ask breathlessly, "How many?"

"Looks to be three," Grant barked, catching her by the elbow and hustling her forward. "Maybe more outside."

Brigid had drawn her blaster as she ran and she muttered, "It's all go on this job."

"Yeah," Grant replied. "Isn't it just."

They reached the control room, and Brigid punched in the 2-5-3 code to close and automatically lock the door. As it rumbled shut, Grant moved to the vid console. On one of the screens, he saw the shadowy figures standing at the corner of the first turn in the corridor. The center Magistrate looked agitated, windmilling his arms, gesturing to his comrades. He tapped the side of his helmet, where the comm-link was placed. The vid's sound pickup didn't work, but something was obviously upsetting them. He doubted catching a glimpse of him was the reason, since they hadn't pursued him to the lower level. On the screen displaying the exterior view of the redoubt, Grant saw moonlight glinting dully from the blunt, armored chassis of a Sandcat, parked just outside of a stand of trees.

Domi entered the jump chamber while Brigid entered the destination code into the keypad control. Once the code was entered, the transit cycle would begin automatically with the closing of the door.

A little confused, but more relieved by the lack of action from the Mags, Grant left the console and joined the two women in the gateway unit. He pulled the door shut, the jump-initiator circuitry on the edge of the door and the frame making full contact.

Almost immediately, the disks in the ceiling and floor exuded a shimmery glow. A low hum arose, rising swiftly in pitch. A faint, fine mist wafted up and down from the hexagonal plates above their heads and beneath their feet. The hum suddenly stopped climbing, dropping down to inaudibility. The floor and ceiling plates lost their shimmer.

The three of them stood motionless in the arma-glass enclosure and exchanged baffled looks with each other.

Grant swiftly opened the door again, pulling it closed with such force the disks trembled slightly under their feet. Once again, the ceiling and floor emitter array glowed, the interphase transition coils hummed. And once more, both the shimmer and the sound faded away.

Grant whirled on Brigid, half snarling, "What's happening?"

In a strained voice, jade eyes bright with a building fear, she said, "I don't know. Something seems to be interfering with the matter-stream transmission cycle. We can't achieve a target lock with the Cer-berus unit."

"Mags do it?" Domi demanded.

Brigid shook her head. "I don't know. I doubt it."

Grant opened the chamber door again. He rum-bled, "I guess we can always ask them. They'll be here in a minute."

Chapter 7

The asphalt ribbon of a road leading to Cerberus skirted yawning, hell-deep chasms and dark ravines. The twisted and cracked blacktop stretched up from the foothills of Montana's Bitterroot Range, wending its way around acres of mountainside that collapsed during the nuke-triggered earthquakes of nearly two centuries ago.

The mountains hadn't been known as the Bitterroot Range since before the nukecaust. Succeeding generations ascribed a sinister mythology to them due to their mysteriously shadowed forests and cloud-wreathed peaks. For close to two hundred years, the range had been called the Darks.

The split, furrowed tarmac curved and looped for mile after dangerous mile, finally broadening at a huge plateau at the base of a great, gray peak. The scraps of a chain-link fence bordered the plateau. It was almost impossible for anyone to reach the plateau by foot or by vehicle, and if anyone dared the near impossible and managed to accomplish it, he couldn't do so undetected. Although an intruder couldn't be seen from the road, an elaborate system of heat-sensing warning devices, night-vision vid cameras and motion-trigger alarms surrounded the plateau.

Planted within rocky clefts of the mountain peak and concealed by camouflage netting were the uplinks with an orbiting Vela-class reconnaissance satellite, and a Comsat.

At the base of the peak, recessed into the rock face, was a massive, vanadium-alloy gate. Operated by a punched-in code and a hidden lever control, the gate opened like an accordion, one section folding over another.

On the wall just inside the massive door, rendered in garish primary colors, was a large illustration of a froth-mouthed black hound. Three snarling heads grew out of a single, exaggeratedly muscled neck, their jaws spewing flame and blood between great fangs. Three pairs of crimson eyes blazed malevolently. Underneath the image, in an ornate Gothic script, was written the single word: Cerberus.

The mythological guardian of the gateway to Hades was an appropriate totem for the installation that, for a handful of years, housed the primary subdivision of the Totality Concept's Overproject Whisper, Project Cerberus.

The researches to which Project Cerberus and its personnel had been devoted were locating and traveling hyperdimensional pathways through the quantum stream. Once that had been accomplished, the redoubt became, from the end of one millennium to the beginning of another, a manufacturing facility.

The quantum-interphase mat-trans inducers, known colloquially as "gateways," were built in modular form and shipped to other redoubts.

Most of the related projects had their own hidden bases, like that of Overproject Excalibur, which was in a subterranean complex in New Mexico. The official designations of the redoubts had been based on the old phonetic alphabet used in military radio communications. On the few existing records, the Cerberus installation was listed as Redoubt Bravo, but the dozen people who made the trilevel, thirty-acre facility their home never referred to it as such.

A masterpiece of impenetrability, the Cerberus redoubt had weathered the nukecaust and skydark and all the earth changes that came after. Its radiation shielding was still intact, and its nuclear generators still provided an almost eternal source of power.

The main corridors, twenty feet wide, were made of softly gleaming vanadium alloy. The redoubt had been constructed to provide a comfortable home for well over a hundred people. Now, most of it was full of shadowed passageways, empty rooms and sepulchral silences.

The redoubt possessed a well-equipped armory and two dozen self-contained apartments. There was also a mat-trans gateway unit, a formal theaterlike briefing room, which was too large to be used, a cafeteria, a decontamination center, a medical dispensary, gymnasium with a pool and holding cells on the bottom level.

The nerve center of the installation was the central control complex. A long room with high, vaulted ceilings, it was lined by consoles of dials, switches and computer stations. A huge Mercator relief map of the world spanned the width of one wall. Pinpoints of light shone steadily in almost every country, connected by a thin pattern of glowing lines. They represented the Cerberus network, the locations of all indexed functioning gateway units across the planet.

For the fifth time in as many hours, Mohandas Lakesh Singh studied the webwork of lines and their glowing termination points. A cadaverous apparition of a man, he ran an impatient hand through his sparse, ashlike hair and sighed in his reedy voice.

From his station at the enviro-op station, Bry said testily, "Sir, I'll let you know if there's any activity on the network."

Lakesh turned toward the small, round-shouldered tech with coppery curls. The man always seemed to be in the control center, monitoring, adjusting, tinkering. Over the past few months, Bry had reached the stage where he viewed the center as his personal domain and looked at anyone who entered unbidden as an interloper—even Lakesh, who had been instrumental not only in the construction of the center, but the redoubt itself.

Lakesh peered over the rims of his thick-lensed glasses with the hearing aid attached to the right earpiece and frowned, though he really felt like smiling.

"As long as I'm in here—again—you might as

well give me a status report." His patronizing tone was deliberate.

Bry bristled a bit, but said, "Kane and Rouch made a clean transit to Redoubt Delta. No activity from the unit there yet. Grant, Baptiste and Domi's jump to Redoubt Tango in Minnesota registered fine, too. Like I already told you."

"And their vitals? The transponders are still transmitting?"

With weary impatience, Bry answered, "I would have informed you if they weren't."

The Comsat kept track of Cerberus personnel when they were away from the redoubt through telemetric signals relayed by subcutaneous transponders. The transponder was a nonharmful radioactive chemical that bound itself to the glucose in the blood and a middle layer of epidermis. Based on organic nanotechnology, it transmitted heart rate, brain-wave patterns, respiration and blood count.

The other satellite to which the redoubt was uplinked, the Vela, carried narrow-band multispectral scanners that detected the electromagnetic radiation reflected by every object on Earth, including subsurface geomagnetism. The scanners were tied into a high-resolution photograph-relay system.

Lakesh grunted in response to Bry's statement and turned back to the map.

Peevishly, Bry continued, "No indexed gateways have been activated in nearly three weeks—not since that little spot registering a materialization in Redoubt Zulu.''

Lakesh nodded, tried to put his hands in his pockets, remembered his white bodysuit didn't have pockets, just flapped pouches, and settled for drumming his fingers atop a nearby computer terminal.

The activity on the Zulu transit line was unusual, but not really anomalous. The united baronial search for him and the renegades from Cobaltville had resulted in the opening of long-sealed redoubts. But the gateways had not been utilized. The mat-trans units were still one of the most jealously guarded secrets of the baronial oligarchy.

When the unit in the Alaskan installation had been activated, the matter-stream carrier wave couldn't be traced. It had originated from an unindexed unit. At first, Lakesh had suspected—feared, actually—that the madly ambitious Sindri was making another incursion from his base on the space station *Parallax Red*.

A little over a month before, the ingenious dwarf had sent them, via the Cerberus mat-trans unit, a taunting message that he was still alive and could overcome their security locks. Sindri's theatrical gesture had consequences. The Cereberus computers analyzed and committed to their memory matrixes the modulation frequency of Sindri's carrier and set up a digital block.

Whoever had jumped into Redoubt Zulu hadn't journeyed from the dark side of the Moon. Inasmuch as Zulu lay within the territorial jurisdiction of Ragnarville, the transmitting unit was probably the one reserved for Baron Ragnar and his personal staff and therefore was one of the unindexed, mass-produced, modular units.

An indexed Totality Concept–related redoubt did exist in Minnesota, and the gateway's sensor feed showed no activity. Therefore, Brigid, Grant and Domi had been dispatched to it as their part of Kane's plan.

If the barons of the nine villes could be kept scrambling and confused long enough, trying to follow up on contradictory reports, then Baron Cobalt might forget all about Redoubt Bravo, the former Project Cerberus installation.

Years ago, Lakesh had used Baron Cobalt's trust in him to covertly reactivate the Cerberus redoubt and turn it into a sanctuary for exiles. He had seen to it that the facility was listed as irretrievably unsalvageable on all ville records. He also had altered the modulations of the mat-trans gateway there so the transmissions were untraceable, at least by conventional means. Sindri had proved there were ways of circumventing those precautions, although Lakesh still had no idea of how he managed to do it.

Lakesh turned back toward Bry, opening his mouth to voice a question. He never had the opportunity. When he saw Bry's eyes widen and fix on a point over his head, he spun toward the Mercator map, his gaze seeking out indications of activity along the quantum-interphase conduits.

When he saw the telltale yellow glowing, he said, "Redoubt Zulu again. Mr. Bry...?"

"On it." The tech's hands rattled over the keyboard as he put the autosequence initiator sensor online. "A dematerialization. Someone jumped from Zulu. Still can't lock on to the destination target code."

Lakesh felt his face creasing in a frown. Half to himself, he murmured, "That means whoever jumped there three weeks ago remained until now. Why?"

Bry didn't answer, nor did Lakesh expect him to. Heeling around to face him, he demanded, "The database was searched for all information pertaining to Zulu, wasn't it?"

Bry nodded. "As per your order. Baptiste did it herself, remember?"

Lakesh scowled, not appreciating the inference— no matter how unintentional—that his memory was faulty. "I may be 250 years old, but I'm not senile yet."

Swallowing hard, Bry stated, "Except for its size, Zulu wasn't exceptional. It appeared to have been built primarily as a shelter and stockpile, like a secondary Anthill complex."

Centuries-old memories slowly trickled back into Lakesh's mind. The Anthill installation in South Dakota was constructed as part of the predark Continuity of Government program, only one of a number of subterranean command posts. The Anthill was the most ambitious COG facility, so named because of its resemblance in layout to an ant colony.

"From what Baptiste found in the records," continued Bry, "Zulu wasn't connected to any Totality Concept projects—at least officially."

Lakesh grunted softly, glancing over to the far wall concealing the mainframe computer, and commented, "What the records don't say is probably far more pertinent and troublesome."

Bry cocked his head at a quizzical angle. "Sir?"

Taking a quick, deep breath, Lakesh said, "Perform another data search. Expand it to include these keywords—Angel, Ionosphere, and..." He paused as he dredged up a name from his memory. "Tesla."

"Tesla?" echoed Bry.

"T-e-s-l-a," Lakesh spelled out. "Get it done."

Bry's eyebrows rose, then lowered. He started to speak, but another voice echoed in the vault-walled room. "Sir! I need you!"

Lakesh turned and looked into the frightened face of Banks. The thin black man was as agitated as Lakesh had ever seen him, and seemed almost on the verge of a faint, using the frame of the control center's open door for support. His face glistened with beads of sweat.

"Banks, what is it?" Lakesh swiftly approached the young man. The distress in the man's voice worried him, although he maintained a poker face and a calm tone. He couldn't recall seeing him so worked up in the four years he had known him.

Try as he might, Lakesh couldn't keep a note of alarm from his voice. "What's wrong with Balam?"

Banks struggled to catch his breath. "You need to see for yourself."

Lakesh realized the man had raced all the way from the holding facility to this part of the complex. "I didn't want to use the intercom...you have to see and experience it in person."

"Very well, lead the way, then," Lakesh said easily. He patted Banks on the shoulder and donned his most friendly codger's smile to soothe the other man's obviously scrambled nerves. "Let's take a look at the little gray bastard together, shall we?"

Banks nodded and walked slightly ahead of Lakesh, turning back and speaking as he retraced his path back to the holding area. "It was the damnedest thing. Business as usual, just like it's been for the last three and a half years. I'd just fed him...." Banks did a poor job of repressing a shudder. "Well, you know what it's like."

"I do indeed, friend Banks," Lakesh replied. Balam didn't eat so much as absorb nutrients through the pores of his skin by a process of osmosis while lying in a liquid mixture of cattle blood and peroxide. It was a sickening sight despite the fact that once a week Banks synthesized the mixture himself.

"He hadn't been in the dip more than a minute," continued Banks, "when he started rejecting it."

Lakesh blinked in surprise. "Rejecting it? How so? By regurgitation?"

Banks nibbled his underlip. "Sort of. Vomiting and—" He broke off. "Like I said, you'll have to see it for yourself. And there's something else."

Lakesh suppressed a sigh. "I was afraid there would be."

"You know how I can tune out his telepathic pressure, resist his mind games?"

Lakesh nodded. Banks was one of two Cerberus personnel adept at tuning out Balam's telepathic touch. Lakesh was the only other one who had successfully learned the trick of focusing past Balam's constant mental urgings, so it was a barely noticeable stimulus on the fringes of his awareness.

Banks went on, "But this...I've never felt him give off vibes like this. What metabolic signs our instruments are able to monitor went off the scale, everything higher than the norm."

The two men stopped at the door leading into the facility housing Balam. Banks reached down and punched in a six-digit number rapidly with his forefinger on the keypad. An electronic buzz sounded, and the lock clicked open.

Banks and Lakesh stepped through the door, closing it swiftly behind them. Lakesh immediately winced at the sensation of queasiness awakening in his belly and the sudden twinge of pain stabbing between his eyes. He shivered, his skin prickling as if ants crawled over it, marching up and down his spine.

Banks asked quietly, "See what I mean?"

Lakesh only nodded, slitting his eyes as he tried to deal with the physical manifestation of psionically transmitted pain. The large, low-ceilinged room looked the same as it had when he had last visited it: computer keyboards and monitors lined up on their own individual desks, along with a control console that ran the length of the right-hand wall. The multitude of telltales and readouts on the console glowed green and amber indicating that the environmental and life-sign controls functioned smoothly. The medical monitor displayed a pair of flashing icons, but since they had been adjusted to approximately read Balam's vitals, their meaning was unreliable.

Lakesh's delicate olfactory senses recoiled from the astringent smell of the peroxide and blood Banks had prepared. The room always smelled vaguely of antiseptic and hot copper as a result of the trestle tables loaded down with glass beakers, Bunsen burners and chemical filtration systems.

The left wall of the room was constructed of heavy panes of clear glass, and beyond that wall in the near darkness was Balam's lair. Lakesh stepped closer to the glass and squinted, trying to see into the crimson-tinged gloom. The indirect lighting provided by a single overhead light strip provided little illumination for human eyes, but Lakesh believed he could discern the shape of Balam's sustenance trough, as well as the head and shoulders of the entity himself. There was no movement.

"Bring up the lights inside, Banks," Lakesh said. "We'll have to forego Balam's comfort for the moment until we can figure out what brought on this condition."

Lakesh spoke tightly, between clenched teeth. Although the sensation of nausea and the head pain hadn't increased, he was starting to feel very ill. Perspiration broke out on his deeply lined forehead, trickling down his seamed cheeks.

Banks stepped over to the master console panel and gently turned a knob in order to boost the lighting system inside the glass-enclosed room. The red illumination brightened and intensified, giving the scene within a properly hellish air.

Balam was seated in a sarcophaguslike tub made of a transparent polymer. Two flexible hoses were connected to it at opposing midway points. The hoses, in turn, were connected to a metal tank with two valve wheels projecting from the top. His slender body was submerged up to the shoulders in dark liquid, the red light making it look rust brown. A string of the thick fluid drooled from the toothless slit of his mouth, and his high, pale gray cranium was covered by a constellation of tiny blood dots, like thousands of pinpricks. The stench of wet cardboard Balam normally gave off seemed unusually pronounced.

Lakesh saw that the bloody mixture was spattered on the floor and walls, trickling down the glass, giving the cell the look of a high-tech abattoir. He was able to catch only a glimpse of the entity's fathomless, tip-tilted eyes and narrow features before Balam erected his hypnotic screen, a telepathic defense that clouded human perceptions and concealed his appearance from the ape kin who held him captive. A shapeless mass of red-hued shadows thickened and seemed to swallow him. The psionic gesture reminded Lakesh of a bather indignantly yanking a shower curtain closed to disappoint voyeurs.

Almost at the same time, Lakesh's nausea and headache abated.

Consulting the medical monitors, Banks announced, "His vitals are returning to normal levels. The high-stress indicator is flattening out."

Lakesh turned away from the glass. "So is my own discomfort. What about yours?"

A little startled, Banks said, "You're right. I feel better." In an uncertain tone, he added, "Maybe we should go in there."

Lakesh didn't reply immediately. The concept of unlocking and entering Balam's cell had never occurred to him in the three years the entity had been at Cerberus. When he thought about Banks's suggestion, fear seemed to paralyze the reasoning centers of his brain.

He had always conscientiously and consciously tried not to view Balam as a monster. An enemy, yes, but not an inhuman, soulless demon, despite the fact the creature patently was not part of humanity—at least humanity as he defined the term.

"Sir?" Banks gazed at him expectantly.

Lakesh shook his head, stepping away from the transparent wall. "I see no immediate need. Whatever crisis Balam underwent, it appears to have passed."

Banks shook his head, frowned. "I've never seen him react to anything like that before. I mean, the synth was literally jumping out of his body, through the pores of his skin. He was puking it up, too. To be on the safe side, maybe DeFore should take a look at him."

Lakesh forced a smile, gesturing behind him to the red-tinged murk. "Take a look at what? She wouldn't be able to see him to examine him. Besides, I think pan-terrestrial biology is a bit outside of the good doctor's field of expertise."

He moved to the door, and Banks called after him, "What do you think happened? Is he dying?"

Lakesh shrugged. "Perhaps. He is exceptionally old, at least on the order of three hundred years. Or perhaps you simply mixed up a batch of synth that disagreed with him." He cast a keen stare at Banks. "Either way, why do you care?"

Banks wet his lips nervously. He answered falteringly, "It's not that I care, exactly…I've just gotten used to him. Sort of."

Lakesh chuckled. "I understand. Sort of. Continue to monitor him. Let me know if there is any change."

As soon he stepped out into the corridor, the smile fled Lakesh's lips. He didn't want to think about Balam or the Archon Directorate, but he couldn't leash his memories or even his theories.

Hundreds of years ago, when humanity dreamed of reaching the stars, speculation about the extraterrestrial life-forms they might encounter inevitably followed. The issue of interaction, of communication with aliens, had consumed a number of government think tanks for many decades.

As Lakesh discovered in the waning years of the twentieth century, all of that hypothesizing was nothing but a diversion, a smoke screen to hide the truth. Humankind's interaction with a nonhuman species had begun at the dawn of Earth's history. That relationship and communication had continued unbroken for thousands of years, cloaked by ritual, religion and mystical traditions.

For that matter, it was still an open question if the Archons were truly aliens, a species apart from humanity, or simply different. No one knew for certain if they had their origins on another planet, another dimension or even another time plane.

Wherever they came from, they didn't refer to themselves as Archons. The term derived from ancient gnostic texts referring to a parahuman force devoted to imprisoning the spark of the divine in the human soul.

Though the existence of the Archon Directorate was a secret known only to a few, it's agenda wasn't a matter of conjecture, and hadn't been in nearly two centuries. Historically, the Archons made alliances with certain individuals or governments, who in turn reaped the benefits of power and wealth.

Following this pattern, the Archons made their advanced technology available to the American military in order to fully develop the Totality Concept. It was the use of that technology, without a full understanding of it, that brought on the nuclear holocaust of 2001.

The apocalypse fit with Archon strategy. After a century, with the destruction of social structures and severe depopulation, the Archons allied themselves with the nine most powerful barons. They distributed predark technology to them and helped to establish the ville political system, all to consolidate their power over Earth and its disenfranchised, spiritually beaten human inhabitants.

The goal of unifying the world, with all nonessential and nonproductive humans eliminated or hybridized, was so close to completion that a counterargument wasn't even an argument; it was hair-splitting.

He easily recalled the telepathic message Balam imparted several weeks ago when Kane had tried to provoke him into a dialogue.

Humanity must have a purpose, and only a single vision can give it purpose...your race was dying of despair. Your race had lost its passion to live and to create. We unified you.

Even after two centuries, Lakesh still felt a near suicidal despair at the memories of the part he had played in that unification. In the late 1980s, after his promotion to Project Cerberus overseer, he was initiated into the covert pact between elements of the military and the Archon Directive, as it was called at that time. Prior to January, 2001, Lakesh moved to the Anthill installation, where he cryonically slept through the nukecaust and skydark.

Revived fifty years ago, he received organ transplants and prosthetic replacements in order for him to best help the Program of Unification go forward. He was not the only predark scientist to be resurrected to aid the final shaping of ville governments.

When he finally understood the full magnitude of the horrors the Archons had wrought on humanity, he determined to fight them secretly. For decades he served as chief archivist in the Cobaltville Historical Division as well as a high-ranking member of the Trust.

He also engaged in highly unethical genetic tampering, hoping to create warriors for his cause, and created a straw adversary called the Preservationists, a fictitious group of scholars and seditionists, to draw attention away from his real work at Cerberus.

Lakesh bitterly turned over the words in his mind. His "real work" was more than likely only a real delusion. As Kane had pointed out numerous times, a war that was already lost couldn't be fought. A new one had to be waged.

Cotta and Farrell passed him in the corridor, but he was only dimly aware of exchanging greetings with them. He was engrossed in reviewing a secret hypothesis he harbored about the Archons and their agenda. He had never spoken of it, or written it down. It usually came to him in the wee, black hours of early morning, the midnight of the soul.

He pondered if the Archons might not be pawns themselves—puppets of vast, dark intelligences toying at will with humanity, wreaking havoc with perceptions and belief systems. He couldn't come up with a why. Perhaps it had simple entertainment value. And perhaps—just perhaps—Balam was only a puppet.

Lakesh had seen his first representative of the Archons in the Dulce installation. In the company of an Air Force general, he peered through an observation port and glimpsed the small, compact creature with huge black eyes set in an equally oversize cranium.

Although he watched the entity for less than a minute, the scene was burned indelibly into his memory for all time. He could easily recall his terror, his incredulity, his denial.

Now he wondered if that Archon might not have been Balam. On a mission to Russia, a colonel in the Internal Security Network had related to Brigid, Kane and Grant how a creature called Balam had been found in a cryogenic-suspension canister at the site of the Tunguska disaster. He had lain buried for over three decades, until the end of World War II. He was revived, spending several years as a guest of the Soviets before being traded to the West.

During the Cerberus team's op to the British Isles, the self-proclaimed Lord Strongbow informed them that as part of his duties as a liaison officer between the Totality Concept's Mission Snowbird and Project Sigma, he dealt directly with a representative of the Archons, a creature called Balam.

It seemed obvious that Balam had acted as something of a liaison officer himself, an ambassador of the Archon Directive throughout the latter half of the twentieth century. In light of the information gathered in Russia and Britain, Lakesh suspected Balam might be something else—the only and perhaps last Archon on Earth.

He knew twentieth-century exobiologists had postulated that all Archons were anchored to one another through hyperspatial filaments of psionic energy, much like the hive mind of certain insect species. He had always assumed the mind link was passive, and therefore Balam couldn't clearly communicate to his brethren of his captivity.

Lakesh contemplated the possibility that Balam no longer had brethren with which to communicate. If such were the true situation, it would explain a great deal, particularly the hybridization program. And if Balam was indeed the last of his kind, then there was no Archon Directorate, just like there was no real group called the Preservationists.

The Oz Effect, Lakesh mused, wherein a single, vulnerable entity created the illusion, the myth of an all-powerful force as a means of manipulation and self-protection.

Lakesh returned to the control center. As soon as he stepped through the door, console lights flashed, power-gauge needles wavered. A humming tone vibrated from the gateway chamber, but it sounded different, with a strange screechy note underlying it. He threw a quick glance at the map and saw two lights glowing simultaneously, thousands of miles apart. The mat-trans units in Redoubts Delta and Tango were both trying to achieve a destination lock on the Cerberus gateway.

Both Bry and Lakesh rushed across the control center and through the anteroom. Facing the deep-brown-hued armaglass door of the jump chamber, they saw swirls of light fluttering on the other side. The droning hum climbed, faltered, then tried to climb again.

"Two conflicting matter-stream carriers," Bry cried. "They're trying to cycle through the materialization process at the same time!"

Lakesh stared, utterly bewildered. A fail-safe device normally came on-line when simultaneous transmits from two different units were attempted, shutting down both gateways for a twenty-minute interval. Through the armaglass shielding, he saw blurred shapes appear, outlines fluttering.

Bry moaned, a sound of disbelief and horror. "The emergency shutdown isn't working. We're losing their molecular resolution."

Whirling on him, Lakesh shouted, "Stop gawking and get to the pattern-enhancement boosters! Move, or we may lose all of them!"

Chapter 8

Kane braced himself on the tabletop, leaning over it, hanging his head and doing his best not to throw up. The few shots of pop-skull he had downed in Boontown percolated in his stomach like lava, threatening to erupt up his throat.

Through the kettle-drum pounding in his ears, he dimly heard Lakesh say, "Damn fortunate the auto-sequence receptors registered your patterns a millisecond before the others."

Kane lifted his head, blinking back the sweat flowing from his hairline and cutting runnels in the layer of mud caked on his face. Foul water dripped slowly from his clothing, beading on the varnished tabletop. Rouch lay in a fetal position on the table, moaning and gagging.

"What do you mean?" he managed to rasp.

In a voice equal parts relief and anxiety, Lakesh replied, "Brigid, Grant and Domi tried to return here at the same time you and Beth-Li initiated the transit cycle. The two carrier waves intersected and overlapped for a microinstant. The timing was in your favor."

Raising a trembling hand to his perspiration-pebbled brow, Kane muttered, "Yeah, I sure feel favored."

DeFore and her aide Auerbach, entered the anteroom. Auerbach rolled a gurney behind him. DeFore's dark brown eyes flicked over Kane and Rouch, then settled on Rouch as the person requiring immediate attention.

Bending over her, DeFore timed her pulse at throat and wrist, peeled back an eyelid, listened to her respiration. Kane pushed himself back from the table. His headache and nausea ebbed a bit, although he still felt rubbery kneed.

"What about Brigid and the others?" he asked.

From the doorway leading to the control center, Bry said, "Their transponders still show strong readings, but their heart rates and blood pressure are a little elevated."

Lakesh glanced to Kane. "They're all right," he said reassuringly, glancing at his wrist chron. "They'll try again. Their unit will automatically reset itself in about ten minutes."

DeFore looked up, her full lips compressed in a moue of disapproval. "Rouch is in a mild state of shock. Mild cardiac arrhythmia. How about you, Kane? How are you feeling?"

"Lousy, but I'll get by."

"You probably look—and smell—worse than you feel." The buxom, bronze-skinned medic turned to Auerbach. "Put her on the gurney and take her to the dispensary. We need to get her heart rate under control.''

Kane didn't feel up to responding to the woman's acerbic observation regarding his appearance and odor. She didn't disguise her dislike of him—or rather, what he represented to her. In her eyes, as a former Magistrate, he embodied the strutting arrogance of ville law enforcement, glorying in his baron-sanctioned power to deal death indiscriminately.

She also believed that because of his Magistrate conditioning, he was unable to reconcile his past with his present and the psychological conflict had him teetering on the brink of nervous collapse. Therefore, Kane couldn't be trusted.

DeFore had presented her diagnosis and prognosis to Lakesh, who had refused to act on it, so she wasn't particularly happy with him, either.

Auerbach gently lifted Rouch onto the gurney and wheeled her out of the room. DeFore regarded Kane with a cold, critical eye. ''I know you could care less, but you need to visit decam and get out of those wet rags.''

Kane only nodded. He had already figured that out for himself. Though the bayou held no dangerous residual radiation, the water he had waded through was probably contaminated with all sorts of chemical toxins.

He began to ask her to keep him apprised of Rouch's condition, but DeFore spun smartly on her heel, presenting him with the intricate French braid at the back of her ash-blond head. She marched away. Kane glared at the braid a moment before turning to Lakesh.

"If they're not back here in a few minutes, I'm going after them."

Lakesh nodded reluctantly. "Let's give them a little while. For now, you should follow the doctor's orders. I think she may appreciate it."

"Yeah," Kane replied with bleak humor. "If I don't, she'll probably use barbed wire the next time she has to stitch me up. But I'll wait a bit longer."

OUT IN THE CORRIDOR, Grant and Brigid listened to the stealthy footfalls of the pointman approaching from around the corner. Both held their blasters ready, though Grant felt Brigid's choice of arms to be so ineffectual against polycarbonate body armor she might as well have brandished a slingshot.

Not only would the .32-caliber rounds not penetrate the Magistrates' exoskeletons, but the targets wouldn't even feel the impacts. As a former Mag, Grant knew all of the armor's weak points, and they were exceptionally difficult to penetrate. After a recent encounter with Cobaltville enforcers, he took pains to load his Sin Eater's clip with armor-piercing rounds taken from the Cerberus arsenal.

They were of predark manufacture, since AP rounds had been outlawed during the unification. For that matter, any kind of blaster, even home-forged muzzle loaders, in the hands of anyone other than Magistrates was a capital offense.

Grant didn't want to engage in a firefight. Although the Mags didn't outnumber the Cerberus team, they definitely outgunned them. Aside from their Sin Eaters, they carried Copperheads, wicked, stripped-down autoblasters capable of firing all of their fifteen 4.85 mm rounds in seconds.

Domi wasn't armed at all. Grant had prevailed on her not to carry her preferred weapon, a .45-caliber Detonics Combat Master. Still recovering from her shoulder injury and subsequent surgery, her slight frame didn't have the strength to handle its recoil. Besides, he hadn't envisioned a situation where she would need it.

He should've know better, Grant sourly told himself. None of the missions he had undertaken since joining the Cerberus exiles had adhered to plan, no matter how intricately they had been constructed.

Straining his ears, he heard the faint squeak of polycarbonate joints and the slight scuff of treaded boot soles on the floor. He heard something else, as well—unsteady respiration, the exhalations and inhalations of air high and irregular. The pointman sounded as if he was more than nervous. He breathed as though he were frightened or dreadfully upset.

Grant didn't hazard a peek around the corner. He kept his eyes on the motion detector, watching the green dot that represented the Mag sliding over the small LCD screen toward the center position.

He tensed, waiting and listening. When he estimated the pointman was less than six feet away from
the bend in the corridor wall, he made his move,
swiftly and smoothly.

Leaning out around the corner, Grant led with his
Sin Eater. The Magistrate was closer than he calculated, barely four feet away. The exposed lower portion of his face showed his mouth twisting in shock.
His voice a low boom, Grant said, "Boo," and
squeezed the trigger.

The round penetrated the red duty badge affixed
to the molded left pectoral, punching a hole through
the hub of the nine-spoked-wheel insignia.

The thunderous crash of the single shot seemed to
shake the walls and ceiling. The reverberations rolled
and surged down the corridor like a wave.

The Magistrate flailed backward, as if he had been
jerked by an invisible cable attached to his belt. The
rear of his helmet struck the slick floor first and skid-
ded along it for a few feet before his body collapsed.
His weapons clattered loudly. A geyser of bright ar-
terial blood squirted up from the perforation in his
badge, splashing the nearest wall with a crimson
streak.

Grant ducked back around the corner, consulting
the motion detector. The LCD showed blank. The
other two Mags remained out of the instrument's sensor range. He hoped if the pointman's comrades were
as distressed as he had been, they'd continue to hang
back.

A second later, the detector uttered a soft beep and a pair of pulsing dots appeared at the far edge of the LCD.

At once a full-auto fusillade of blasterfire burst down the corridor. The Copperheads stuttered, sending a hailstorm of lead spattering against the walls, striking sparks from the vanadium sheathing, ricocheting with wild, keening wails.

Grant turned his back, hunching his head between his shoulders so the wide collar of his coat would offer some protection for the back of his head. Brigid crouched down, grimacing at the racket and the astringent, sweetish odor of cordite.

A ricocheting bullet plucked at Grant's coat sleeve. The Mags seemed determined to empty their subguns, but Grant didn't sense they did so out of fear. Rage drove them.

The dry snapping of firing pins striking empty chambers replaced the double trip-hammering and the shriek of ricochets. Empty shell casings clanked against the floor. A few seconds later came the mechanical clicking sounds of spent clips being ejected and fresh ones jammed into place.

A voice hoarse with fury bellowed down the corridor, echoing hollowly. "You fuckin' traitor, you fuckin' slaggin' assassin, you ain't walkin' away from this!"

Another voice, deeper but no less quivering with outrage, roared, "Think you can chill a baron and live to laugh about it? It won't happen, you bastard. You hear me? *It won't happen!*"

Grant's and Brigid's eyes met, widening in confused astonishment. She straightened up and, before Grant could stop her, she shouted, "What are you stupes talking about?"

Growling a curse, Grant gestured sharply for her to keep quiet. He had wanted the Mags to think they had cornered only one man. Brigid and her Mauser weren't much in the way of backup, but they were better than nothing.

The sound of the female voice seemed to surprise the Magistrates, then galvanize them to even greater heights of anger. The first man who had spoken shrieked, "You got the *woman* with you? The fuckin' bitch who chilled Baron Ragnar herself?"

A tremor of fear undercut the man's tone, but fury overwhelmed it.

Grant called, "You stupes are fused out. We don't know anything about your baron."

As his voice rebounded from the walls, he waited for the Mags' reaction to his words of denial. He didn't have to wait long. With howls of homicidal lust, the Magistrates charged down the corridor, both of them firing their Sin Eaters and Copperheads in a simultaneous frenzy.

The reports blended, mixed, creating a deafening cacophony. Rounds struck the walls, gouging them with shiny smears, chipping out fragments from the corner. Grant snarled in wordless frustration and pushed Brigid ahead of him toward the open door of the mat-trans control room.

He wasn't about to stand his ground and exchange fire with a pair of berserk Mags, AP rounds or not. Chances were he might get one of them, but chances were far greater that one of them would get him.

They reached the doorway, and Brigid hastily keyed in the close code. As the portal slid shut, at least a dozen bullets struck it, sounding like a work gang pounding on it with sledgehammers.

Fearfully, Domi peered around the open door of the jump chamber. "We're safe in here, right?"

"I'm sure they've been briefed on the entry codes," Brigid replied. "They can get in here if they want to."

Another, heavier storm of slugs clanged against the door.

"And they really want to," remarked Grant darkly.

"Even if we can't make a jump," stated Brigid, trying to suppress the quaver of fear lurking in her voice, "we can hold them off in the chamber. They probably don't know about the gateways at all, certainly not about the security lock code. And they can't shoot through the armaglass."

"No, but they can starve us out," Grant retorted. "Or call in reinforcements with high explosives and blow our asses out of there."

"I can always enter the destination code for an

alternate unit,'' Brigid said, eyeing the keypad. ''Jump luck.''

The blasterfire stopped. Grant glanced to the vanadium door. The Mags had leashed their emotions and were probably discussing strategy on the other side of it.

''I doubt we'll have more than one chance to get out of here,'' he said grimly. ''Once the Mags get in, we'll be stuck in the chamber.''

Curtly, Domi declared, ''Whatever we're going to do, let's do it.''

Brigid sank her teeth into her lower lip. ''Cerberus, then.''

The three people entered the gateway, Brigid pausing momentarily to punch in the lock code. As Grant sealed it, he heard the pneumatic hissing of the sec door at the control room wall. He stayed where he was, head pressed against wall, listening.

The humming drone arose as circuitry engaged. The hexagons shimmered and danced with silver. Outside the chamber, the blasterfire began anew. Bullets smashed themselves into shapeless blobs, black against the red of the armaglass walls. Grant stepped back, wondering briefly if this situation qualified as a one-percenter.

Chapter 9

Bry called from the control center, "Activity on the unit in Redoubt Tango. A dematerialization."

Kane glanced toward the brown-tinted armaglass enclosing the jump chamber and waited for it to do something. When it didn't, he cast an impatient, questioning glance toward Lakesh.

Striving for a tone of reassurance, Lakesh said, "You know traversing the quantum pathways isn't necessarily instantaneous. Sometimes it is, sometimes it isn't."

Kane didn't reply, but he knew from experience that mat-trans jumping occasionally resulted in minor temporal anomalies—like arriving at a destination three seconds before the origin jump-initiator had actually engaged. Lakesh had stated more than once that the nature of time couldn't be measured or accurately perceived in the quantum stream. That brief temporal dilation was the primary reason Overproject Whisper's Operation Chronos had used reconfigured gateway units in their time-traveling experiments.

From the jump chamber, a sound like a fierce rushing wind grew, rising louder and louder. Bright light flashed behind the armaglass, swelling in intensity and in tandem with the hurricane noise. Within seconds, both the light and sound faded.

Kane grabbed the door handle, ignoring the weak jolt of static electricity shooting through his fingers, and wrenched up on it. Through the curling fingers of dissipating white mist, he saw two blaster bores pointing up at his head. The tense, grim faces of Grant and Brigid appeared behind them. Their tight expressions almost immediately went slack with relief, and they lowered their weapons.

"What's with the guns?" Kane demanded.

"Sorry," Brigid replied, pushing herself to her feet. "Couldn't see the color of the armaglass for a couple of seconds. Thought the demat cycle might've failed and we were still back in Tango."

The unholstered Sin Eater in Grant's hand was a definite violation of basic security precautions. The Sin Eaters weren't equipped with safety switches, so a reflexive jerk of the finger while reviving from the transit process could result in fatal consequences for the rest of the jump team. But he knew Grant wouldn't have disobeyed the protocols unless the circumstances were extreme.

He stepped aside, allowing Brigid, Grant and Domi to exit. If any of them found his odor disagreeable, they were too polite to comment on it. In Grant's case, his sense of smell was too impaired, inasmuch as his nose had been broken three times in the past and never properly reset.

"Thank God," Lakesh said fervently. "Thank God you made it back."

Grant glared at him as he pushed his blaster back into its holster under his coat sleeve. His distrust of the mat-trans units was only a little weaker than his suspicion that Lakesh didn't know as much about them as he claimed.

"We damn near didn't," he rumbled. "The piece of shit in Minnesota malfunctioned on us."

"It didn't malfunction," Lakesh retorted, a bit peeved by having one his creations compared to excrement. "It functioned according to design."

Brigid quirked a challenging eyebrow at him. "How so?"

He curtly explained about the fail-safe devices installed in the gateway operational systems. "It's a standard safety feature, developed with the prototype."

"Wasn't safe for us," piped up Domi. Now that the danger was past, she was in a cheery humor. "Nearly got us chilled by Mags."

"Mags?" Kane echoed.

Grant nodded grimly. "A three-man recce squad. Lousy timing all around."

Brigid unbuttoned her jacket. "Something else, too. They accused us of assassinating Baron Ragnar."

Grant frowned toward her. "It was more like they accused you."

Brigid's announcement put expressions of incredulity on the faces of Lakesh and Kane. It required both men several moments to speak.

"Assassinated?" Lakesh's reedy voice held a strident, skeptical note.

"Evidently by a woman," Brigid replied stolidly. "They didn't supply details. They were fused out, almost hysterical."

Grant pursed his lips contemplatively. "Now that I think about it, I get the impression they'd just learned about it...right after they entered the redoubt."

"You're right," Brigid agreed. "They spotted us, but didn't seem inclined to chase us for a few minutes. Maybe the information was relayed to them right after they saw us."

Impatiently, Kane said, "Just what went on in there?"

Grant nodded to Brigid, who supplied a full report.

Afterward, Lakesh shook his head, dumbfounded. "A baron hasn't been murdered since—well, never. Not since the advent of the unification program when the oligarchy was established. For that matter, I don't think a baron has even died of natural causes."

No one commented on Lakesh's words. If the nine barons weren't immortal, they were as close as a flesh-and-blood creature could come to it. Due to their hybrid metabolisms, their longevities far exceeded those of humans. Barring accidents, illnesses—or assassinations—the barons' life spans could conceivably be measured by centuries. Even Lakesh wasn't certain how long they lived.

But the price paid by the barons for their extended life spans wasn't cheap. They were fragile physically, prone to lethargy. Their vitality had to be sustained during annual visits to the Dulce installation. There they underwent medical treatments to reverse deterioration of their mingled genetic material. The entire scope of the procedures and treatments was unknown even to Lakesh.

Squinting at Brigid, he inquired, "You say a woman killed him?"

"That's what one of the Mags said—or rather, screamed."

"Could an insurrection be brewing?" Kane asked.

Lakesh's furrowed brow acquired new and deeper grooves. "Anything is possible. But for a baron to be murdered within his own ville—presumably inside the Administrative Monolith—it just doesn't seem likely."

All of them understood what he meant. One of the reasons the barons were such mysterious, awe-inspiring figures was that they rarely left their impregnable aeries. Only a month before, the deranged Baron Sharpe had accompanied a Magistrate squad on an incursion to Redoubt Papa.

Although he had been tricked into it by a vengeance-minded councilor, circumstances put him under Kane's gun. As of yet, no Intel had filtered in from Sharpeville indicating whether the baron had survived the encounter.

Grant declared, "Every defense always has a hole in it. Somebody found it, that's all. The question is who."

Lakesh shook his head in disgust. "The other barons won't ask that question. They already have their answer. No doubt you, Kane and Brigid will be named as the culprits."

He gusted out his breath in a sigh. "And thus your legend grows. From turncoat seditionists to baron-blasters."

Kane shrugged, and drops of foul-smelling water dripped from his clothing. "I don't mind taking credit for blasting a baron."

Domi asked, "What will happen in ville now, with baron chilled?"

Lakesh imitated Kane's shrug. "As far as I know, there is no proviso for dealing with a power vacuum in the ville chain of command. Presumably, the highest ranking member of the Trust might assume the post temporarily. But—"

He shook his head again, his voice trailing off.

"You don't know?" Grant asked, a taunting note in his voice.

A bit resentfully, Lakesh admitted, "No, I don't. I suppose since genetic samples of all the barons are in storage at Dulce, a duplicate of Baron Ragnar might be developed through a form of cloning. But that is only supposition."

"Or," Brigid ventured, "the Archon Directorate might actually take an active hand."

Lakesh's usually slumped posture straightened, his rheumy blue eyes glinting behind the lenses of his spectacles. He swiftly consulted his wrist chron. "The timing seems about right. It can't be a coincidence."

"What can't?" demanded Kane.

"About forty minutes ago, Banks reported highly unusual behavior in Balam. As best as I can describe it, Balam underwent a short period of traumatic shock."

"So?" Grant asked.

"As you know, the standard theory is that Archon minds are linked in a psionic community."

Brigid frowned slightly. "A passive link, an almost subliminal awareness of one another, right? You said they would sense the absence of another mind filament. Are you suggesting that Balam reacted to the death of Baron Ragnar? But he's not an Archon, not really."

"It's only one solution that fits the provisional facts," Lakesh replied. "And it makes perfect sense that such a psi-link would be bred into the barons— more of a puppet string leading directly to the puppet masters than a channel of communication."

"This is all very fascinating," said Kane dryly, "but I think the next course of action undertaken by the barons should concern us the most."

"They may have to consult with the Directorate itself before they do anything," Brigid argued.

Lakesh muttered, "If there indeed truly is such a thing."

All eyes fixed on him with intense, questioning gaze. Lakesh cleared his throat uncomfortably. "Strike that last. Yet another of my endless theories. Friend Kane, you need to visit decam. Dearest Brigid, there's a matter I want to discuss with you."

He gestured dismissively to Domi and Grant. "Be about your business. Welcome back, and all of that."

Taking Brigid by the elbow, Lakesh led her out of the anteroom.

Kane commented snidely, "He's given us our marching orders for the rest of the day—or night."

If Lakesh overheard, he gave no indication.

They strode through the sweeping expanse of the control complex. Brigid, Bry and Lakesh were already huddled around a computer terminal at the far end of it, paying no attention as they passed by. Kane tried not to feel irritated. Unless risk taking or blood-letting was pending, Lakesh often behaved as if he had no use for any of them but Baptiste. The woman could do no wrong in the old man's eyes, even though Kane knew the two had argued bitterly over matters of Cerberus policy in the recent past.

Most of the time, Kane attributed Lakesh's marked favoritism for Baptiste to their long relationship in Cobaltville's Historical Division. Lakesh had held senior status there, and Baptiste was one of his subordinates. He had selected her to join the resistance group in the redoubt.

But on occasion, their relationship seemed far deeper than that of a mentor and student. Certainly it was not sexual in nature—it veered very close to the paternal, and was markedly different from the fondness Lakesh displayed toward Domi.

Kane shrugged mentally as he, Domi and Grant exited into the corridor. "DeFore ordered me to decam," he told them. "What about you two?"

Grant shook his head. "We're clean, which can't be said for you."

"That for sure," Domi said vehemently. "Way you smell, make me homesick."

Home for Domi had been a squalid Outland settlement on the banks of the Snake River in Hell's Canyon, Idaho.

Kane took a strip of hanging cloth and squeezed it, wringing out a flow of rancid water. Grant and Domi made an exaggerated show of stepping around it and continuing on their way.

The albino girl's unabashed devotion to Grant was the source of whispered jokes and rumors among the redoubt's personnel. She was enamored of Grant and very jealous if she perceived he paid attention to another woman—or if she suspected another woman paid attention to him.

Even Kane, who had been partnered with Grant for over a dozen years, wasn't sure of the true extent and nature of their relationship. He sourly reflected that he wasn't sure of the true nature of *anybody's* relationship, including his and Baptiste's.

The dispensary was adjacent to decam, so he entered to check on Rouch's condition. Only Auerbach was there, adjusting the height of one of the three examination beds. To Kane's question, the burly, red-haired man replied sullenly, "DeFore checked her out a few minutes ago."

"She felt better, then?"

Auerbach grunted, not deigning to look in his direction. "Suppose so."

Kane felt a flash of annoyance at the man's disinterested tone and manner, as if he begrudged every word he spoke to him. He had heard that Auerbach had an unrequited crush on Baptiste, but due to his fear of Kane he never acted on it. And since Rouch was fairly up-front about her mission to bear Kane's child, the opportunities for the other men in Cerberus were limited.

Auerbach probably felt—and justifiably—that Kane didn't deserve such an embarrassment of carnal treasures, regardless of whether he took advantage of them.

Decam was a wide, white-tiled shower room with four partitioned cubicles. Wegmann was pulling attendant duty and he held his nose as Kane stripped off his muddy garments and dropped them in a receptacle. Standard procedure was to decontaminate clothing, too, but the balding man eyed the rags with loathing. "Surely you don't want to keep those nasty-ass things."

Kane thought about the likelihood of impersonating a swamp-dweller again in the near future and shook his head. "Take them down to maintenance and use them to wipe the machines."

"Like hell," Wegmann retorted. "It's already filthy enough down there. I'll burn 'em instead."

In the shower stall, a warm mixture of liquid disinfectant and sterilizing fluid sprayed from the faucet. The needle of the rad counter affixed to the tiled wall registered only low-yellow readings. Kane massaged the decam stream into his body and made a shampoo out of it for his hair.

Dark puddles formed at his feet, swirling down into the floor drain. He stayed beneath the shower longer than was necessary, even after the rad counter's needle flicked over into the green band. He felt more than dirty; he felt defiled and he wanted to scrub every microscopic bit of the bayou from his pores.

When his fingertips wrinkled and turned pink, he decided he was as decontaminated as he was likely to be. He rinsed himself with jets of cold, clear water.

He felt much better when he stepped out of the cubicle and put on a robe. He walked to his private quarters, a four-room suite substantially larger and better appointed than his old flat in the residential Enclaves of Cobaltville.

In the bathroom, Kane shaved away the three-day

growth of beard stubble. Patting his face dry with a towel, he walked into his bedroom. He didn't immediately see Rouch there.

She sat on the edge of the bed, dressed in a form-fitting white bodysuit. In Rouch's case, it seemed to fit her form tighter than usual.

"I knocked," she said, "but when no one answered, I let myself in."

Although the door to Kane's living quarters had a lock, his flat in Cobaltville didn't. He had never acquired the habit of locking his door.

"I checked on you," he said, discreetly making sure his robe was closed. "Auerbach said you were feeling better."

Rouch chuckled warmly. "A lot better. Tell me something—did you really knife a slagger in the swamp?"

Kane favored her with a sudden slit-eyed stare. "Why do you ask?"

She tossed her fall of jet-black hair behind her shoulders. "Think about it—you end a life, and here I am so you can start a new one."

Kane didn't respond, but it required all of his self-control not to roll his eyes rudely ceilingward. He bore no personal grudge against Rouch, but Lakesh's interest in improving the breed and turning Cerberus into a colony was a different matter. To Kane, it was a continuation of sinister elements that had brought about the nukecaust and the tyranny of the villes. The Totality Concept's Overproject Excalibur dealt with bioengineering and one of its subdivisions, Scenario Joshua, had sprung from the twentieth century's Genome Project. The goal of this undertaking was to map human genomes to specific chromosomal functions and locations in order to have on hand in vitro genetic samples of the best of the best, the purest of the pure.

Everyone who enjoyed full ville citizenship was a descendant of the Genome Project. Sometimes a particular gene carrying a desirable trait was grafted to an unrelated egg, or an undesirable gene removed. Despite many failures, when there was a success, it was replicated over and over, occasionally with variations. Lakesh had admitted that Kane was one such success, one that he himself had covertly been involved with.

Some forty years ago, when Lakesh determined to build a resistance movement against the baronies, he riffled Scenario Joshua's genetic records to find the qualifications he deemed the most desirable. He used the Archon Directorate's own fixation with purity control against them. By his own confession, he was a physicist cast in the role of an archivist, pretending to be a geneticist, manipulating a political system that was still in a state of flux.

From a strictly clinical point of view, what Lakesh wanted to do now made sense. To ensure that Kane's superior qualities were passed on, mating him with another woman who met the standards of purity control was the most logical course of action. Without access to the ectogenesis techniques of fetal development outside the womb, the conventional means of procreation was the only option.

However, Kane couldn't view the situation as clinically as Lakesh or as expectantly as Rouch. Far too many emotional factors were at work.

"Listen, Rouch—" he began gently.

She broke in, "Call me Beth-Li, please."

Kane nodded and continued, "What Lakesh wants is what Lakesh wants. Neither one of us has to go along with it."

She uttered a low laugh and stood up, languorously unzipping the front of her bodysuit. "It's what I want, too."

Rouch wore no underclothes, and Kane wasn't surprised. She stepped out of the one-piece garment and approached him with a feline grace, smiling in such a way that showed she knew he found her beautiful.

Kane couldn't help but find her slender, compact body beautiful. He flicked his gaze over her firm, pear-shaped breasts with their hard, dark nipples, her flaring hips and flat-muscled belly. The dark tuft at the juncture of her thighs was a perfect triangle.

She stared at him boldly. "It's been a long time since I had a man, Kane. And you haven't touched a woman since you came here."

He ruefully thought back to his brief dalliance with Morrigan aboard the *Cromwell,* and his even briefer encounter with the mad Fand in Ireland. So, technically, Rouch was wrong, but he didn't feel inclined to correct her.

The sweat of tension formed on his body, and he felt the physical stirring her naked proximity and sensual voice invoked in him. "What makes you so sure of that?" he asked gruffly.

She laughed again, fingers insinuating themselves under his robe and lightly caressing his chest. "I can see it in your eyes. You're suffering. Let me ease it."

Kane felt a longing come upon him, a longing he had put aside every day, every night for months. But it wasn't a longing for Rouch.

"Is it me?" he asked, "or the fact that I spilled a poor mutie bastard's blood that's making you hot?"

"Both do," she replied, cupping his face with her hands. She stared up at him levelly. "I know men like you want a fuck-dessert after a blood feast."

Despite himself, Kane felt his body responding to her, to the musky scent and heat radiating from her body. He hardened and rose and he had difficulty breathing.

As his hands reached for her, he thought again of Morrigan, of Fand and of Baptiste. What he did next was not easy, but it was the only thing he could do. He thrust Rouch away from him, but not without a pang of regret that was almost painful.

Matter-of-factly, he said, "I don't need this complication."

Her dark eyes flared in anger. "What's complicated about it? Plant your seed in me, let me carry it. We can have fun doing it. No other woman here is suited for you. Baptiste can't bear your offspring even if she wanted to.''

He was so occupied trying to get his body's reactions under control, the oddity of Rouch's comment didn't penetrate for a moment. When it did, his fingers tightened on her bare shoulders. She winced, but made no attempt to twist out of his grasp.

''What do you mean?'' he demanded.

Rouch started to speak, but the warbling from the trans-comm unit on the wall cut her off.

Brigid Baptiste's voice floated out of it. ''Kane, are you there?''

The Cerberus trans-comm channels were voice activated, and Rouch knew it. She turned her head toward it and called, ''He's busy. Leave us alone.''

Kane growled, ''You little bitch,'' and stepped to the unit. ''What is it?''

The response was so long in coming Kane almost repeated the question. When Brigid spoke again, her tone was ice-cold. ''We've found something that might have bearing on Baron Ragnar's assassination. It'll keep until you're not busy.''

''I'll be there in a couple of minutes.''

''Take your time. I want to change clothes and have a bite to eat.''

She closed the channel with a preemptive click.

Rouch put her hands on her hips and threw him a smugly triumphant smile. ''Now that she's given you her permission, can we get on with it? We can take as much or as little time as you want.''

Kane glared at her. Under the icy intensity of his eyes, the smile faltered, then left her lips. ''Get out,'' he grated.

A stricken look crossed her face. ''But—''

Bending down, he snatched up her bodysuit and flung it at her. ''Get dressed and go. Or don't get dressed. Either way, go.''

Anger flared in her dark eyes, twisted her features. ''You'll regret this, Kane.''

He bestowed a hard, cold smile on her. ''Be careful what you say, Beth-Li. Almost everyone else who directed that lousy cliché at me boarded the last train West.''

For an instant, Rouch appeared confused, not understanding the old Deathlands jargon. When she grasped the context, she hugged her clothing tightly and took a backward step. Her sudden fear seemed a little exaggerated.

''Are you threatening me? I'll tell Lakesh.''

''I'm not threatening you. And there's no need to tell Lakesh. I'll speak to him myself. And I'll tell him this, too—if he wants Cerberus to become a colony, that's his business. But participation is voluntary. I'll be the one to decide if I want my seed spread and who carries it. Not him or you.''

Rouch whirled away, hissing over her bare shoulder, ''There are other men here, Kane. I'll visit one of them.''

She stalked out of the bedroom with an arrogant twitch of her backside. Kane wondered if she would get dressed before leaving his quarters, but when he heard the door open and click shut, he knew she hadn't bothered. Domi had been known to stroll nude through the redoubt, so if Rouch wanted to do the same, it wasn't without precedent. He thought it probable she hoped to bump into Baptiste on her way to her own quarters.

Swallowing a weary sigh, Kane went to the closet and removed a bodysuit from a hanger, a bit surprised he felt so little genuine anger toward Rouch and even less toward Lakesh.

The cooperation among the Cerberus exiles was only a spoken agreement; there were no formal oaths or vows like the ones he and Grant had taken upon admission into the Magistrate Division. There was no system of penalties or punishments if cooperation was not given.

There were security protocols to be observed, certain assigned duties that had to be performed, but anything other than those was a matter of persuasion and volunteerism.

Kane had certainly not volunteered to take part in Lakesh's breeding plan. Still, he couldn't help but wonder why he felt a twinge of jealousy at Rouch's statement about other men.

Chapter 10

Shortly after the lifting of a frosty dawn, the storm moved into Ragnarville. That in itself wasn't unusual. Ice storms with 250-mile-per-hour winds once roared out of Canada, and toxic, acidic rains used to lash the landscape with a seasonal frequency. The aftereffects of skydark still lingered in some regions.

Though weather patterns could only be counted on to be capricious, this storm was different. A mountainous thunderhead skimmed out of the north on a direct course with the ville, blotting out the sky above the spire of the Administrative Monolith. The floating, billowing mass thickened rapidly, casting deep shadow over the entire perimeter of Ragnarville, bringing a sudden and oppressive gloom. The atmospheric pressure seemed to increase, pressing against eardrums, making respiration labored.

Down in the Tartarus Pits, eyes still blurred from sleep turned upward from the muddy streets to watch the stormy blackness slowly lowering and spreading like a blanket. Strange luminescence flashed within its roiling center, like arcs of heat lightning. A hollowly booming thunderclap made the ramshackle buildings tremble.

The underside of the cloud surged out, belling downward. From this sparkled glowing motes, showering down like a glittering snow flurry. As the motes fell, tiny whistling noises cut through the chill air. Black-rimmed holes appeared in the white rockcrete facade of the monolith, little curls of smoke rising from them.

A Pit dweller, face upturned, suddenly screamed in agony. He dropped to his knees on the sludge-covered lane, clawing at his face, smoke wisping from the black, empty socket of his right eye.

People echoed his scream, stampeding for shelter, jerking with the impact of the tiny, glowing drops. As the drops fell, they became globules, hissing and sending up clouds of steam as they struck the wet streets. Flames exploded on the dry-rotted roofs of some of the older squats. Crowds herded to any cover they could find, the panicky crush a near riot. Children were bowled off their feet, trampled and kicked as the air fogged with the falling, fiery globules.

A thread of writhing white fury emerged from the boiling center of the cloud and caressed the exterior of the Administrative Monolith, between Levels A and B. Several square yards of rockcrete erupted from its columnar surface, the glass panes in two of the slit-shaped windows bursting inward. Thunder boomed and echoed.

The storm slowly began to drift away from Ragnarville, nudged by the wind. On Level C of the monolith, a wide, square section of the facade rose.

As it ascended, giant groaning gears and squealing pulleys extended a long flat slab like a metal-riveted, squared-off tongue. Three Deathbirds rested upon it, secured by cables attached to eyebolts sunk deep in the slab. All three of the helicopters were sleek, compact and streamlined, painted a matte-finish, nonreflective black. The curving forward ports were tinted in smoky hues. The metal-sheathed stub wings carried thirty-two 57 mm unguided missiles, two full pods to a wing. Multibarreled .50-caliber miniguns protruded from chin turrets beneath the cockpits.

Mechs scurried out of the cavernous opening on the side of the tower, unhooking the cables from the landing skids on the center Deathbird. Two black-armored Magistrates, a pilot and his gunner, climbed into the cockpit and keyed the engine to life. The rotor blades whirled, inscribing a hazy circle.

The aircraft lifted from the pad, turned and streaked over the walls in pursuit of the cloud. It reached the trailing edge of the dark mass and cut a circling course around it.

The chopper suddenly swerved as if caught in a blast of wind sweeping out of the thunderhead. Bucking up and down, wobbling to and fro, the pilot fought the controls, attempting to level off the Deathbird and move away from the cloud at the same time.

For a long span of seconds, the aircraft seemed to hang, floating suspended in the sky. Then, with a whine of overstressed engines, it managed to bank swiftly away. Ascending at a sharp angle, it leveled off a hundred feet above the cloud and assumed a hovering position.

Crooked flares of white lightning erupted out of the top layer of the cloud formation. They whiplashed around the belly of the Deathbird, and for an instant a skein of electricity danced over the fuselage like a crackling web.

The helicopter heeled over and plunged straight down, tumbling into the thunderhead itself. It vanished, swallowed up by the billowing darkness.

When the Deathbird reappeared, it was tearing through the bottom layer of the cloud formation, spilling downward in a wild, gyrating spin. The portside stub wing buckled back as it plummeted.

The Deathbird spiraled down, tail assembly grotesquely pointing at the underside of the cloud, foreport on a direct vertical line with the ground. It plunged to the horizon. A faraway concussion shook the air. A burst of smoke, a tongue of orange flame and flying dust mushroomed up in a plume.

TERRIFIED CRIES TORE from the lips of the onlookers assembled at the open hangar door. Royce muttered breathlessly, "What could have done that? Lightning that strikes *up?* It's like the cloud—"

He broke off as Barch turned and looked at him. He asked, "The cloud was like what?"

Royce tried to meet Barch's one-eyed stare, but he couldn't. "Like nothing, sir."

"Go ahead," Barch urged in a surprisingly soft voice. "Speak."

Hoarsely, Royce said, "Like the storm was intelligent—or controlled."

A hard, humorless half smile quirked the corner of Barch's mouth. "Do you think that's possible?"

Royce shook his head. "I don't know. I didn't think it was possible for the baron to be fried in his bed, either."

Bleakly, he added, "Maybe there's a connection. Maybe the ville is cursed—"

He broke off, realizing he was voicing private fears and how foolish they sounded. He waited for a stern rebuke from Barch, but it didn't come. Instead, his superior barked orders to the milling Magistrate Division personnel to retract the pad, close the hangar bay doors and dispatch a squad to the crash site.

Royce watched him and listened to his commanding tone and he wondered, just for a moment, why Barch had ordered the Bird flyover of the storm and why he didn't appear more distraught about the loss of one of the rare aircraft—not to mention a pair of highly trained Bird jockeys. Neither the Deathbirds nor the men who knew how to fly them were commonplace.

But, since now Barch claimed to be in command of Ragnarville, no one questioned him. Certainly none of the other division administrators had lodged objections to his assumption of authority. They were relieved someone had.

As the huge hangar door rumbled down, Barch imperiously gestured for Royce to follow him as he walked through the cavernous bay. They passed the two Deathbirds remaining in Ragnarville's fleet, and exited into the main corridor. Royce trailed Barch past the office suites, training rooms and the Intel section.

When they entered Royce's small, oval-shaped office, Barch took the chair behind the desk. He waved him to the only other chair and, after Royce seated himself, he announced without preamble, "I'm appointing you Magistrate Division administrator."

Royce's mind froze in stunned disbelief. True, he had reached the age where the mandatory transfer to an administrative position was pending, but to be given the power and responsibility over the entire division wasn't a promotion he had ever dreamed could happen. On reflection, he wasn't certain if he wanted it to happen.

After several false starts, he managed to get his tongue, voice box and brain working more or less in tandem again. "Sir, *you're* the administrator."

Barch leaned back in the chair, linking his hands behind his hairless head. "As of today, I'm relinquishing that post and assuming authority over Ragnarville and its territory. You're one of my own, Royce, and I need one of my own to take over as administrator. I don't trust anyone else."

Royce coughed self-consciously. "Is this only a temporary arrangement, sir?"

Barch narrowed his eye. "Temporary?"

"Until a new baron is named."

A grin stretched Barch's lips. "For all intents and purposes, I am the new baron. Wouldn't you agree?"

Royce's shocked mind wheeled with questions, alarm and conjecture. All he really knew about the barons was that they were part of an oligarchy, elevated and removed from the common human herd. For a man he had known for years—a man he respected as intelligent, resourceful—to proclaim himself baron smacked of heresy. Barch, for all of his gifts and abilities, was still only a human like himself.

The grin disappeared from Barch's face. In a steel-edged voice, he repeated, "Wouldn't you agree?"

Royce nodded. "I would."

Barch continued to stare at him, his cyclopean gaze unblinking and menacing.

Royce groped for the right words, then ventured, "My lord baron."

Barch laughed and leaned forward, propping his elbows on the desk. "Of course, I don't expect you to address me that way in public—at least not right away. First things first. I want you to select a dozen of the bravest and the brightest from the division ranks. Are all of our officers accounted for?"

"All but three. Hadley, Brewer and Arnam. As per our orders, I sent them to recce the redoubt—" Barch's eye flickered with a fleeting, indefinable emotion, but Royce plunged on "—where they encountered two, possibly more intruders. One was a woman.''

Barch's face locked in a tight, grim mask. ''Outlanders, probably.''

Royce shook his head. ''No, sir. One of them chilled Arnam. According to the radio report I received, he was chilled with a Sin Eater.''

Barch's reaction wasn't what Royce expected. The grim mask of his face didn't alter. ''Were the intruders apprehended?''

Royce fidgeted in his chair, not knowing how or even wanting to answer the question. ''Permission to speak freely?''

Barch inclined his head a fraction of an inch in a nod.

Inhaling a deep breath, and then exhaling it, Royce stated as unemotionally as he could, ''According to Brewer and Hadley, the intruders escaped by a means they could not understand or even really describe in a way that made sense. If I hadn't seen you step out of that armaglass chamber on Level A, I wouldn't have known what they were talking about.''

Barch steepled his fingers under his chin. Very quietly, he said, ''A gateway unit. You and your recce squad saw something not meant to be seen by uninitiated eyes.''

Royce uneasily recalled Barch's recriminations to Walsh only a few hours ago about the violation of protocol. At the time, he didn't know what he meant, but now a fearful understanding crept into his mind.

"Fortunately for you," Barch continued smoothly, "as administrator of the division, you will be initiated."

Royce didn't feel relief. Not responding to the comment, he said, "The intruders had something to do with the baron's death, or they were the assassins themselves. I ordered Hadley and Brewer to remain there until further notice. They have two days' worth of rations in the wag."

"Under the circumstances, you made the correct decision," Barch replied. "However, I don't think the intruders in the redoubt need concern us overmuch. If they are part of a larger conspiracy to overthrow Ragnarville, they are only pawns."

"Conspiracy?" Royce echoed.

Barch spread his hands wide. "What else could it be? The baron and one his guardsmen murdered, a bizarre storm. None of these events can be coincidental. That's why I want the formation of a task force so we can not only ferret out the conspirators that may be in our midst, but also to act immediately if and when another assault comes our way.

"They don't have to be blooded hard-contact Mags, but I prefer that they are. I also need a halfdozen tech-heads, the higher the seniority the better. After you've made your choices, send their psych profiles to me for review."

"You suspect traitors in Ragnarville?" Royce tried to smother the skepticism in his tone, but he knew he only half managed it.

"An inside job is the only explanation. A small handful of seditionists within the ville are colluding with the Preservationists."

Every Mag in every ville knew about the Preservationists. They had served as a culprit for a variety of crimes for decades, a shadowy menace drifting in and out of the baronies like smoke.

Royce nodded. "I understand. How soon do you need the profiles?"

Barch heaved himself out of the chair with a screech of springs. "I needed them about three weeks ago. I'll settle for two hours from now."

Royce stood up as Barch moved around the desk. Barch clapped him on the shoulder as he walked to the door. "The next few days will be tough, but if you believe in me, I promise you the rewards will be more than worth it."

Royce waited until Barch strode into the corridor before murmuring, "That's what the fuck I'm afraid of."

Chapter 11

From his chair in front of the VGA monitor screen, Lakesh said, "We've discovered...something." He fell silent.

Kane waited. He looked over to Bry, who was hunched over a computer terminal on the far side of the control complex, then cast his eyes over to Grant. He saw the mental shrug in his otherwise expressionless eyes. Apparently, Grant was going to remain quiet and let Lakesh move forward with his discovery when the old man was good and ready.

Kane was not so patient. He prompted, "Discovered what? Baptiste said you'd come across something that might connect to Baron Ragnar's death."

"I'll explain in a moment, friend Kane. As soon as Brigid arrives, we'll hold a full briefing."

As Lakesh spoke the last word of the sentence, Brigid strode in with her characteristic mannish stride. A few wisps of her red-gold hair peeking out of the severe bun at the back of her skull were the only evidence she'd been hurrying. She had changed into a bodysuit that clung in all the right places to her tall, willowy body. She wore the badge of her former office as an archivist, a pair of wire-rimmed, rectangular-lensed spectacles.

"You're late," Kane groused.

Brigid didn't respond, keeping her attention on the seated Lakesh. "Sorry."

"Nonsense, you're right on time," Lakesh said with a broad smile. "For a change, friends Kane and Grant were early."

Brigid cast a cool glance toward Kane. "I told you to take your time. I figured you and Rouch would be busy for a while."

Kane scowled at her and opened his mouth to say something profane. Lakesh interjected hastily, "Yes, well, perhaps later you and Brigid can discuss your differing interpretations of 'busy.' At the moment, there is something else to consider."

Kane closed his mouth. Rather than argue, he waited for the cadaverous man to reveal the reason the three of them had been summoned to the control center.

"So, what's wrong up there?" Brigid asked the room.

"Where?" Kane growled.

"There," she replied, pointing a finger at the upper corner of the Mercator map. "In Alaska."

Kane felt as though he and Grant were both unruly students trapped in some godawful geography class, with Baptiste standing tall and proud as the teacher's pet.

"There's a problem in Redoubt Zulu?" Grant

asked, taking note of the winking light that was alternating between the colors of amber and green.

"Of a sort," Lakesh told him. "In some ways, more of a mystery, but it could have a promising, perhaps even beneficial solution."

"How so?"

"As we know, someone visited the redoubt some three weeks ago. Only a couple of hours ago, coinciding with the alleged murder of Baron Ragnar and Balam's outburst, the sensors registered new activity on the mat-trans jump lines. A demat and a mat."

"Seems like more and more people are becoming aware of what was once a secret method of getting around," Kane remarked.

"All of the barons are aware of the units, and in order to carry out searches, others must be informed. Such is the way. And someone perhaps abusing those secrets is also the way."

Grant turned to Lakesh. "Is there anything in that redoubt worth abusing? According to the Intel you pulled from the database, it was built to be a stockpile...and it was cleaned out during unification."

Lakesh consulted a sheaf of printout. "We performed a deeper, more comprehensive search, using other keywords. From the classified information we've been able to access from the database, Redoubt Zulu also served as a primary HAARP installation."

Kane and Grant stiffened at the mention of the word *harp*.

"Harp?" Kane demanded. "Did I hear you right?"

The word held unpleasant connotations for them, instantly bringing to mind their painful encounters with infrasound weapons in the shape of the musical instruments.

"Obviously, HAARP is an acronym, Kane," Brigid stated with only the slightest dash of dry sarcasm. "It's got nothing to do with the Danaan. Or Martian trolls."

"That's good to know, Baptiste," Kane retorted curtly. "I was afraid we might have to hang up our blasters and go out into the field armed with tubas." He hated himself for being baited, and hated himself even more for allowing his voice to rise in timbre when he snapped back at her.

Before Brigid could select from the half-dozen or more rejoinders that appeared on the slate of her fertile mind, Lakesh broke in quickly, "HAARP is indeed an acronym. It stood for 'High-frequency Active Auroral Research Program.'"

"Which still tells me nothing," said Kane.

"That makes two of us," Grant agreed.

"Allow me to enlighten the pair of you, friend Grant. After all, that is the reason for a briefing session, is it not?"

Grant nodded affirmative and kept silent, his heavy-jawed black face set in a frown. Lakesh took the silence as a cue to continue, using his free hand to reach over and click a small switch on the tabletop, which caused the four-foot-square VGA monitor screen to flare into life. On it appeared a predark map of the most northward addition to the United States, the landmass of Alaska.

"During the early part of the nineties," he said, "a decade or so before the nuclear conflagration, the HAARP facility was assembled on a military base in Alaska. This was a joint project between the Air Force and the Navy, at least, a joint project for cover-story purposes. In actuality, the United States was working closely with a Russian team, who had their own version of HAARP, known as SURA."

"Once a pissing contest, always a pissing contest," Kane said sourly.

"Quite the vulgar simile, friend Kane. But also quite true. HAARP had several parts, most interesting being the IRI, or Ionospheric Research Instrument. At the time of its construction, the IRI was the largest high-frequency radio transmitter ever built."

"Purpose being communications?" asked Grant.

"Not exactly. It was designed to concentrate several thousand megawatts into an intense beam of almost unimaginable strength, transmitted through miles of planar antenna arrays on the shortwave band."

"And then?"

"HAARP was able to facilitate enormous changes to the upper atmosphere with a focused and steerable electromagnetic beam, generating enormously high degrees of heat. In fact, according to the documentation of the time, HAARP was better known and described as being an ionospheric heater."

"A heater." Grant repeated. He cast an incredulous look at Kane.

Lakesh caught the eye exchange and said impatiently, "Of the ionosphere, yes. Almost a reversal of what a radio telescope is—the HAARP antennaes send out signals instead of receiving, and their destination is very close to home."

"So the ionosphere is what, part of the atmosphere?" Kane asked. Both he and Grant were far from being dense, but parts of Lakesh's dissertation fell on dead zones in their limited educations. "What's this thing good for? Heating up cold spots or something?"

"Close, friend Kane. The ionosphere is the electrically charged sphere surrounding Earth's upper atmosphere. Understand, the ionosphere is an active electrical shield protecting our planet from the constant bombardment of high-energy particles from space. Working in conjunction with the Earth's magnetic field, all sorts of harmful types of cosmic radiation are prevented from coming down below.

"Usually, the ionosphere is approximately forty to sixty miles above the surface of the planet, keeping the danger away. However, full activation of the HAARP project would have brought this much closer to home. And as such, was considered fair game for the military. The former Department of Defense believed that the HAARP project would give them incredible means of communication far beyond their current capabilities.''

"All of this talk reminds me of a banned book I once read during a slow moment in the Cobaltville archives,'' Brigid said thoughtfully. "A man named Gordon J. F. MacDonald wrote and published a book entitled *Unless Peace Comes*.''

"Ah, Professor MacDonald. I met him once,'' Lakesh said. "Back in the 1960s, he was associate director of the Institute of Geophysics and Planetary Physics at the University of California. He was quite keen on the use of environmental-control technologies for military purposes. Hadn't thought about the fellow in years, but now you've jogged my memory.''

"There was a chapter in his book called 'How to Wreck the Environment,' '' she stated. "He described something similar to HAARP in order to affect and control the weather, climate modification, polar ice-cap melting or destabilization, ozone-depletion techniques, earthquake engineering, ocean-wave control and even brain-wave manipulation using the earth's energy fields.''

"There you go.'' Lakesh leaned back in his chair and folded his arms over his chest.

"Well, if this HAARP thing can do all of that,'' Kane demanded, "why wasn't it ever used?''

"Who's to say it wasn't?'' the old man said. "I imagine it was buried under the usual reams of paperwork and misinformation. Unlike the Totality

Concept projects, which none but politicians and military personnel with the highest classifications were aware of, HAARP was an open book, at least, superficially. The more informed public minds knew it was there, and it scared the hell out of them, but since the military had taken great pains to hide the secret in plain sight, not much was ever accomplished.''

"The 'Purloined Letter' principle," Brigid commented with a wan smile.

Neither Grant nor Kane knew what she meant, but Lakesh chuckled appreciatively.

"Just so. My theory is that while the capabilities of the HAARP installation might have been tested in some degrees, the full capability of the antenna array was never fully utilized. There wasn't enough time. Lack of funds and lack of time.''

"So it wasn't part of the Totality Concept?" asked Kane.

Lakesh shook his head. "The scientific background of HAARP predated the Totality Concept by decades.''

He rapidly typed a few commands on the keyboard of the terminal before him. The screen cleared of the Alaskan map, and a photograph replaced it. It was the image of a man with a mustache and hairstyle that hadn't been worn in over three hundred years. The man looked bemused, looking off camera at something only he could see. From the black-and-white tones of the photo, the period dress, and the man's appearance, Kane knew he looked at someone dead long before the nukecaust.

"Nikola Tesla," Lakesh announced. "Arguably, the greatest inventor who ever lived. He shares credit with his student, Marconi, for the invention of radio and he also discovered alternating current. Back in 1899, Tesla built a transmitting tower on top of a Colorado mountain as his first experiment in utilizing the electromagnetic radiation of Earth to provide a free energy source.

"His intent was to use the Earth as a huge resonant system, his writings contain references to 'the terrestrial stationary waves,' a resonant excitation of the ground, the magnetosphere or even the 'wave guide' between the two. Tesla boasted that he'd done this on a trial scale, using superpowerful 'magnifying transformers' like his tower in Colorado.

"Around 1901, Tesla proposed his 'world system.' Specifically, Tesla anticipated very-low-frequency global navigation, radar, Morse telegraphy with ships at sea, multiplexing, remote-controlled weapons and pretty much the rest of the terrestrial postmodern technosphere."

Grant crossed his arms over his broad chest. "Did any of this really work?"

Lakesh shrugged. "Twentieth-century conspiracy theorists claimed Tesla's wireless power distribution actually worked too well. It's one of those great, unprovable, Frankenstein tales, half antigovernment paranoia, half fear of science."

Kane shifted his feet impatiently. "Assuming Redoubt Zulu was part of the HAARP project and assuming someone is visiting it, why is that supposed to concern us? Even if the antenna array still exists, so what if it's put back on-line?"

Brigid spoke up matter-of-factly. "If the apparatus for HAARP is still operable, it will function like the reversal of the old radio telescopes. It focuses a giant gigawatt electromagnetic beam on the ionosphere, which bounces back to Earth and penetrates everything. The reflected beam can travel along the planet's magnetic mantle, and the impulses will vibrate geomagnetic flux lines. If aimed and pulsed with the proper precision, you'd have an instant earthquake."

"Or," interjected Lakesh, "the lower atmosphere can be disrupted to create weather from hell, of the likes not seen since skydark."

Grant's eyes narrowed with suspicion. "Weather control?"

"Weather warfare," Lakesh replied. "For decades, the Department of Defense developed methods to manipulate storms in Projects Skyfire and Stormfury. In 1994, they announced a master weather-control program called Spacecast 2020. Is it a coincidence this program dovetailed with the completion of the HAARP installation?" He shook his head. "I don't think so."

"There's more to it than that," declared Brigid.

Kane didn't bother to suppress an exaggerated sigh. "Isn't there always?"

Affecting not to have heard the comment, she continued, "Pulsed-radio-frequency radiation, the very stuff HAARP is based on, can disturb and manipulate human mental processes. In other words, mind control. Electromagnetic waves can produce mild to severe physiological disruption or perceptual distortion."

Grant shook his head. "All right, you've convinced me that HAARP could be put to destructive uses. *Could* be. I'm still waiting to be convinced that this somehow connects to Baron Ragnar's death and the activity at Redoubt Zulu's mat-trans unit."

Lakesh regarded him stonily. "I don't believe in coincidence, friend Grant. Baron Ragnar's apparent assassination at the hands of parties unknown coming on the heels of transit-path traffic to and from Zulu— a redoubt under Ragnarville's jurisdiction—points to something other than mere happenstance. It demands investigation."

Grant thrust his jaw out truculently. "The last time we investigated activity in a redoubt, we ended up on Mars."

Both Kane and Brigid couldn't help but smile, and after a moment, Lakesh did, too. "I can't offer absolute assurance that you won't visit another celestial body, but I can assure you that the implications of an operational HAARP are worse than dire."

"Hell," snapped Kane, "you say that about every op you plan for us."

"Haven't they been?" Lakesh challenged. "Or rather, once you've undertaken them, they prove to be worse than I initially outlined?"

Kane mentally reviewed all the prior ops he, Brigid and Grant had performed since arriving at Cerberus. Grudgingly but silently, he admitted the old man was right.

"Perhaps we have some recent satellite pix of Redoubt Zulu's region," Brigid suggested. "That might give us an idea of anything going on there."

Lakesh gestured in Bry's direction. "Mr. Bry is working on that now. However, our first step in the investigation isn't Alaska. It's Ragnarville. Friend Kane, friend Grant, you need to go there."

Grant stared at him as if he had suddenly gone insane. "Oh, no. No way."

"Grant and I are criminals, remember?" Kane said hotly. "We're wanted in all the villes. And we're suspected of chilling Baron Ragnar."

"If we want to know more details about the assassination," said Lakesh, "what better place to find out than in the ville itself, and who better to ask the questions than a pair of Magistrates?"

Grant rumbled, "'What better place to stumble around, get made and chilled?' is more like it."

"You walk the walk and talk the talk," countered Lakesh. "Go in, be discreet and get out."

"How do you expect us to get there so we can

walk the walk and talk the talk?'' demanded Grant. "We'll have to jump to Redoubt Tango and it's what—'' he glanced toward Brigid "—thirty miles from the ville?''

Brigid nodded. "A long way to walk the walk this time of year that far north.''

"More than likely,'' Lakesh said, "guards have been posted at the redoubt since your encounter. If so, they have a vehicle you can commandeer.''

"If so,'' growled Kane, "the guards will blow us to itty-bitty pieces as soon as we step out of the jump chamber.''

Lakesh chuckled. "Not if you step out as Ragnarville Magistrates. They'll challenge you certainly, but just say, 'Barch sent us.'''

Recognition flickered in Grant's eyes. "Barch... isn't he their division administrator?''

Though all the villes and their respective divisions operated independently of one another, there was still an exchange of information about personnel between them, particularly so in the Mag Divisions.

Lakesh nodded. "If nothing else, invoking his name will buy you some time to either bluff your way through or...overpower the opposition.''

Kane and Grant stiffened at the euphemism. "No need to pretty it up,'' Kane said harshly. "You mean chill them.''

Although both men were uncomfortably aware that terminate-on-sight warrants had been issued against them, directing violence against members of their former brotherhood still caused them pangs of guilt. They retained vivid memories of the firefight with Cobaltville Mags when they made their escape. Neither man relished them.

"I meant overpower," Lakesh stated doggedly. "There are a few nonlethal weapons in the armory."

Grant thought of the Cerberus arsenal, with its number of subguns, semiautomatic pistols, explosives, bazookas, tripod-mounted M-249 machine guns and grenade launchers.

"There are?" Grant asked doubtfully and sardonically.

"Admittedly only a few. They would not have been much use to you on your previous field trips."

"What if there are no guards and no means of transportation to Ragnarville?" Kane wanted to know.

Lakesh gestured negligently. "In that eventuality, return here. Cerberus can't afford your absence for the length of time it would take you to hoof it to the ville."

Grant angled an eyebrow at him. "But it can afford our absence if we make it there and are captured and chilled?"

Lakesh smiled, but this time it held no warmth or humor. "In that case, at least your fates will be in the line of duty. You should find some comfort in that."

Chapter 12

The eyes of the Ragnarville Trust glittered under the muted lights. Although the seven faces turned toward Barch held wariness or suspicion or a combination of both, he knew he had their attention. A mere human daring to sit down in the baron's chair was bound to have that effect.

Barch knew full well the risk he was taking by planting his buttocks in the over-padded seat of Baron Ragnar's ornate chair at the head of the long table. Still, he wasn't acting recklessly. He had calculated all the elements of risk.

Since the baron had been slightly smaller than even the shortest member of the Trust, his place of honor had been designed to elevate him several inches above everyone else when the Trust convened. It was the cheapest of psychological ploys, but because Barch was over six feet tall, he felt a trifle ridiculous towering over the table.

Of course it wasn't just taking the baron's chair that sparked the suspicion. Calling an emergency meeting in the room exclusively reserved for the Trust's councils and assuming the place of such an elevated personage wasn't just arrogance—it bordered on blatant heresy.

As yet, no one had commented or affected to notice the egg-shaped object placed on the table in front of Barch. It was small, no longer or broader than his hand, and balanced on the broad end by a spindly tripod. The shell of the egg appeared to be made of a coppery opaque substance, like metal or plastic.

When all the members of the Trust had seated themselves, Barch casually fingered the egg. A horizontal crack appeared about its middle, and the upper half of it rose vertically, rotated on delicate pivots within the shell and pointed toward the assembled men. They all eyed it with dull curiosity, but nobody said anything. They were too busy staring with outright suspicion and hostility at Royce.

His presence, as he stood at stiff and nervous attention on Barch's right side, only added to the atmosphere of tension thickening in the room.

Silently surveying the faces on either side of the table, Barch wondered which man would be first to lodge an objection, and subsequently be the first to die. All the faces were different in features and complexion, but they were markedly similar in expression—a certain pride, a diffident superiority. They were the elite of the ville's caste-based society.

They were the Trust, and as such they were the keepers of the deepest, darkest secrets of humanity's past, present and future.

Every ville had its own version of the Trust. The

organization, if it could be called that, was the only face-to-face contact allowed with the barons, and the barons served as the plenipotentiaries of the Archon Directorate.

The Trust acted as the guardians of the Directorate, and its oath revolved around a single theme— that the existence of the Directorate must not be revealed to humanity. If their presence became known, if the truth behind the nukecaust filtered down to the people, then humankind would no doubt retaliate with a concerted effort to throw off the harness of servitude—and the Directorate would be forced to visit another holocaust upon the Earth, simply as a measure of self-preservation.

So, to prevent another apocalypse, maintaining the secrecy of the Directorate and their work was a sacred trust. It was a sworn and solemn duty, offered to very few. The Trust was the latest in a long line of secret societies that held and concealed the knowledge of the Archon Directorate from the world. Barch had been told that the Trust had its roots in ancient Egypt, Babylon, Mesopotamia, Greece and even Sumeria. Throughout humankind's history, secret covenants with the entities known as Archons by kings, princes and even presidents, were struck.

Exhaling a slow, deliberately worried-sounding breath, Barch said, ''Our world is threatened by darkness, by the storms of strife. Enemies conspire for our destruction. The winds of chaos build in strength to sweep away the reign of order. The laws of our society begin to crumble."

His voice climbing in volume, deepening in timbre, he declared, "We must draw a line in the sand and proclaim, 'This far and no farther!'"

He slapped one big hand against the tabletop. "We must all work together to draw the line. There can be no dissent, no doubt, no individual ambitions. Otherwise, all of the good accomplished by the Program of Unification will be undone. The world will return to the madness and anarchy of the Beforetime, of skydark, of the savagery of the Deathlands."

Barch paused, allowing his words to sink in.

Zaprado, the Historical Division's administrator, broke the spell. "Inspiring words," he said dryly. "But with very little focus on the truly important issue—namely, what progress has your division made in apprehending Baron Ragnar's assassin?"

Barch answered sternly, "At this moment, laying our hands on the baron's actual murderer is of secondary importance."

Outraged gasps tore from seven throats. Timid little Walsh said hoarsely, "How can you say that? As Magistrate Division administrator, it is your duty to find our lord baron's killer. Zaprado raised a valid point."

Barch favored him with a patronizing, almost pitying half smile. "My duty, first and foremost, is to protect the ville. That is why we must keep the news of the tragedy from leaking down into the Pits or to the Outlands. If the poison of insurrection is being brewed, knowledge of the baron's death will cause it to boil over."

"But," pressed Walsh, "shouldn't the Magistrates devote all their efforts to capturing Baron Ragnar's killer? That would nip a revolt in the bud."

Smoothly, Barch replied, "The responsibility for the Magistrate Division is now in the more than capable hands of Royce. Direct your questions and suggestions to him."

The men at the table stirred fitfully, gazing at Royce. He shifted his feet uncomfortably and found a spot on the floor that seemed to fascinate him.

Thick-bodied Whitney, administrator of the Manufacturing Division, said bluntly, "He has yet to be initiated into our order. According to our rules of procedure, initiation must precede such a promotion."

Barch's voice became silky soft. Barch replied, "That is why he is here. To be inducted. I've already briefed him about the Directorate. All that remains is the ceremony itself. I intend to follow our protocols."

He slitted his one eye toward Walsh. "Unlike you, who permitted Royce to see the gateway unit. His initiation began at that second, whether you wanted it to or not."

Walsh's face screwed up, as if he were about to burst into tears.

Garrick, a member of the baron's staff, raised himself from his chair. "The baron presides over the induction process and the ceremony," he half stammered, half spluttered. "It is he and he alone who makes the choice of who joins us. What you propose is—is..."

His words trailed off as he groped for the proper descriptive adjective.

"Presumptuous?" Zaprado supplied helpfully.

"Exactly!" Garrick snapped. "Presumptuous and high-handed. The Directorate will never recognize your authority!"

Barch said quietly, "Take your seat, Garrick."

The man tried to meet Barch's obsidian, intimidating gaze, but he blinked, then wilted back down in his chair.

Barch said, "How do you know the Directorate will not recognize me? To inform me of that, must they not contact me?"

Exner, administrator of the Food Preservation and Distribution Division, said falteringly, "Baron Ragnar must have some means of communication with the Directorate."

"Which is?" challenged Barch.

Exner passed a hand over his balding scalp. "I don't know. Only the baron knows that."

"And of course," Barch said, "with him dead, the channel of communication—if such a thing exists— is only one-way."

Blinking his eyes rapidly, Walsh asked, "What are

you saying? That the Directorate is not aware of what has happened? Surely they must be!''

''Why must they?'' Barch challenged.

Walsh's lips worked as he tried to find words to put on them. After a moment, he gave up and shook his head in grieved frustration.

Zaprado fixed an inquisitive, unblinking stare on Barch's face. ''You were gone from Ragnarville for several weeks, ostensibly on a mission for the baron.''

Barch didn't respond. He met the archivist's direct gaze with his own.

''You took one of my historians with you,'' continued Zaprado, ''Berrier, by name. Yet you returned without her. I find that highly questionable.''

Barch still did not speak.

''Even more questionable is the purpose of the assignment you gave her. As was my right as senior archivist and Berrier's superior, I attempted to review her work on the historical database. I say 'attempted' because my efforts were blocked. Someone had authorized the insertion of a new, nonstandard encryption key into her files. I was locked out.''

Zaprado paused, still staring, waiting for a reaction or a comment from Barch. When one wasn't forthcoming, he demanded, ''Did you authorize the encryption?''

Lips barely moving, Barch replied slowly, ''Of course I did. The baron's mission was classified at such a high security level that not even you with your Xeno clearance were allowed to be privy to it."

Zaprado nodded, as if in satisfaction. "And now Baron Ragnar is dead, and he cannot speak of the purpose of your mission. But you can and you shall."

Barch shook his head. "That I will not do. The mission is ongoing, and its successful completion will determine our victory over the conspiracy. If it is compromised, the dark forces gathering around us will swallow us whole."

His lips twitched in a smile. "But you know that, don't you?"

Zaprado chuckled, a harsh, humorless rasp. "It's beneath you, Barch, to employ such an old trick. Don't try to misdirect suspicion onto me."

He turned in his chair, sweeping his flinty gaze over the faces of the men at the table. "I submit that Barch was somehow involved with the murder of Baron Ragnar. I further submit that if there is a conspiracy, he is the brains behind it. He should be stripped of his rank and removed from the Trust and held in detention until his actions can be properly investigated."

The archivist fixed his gaze on Royce. "As the Magistrate Division commander, I charge you with placing Barch under immediate arrest."

Royce's tongue touched his lips. He didn't move or lift his eyes from the floor.

"Royce!" Zaprado raised his voice in a sharp, imperious command. "Do your duty or share Barch's fate!"

Royce cast a sidewise glance toward Barch. The one-eyed man sighed as if in resignation. "Do as he says, Royce. Your duty, as per your orders."

No one saw Royce tense the tendons of his right wrist, but they all heard the faint drone of a tiny electric motor and the solid slap of the butt of the Sin Eater sliding into his hand.

The atmosphere of the room seemed to shatter at the bellowing roar of the shot. The high-velocity round took Zaprado in the forehead, punching a neat, blue-edged hole barely half an inch above his right eyebrow. His head snapped back violently as the rear of his skull exploded, splattering the back of the chair with a slurry of blood and grayish pink brain matter.

The raised arms and high back of his chair kept Zaprado from falling, though his body sagged down toward the floor. There was a soft thud when his chin struck the edge of the table as he slid down. Cordite stung the eyes and nostrils.

Barch slowly rose to his feet, levering himself upright by hands pushing against the tabletop. His calm gaze met the stares of shocked faces. "Does anyone else care to comment on my duty?"

There was no answer, and at a nod from Barch, Royce replaced the Sin Eater in its forearm holster.

"Don't fear that Zaprado's sudden vacancy will create a vacuum in the Trust. Royce will take his chair." Barch grinned suddenly, teeth flashing in his dark face. "After it's cleaned up, of course."

The door to the council chamber swung open. A blond-haired Baronial Guardsman entered. He gazed at Barch impassively. Barch gestured to Zaprado's body. "Get him out of here. Take him to the processing bin on E Level."

Barch nodded in Whitney's direction. "With your permission, of course."

Whitney returned the nod, with a wobbly jerk of his neck. E Level was Whitney's domain. Corpses of the executed were placed in a bin so they might be rendered down into their useful chemical components. Nothing went to waste in the villes, not even the body of a division administrator.

The guardsman pulled Zaprado's chair back. As the corpse fell, the man fitted his huge hands under its arms. Effortlessly, he swung up the corpse and placed it over the wide yoke of his shoulders. As he crossed the room, blood from the archivist's bullet-broken skull drained down, spattering a wet crimson trail to the door.

Nobody spoke or even dared sniff. Barch's soft, even voice broke the silence. "As I said, there can be no dissent or doubt. I was not making a request."

He gestured. "Everyone will rise to induct our newest member into our sacred order, as I administer the pledge of eternal fealty."

The six men at the table pushed their chairs back and approached Royce, standing in a semicircle around him. Barch stepped forward, placed his right hand on Royce's breast, over his heart. Royce imitated him, laying his own hand flat against Barch's chest.

In a deep voice, Barch announced, "You are about to take the oath of the Trust. You are expected to obey its conditions. There are sound reasons behind the oath, and it is easy to see why it is necessary, but not so easy to see how you can live up to it. But live up to it you must and that means you must make difficult choices. All former loyalties are superseded, swept aside by the oath. Do you understand?"

Royce said, "I understand."

"Repeat after me." In ringing tones, Barch declaimed, "'Resolve is our armor, will is our weapon, faith is our mission. Personal ambition is our scourge.'"

Royce repeated the words Barch spoke. "'We solemnly vow that we will face death rather than disclose the secrets we learn here. We sanctify ourselves in the service of humanity. We accept our responsibilities in the world as ministers of the Archon Directorate. We promise to discharge our duties as befits servants of the future and to hold our knowledge sacred and inviolate.'"

Once the oath was completed, Barch moved aside and Walsh took his place, repeating the same vow, and Royce repeated it back.

Stepping aside, Barch leaned against the table, folded his arms over his chest and tried not to look as bored as he felt. He made sure he was out of the field effect of the miniature microwave oscillator, what Berrier had described as an updated, state-of-the-art Tesla Coil. He let it continue to expose the men to its invisible wavelengths of radiation. He was a little disappointed that it hadn't worked on Zaprado as effectively as it had on Royce. Zaprado would have made a far more useful lieutenant than dull-witted Royce.

He had certainly been an easy mark for the coil's resonant ELF field, but Zaprado had been made of sterner stuff. Regardless, the first step to assuming power was to have people already in power to acknowledge that assumption.

Forcing the induction ceremony upon the members of the Trust was a strong first step.

Rituals and oaths were only tools to construct the kind of political machine he had in mind. The members of the Trust were only cogs, and as far as he was concerned, they were interchangeable. As long as they functioned according to his design, he would pretend he still believed in the Archon Directorate.

Soon, they would believe only in him.

Chapter 13

Hadley didn't like the redoubt, not a bit. He wished he were outside in the Sandcat, but keeping company with Arnam's corpse in its body bag spooked him even more than the hollowly echoing corridors. Besides, it was dangerously cold outside, despite the insulation provided by his armor and the Kevlar undersheathing.

He could have said he would guard the entrance, but Brewer would accuse him of being afraid of shadows. Hadley eyed the closed door that sealed off the strange control room. The people—two of them, maybe more—had disappeared like shadows. They had entered the six-sided booth with its glossy, bulletproof walls and vanished.

When Brewer trans-commed Royce in Ragnarville to report what had happened, Hadley feared their superior officer would accuse them of being fused out, juiced up on jolt or worse. He was astonished when Royce didn't question the story and dismayed when he ordered them to stay put until further notice. He added he was conveying a command from Barch himself.

Brewer never disobeyed an order or complained

about one, either—it was Arnam who used to grumble about orders, though he was usually circumspect about whom he griped to.

He hadn't griped when Brewer instructed him to take the point position. He had been too scared, too numb with disbelief after the news of Baron Ragnar's murder to balk or argue. He had obeyed, walked point and was chilled.

Hadley studiously averted his gaze from the smear of drying blood on the floor and lower section of the wall. The armor-piercing round had done more than snuff out Arnam's life in an eye blink—it shook Hadley to the roots of his soul, made him question the reasons he was a Magistrate, made him fear that no real reasons existed.

He had had no choice about joining the division when he came of age to do so. Magistrates followed patrilineal traditions, assuming the duties and positions of their fathers before them. They didn't have given names, each taking the surname of the father, as though the first Magistrate to bear the name was the same man as the last.

Now it appeared the Mags had no choices in the matter of their lives and deaths. Since the advent of the Program of Unification and the disarmament of the people, no Magistrates had confronted adversaries better armed than they were. The majority of hard contacts went smoothly due to their reputations, the fearsome images the Magistrates went to great effort to maintain.

It simply hadn't occurred to Hadley, Brewer and certainly not to Arnam that they might encounter opposition from enemies who had the means and the motives to chill them on the spot.

There were precedents in history, particularly in predark days. He remembered reading about the Magistrate's organizational antecedents, and about an incident that had happened only a few years before the nukecaust.

A raid on a slaghole had gone terribly wrong because the 'forcers hadn't expected to meet equal firepower, or come face-to-face with people who weren't impressed with either their authority or reputations. The arrogant assumption on the part of the 'forcers that they were invincible and their adversaries were incompetent jolt-brains had cost many lives. Waco, he thought the name of the place had been.

Hadley marched along the corridor, away from the doors and the strange room and mysterious booth behind them. As he passed a bunk room, he heard Brewer's snores. The sound reminded him of how tired he felt, but he knew that when his turn came to sleep, his tension would probably keep him awake and staring at the ceiling.

He could not imagine a single logical reason for Royce to station him and Brewer out here, not when the most monstrous crime in ville history had just been perpetrated. If news of it filtered down to the Tartarus Pits, disorder and maybe even an uprising would erupt. In that instance, every Mag, regardless of experience, needed to be on hand.

Turning the corner, he glanced at all the dents and pocks made by the bullets he and Brewer had indiscriminately hosed around. He felt a twinge of shame. They had allowed their emotions to control them, their surprise and anger over Arnam's murder and the news about the baron sweeping them away from reason.

Hadley still couldn't comprehend all the events of the past thirty-eight hours. He had been briefed about the renegade Magistrates from Cobaltville, of course, how they had abducted Baron Cobalt's favorite adviser and were using the redoubts as bolt-holes. What he didn't grasp was the means employed by the fugitives to penetrate Ragnarville's impregnable Administrative Monolith, assassinate the baron and then escape.

Replaying the exchange of words with the intruders, Hadley experienced a niggling doubt. The man—who might have been Kane or Grant or someone else entirely—definitely expressed surprise at the accusation he had chilled the baron. The woman, too, who Brewer was totally convinced was the actual hands-on assassin, denied the charge.

If the assassination had been politically motivated, then it seemed to him that the murderers would have gleefully taken credit for it, not vehemently claimed they knew nothing of it.

The vanadium walls threw back his sigh. Whoever

they were, they were gone, and it seemed resources and time were wasted keeping him and Brewer out here on the astronomically slim chance they might return.

Reaching the foot of the stairwell, Hadley paused to consider going up to check the main entrance, thought better of it and turned to retrace his steps.

He hadn't gone far when he heard the steady, measured tramp of booted feet echoing around the corner. He came to a sudden halt, heartbeat speeding up. For a second, he thought—he hoped—it was Brewer, but the sound was made by two pairs of feet.

Into the comm-link of his helmet, he whispered, ''Brewer? Brewer!''

No response filtered in through the transceiver. Brewer had removed his helmet when he stretched out on the bunk and so couldn't hear the comm-call. At least, Hadley prayed that was the reason.

Fisting his Sin Eater, clutching the grip of the Copperhead, he sucked in a deep, fortifying breath and stepped swiftly around the bend in the wall. He had prepared himself to bellow ''Freeze, slaggers!'' but instead he uttered a bleat of wonder and relief.

Two Mags in full armor strode down the corridor, and their measured gait didn't falter even when they caught sight of him. He scanned the jawlines visible under the red-tinted visors, tried to match them with ones in his memory and then found that he couldn't.

A very distant alarm bell rang in the recesses of his mind, but at the moment he was too relieved to pay it much heed. One of the Mags asked sternly, "Where's your partner?"

Hadley walked toward them. "Catching some shut-eye. Where'd you two come from?"

The larger of the pair, a black man, casually hooked a thumb over his shoulder toward the door leading to the control room. His companion asked acidly, "Where do you think? Ragnarville."

Hadley's mind reeled with fragmented questions and conjectures. Royce hadn't wanted to hear about the six-sided chamber that made hurricane noises and lightning flashes and apparently swallowed up the intruders.

Although he hadn't sounded incredulous, Royce had seemed uncomfortable with the topic. Hadley now demanded, "How did you get here?"

"How do you think, pissant?" growled the white Magistrate.

Hadley didn't like the disrespectful tone, but he noted that neither Mag had drawn a weapon, though the black man had his right fist clenched.

Lifting the barrel of the Copperhead, Hadley said, "That's the point. I don't think I know how. Maybe you'd better tell me."

The Mags kept coming. "Need-to-know basis. Barch sent us because we're on his need-to-know list. You and your partner aren't."

At the mention of the administrator's name, a bit of the suspicion flooding through him ebbed away. Hadley knew that some Mags were attached to secret

Intel section duties, but that still didn't explain why he didn't recognize these men or how they had arrived.

"What are your names?" Hadley snapped.

"I'm Howard." The Mag pointed to the black man. "This is Fine."

They kept coming, and Hadley realized the two men intended to march right past him.

"Understand you have a casualty?" Howard inquired.

Hadley nodded. "Yeah, an AP round dropped him dead. Right through the badge."

As he spoke, his eyes flicked automatically to the red badge affixed to Howard's molded pectoral, flicked away, then returned. The Mag's disk-shaped badge with its stylized scales of justice superimposed over a nine-spoked wheel didn't look quite right. It would pass a superficial visual inspection, but on a second, closer look, it had an odd, unfinished quality to it, almost a crudity. It looked more like a plastic imitation instead of being manufactured out of metal.

Hadley suddenly realized he had stared at the badge too long and he started to speak. Fine's right arm whipped up, a short, thick metal cylinder extending from his fist. Hadley tried to lunge backward, but a stream of white liquid jetted out of the rod and into his face, up under his visor.

Hadley tried to trigger his Sin Eater, but for a moment he lost all coordination, aware of nothing but the burn of the fluid on his skin, blinding his eyes, filling his nostrils.

He felt himself being pressed tightly between the two Magistrates, his arms pinned in hammerlocks, his index finger cruelly bent away from the trigger of his Sin Eater.

A cold blaster muzzle touched his chin. "Don't move, stupe," said a rumbling, familiar voice. "I don't need AP rounds this time."

Hadley recognized the voice and he felt his strength seep out through the soles of his feet. He stood motionless as he was swiftly and efficiently disarmed. Muscular control returned to his limbs, but his eyes and mucus membranes still burned.

The men released him and he swayed. Blinking back tears, he asked, "What was that stuff?"

"Some kind of mild nerve gas, I'm told," Howard replied casually. "It's absorbed through the skin, disrupts the nervous system for a while. You'll recover."

He reached over and unsnapped the under-jaw locking guard of Hadley's helmet. As he tugged it off, he asked, "What tipped you off? The badge?"

Hadley replied quietly. "Yes."

"Knew it," Howard said with a touch of bitter triumph, placing the helmet on the floor and drop-kicking it down the corridor.

Hadley swallowed the hard, bile-tasting lump creeping up his throat, brushing away tears. He managed to husk out, "You're them, aren't you?"

"Them?" echoed Fine.

"Kane and Grant. The renegades from Cobalt-ville."

Neither of the armored men responded with a confirmation or a denial. The black man used his free hand to remove a pair of nylon wrist binders from a compartment on his web belt. The other Mag twirled Hadley around and pushed him against the wall, jerking his arms back and affixing the cuffs to his wrists. As he did so, he said softly, "Yeah, we're them. I'm Kane."

Hadley felt his heart begin to thud with a painful surge of fright.

"But we don't want to chill you or your partner," Kane continued. "You're just doing your duty."

"Why are you here?"

Kane pulled him away from the wall. "We're doing *our* duty. What's your name?"

"Hadley."

"And your partner's?"

"Brewer. Guess he's still asleep."

Grant declared, "Let's go wake him up. Don't yell or try anything brave. We may not want to chill you, but we will if you force the issue. Believe it."

Hadley believed it and didn't resist as Grant prodded him forward with the barrel of his Sin Eater. They entered the dimly lit bunk room. Brewer still lay on a cot, helmet on the floor beside it, mouth opened as he snored. His hands were folded over his chest.

Grant glided across the floor on the balls of his feet. He placed the heel of one hand over the man's mouth and squirted the fluid onto his face. Brewer came to a thrashing, convulsing, choking consciousness. His Sin Eater's tiny electric motor droned, and the blaster sprang into his palm. He couldn't crook his finger around the trigger, and Grant took a firm, painful grip on it.

Brewer's struggles subsided slowly. Maintaining a firm grip on his index finger, Grant said coldly. "I'm going to unbuckle your holster. Don't try anything or I'll give you another dose. You'll die quick but you'll still die."

Brewer didn't move, his eyes reflecting his terror of the black-clad man looming over him. Grant loosened the buckles and yanked the holster and blaster over the man's wrist and hand.

He stepped backward. "Stand up. Hands behind your back. Face the wall."

Brewer unsteadily obeyed, and Grant bound his wrists with another set of cuffs. Kane pushed Hadley down on the bunk and Grant directed Brewer to sit down beside him.

"Where are the keys to the Cat?" Kane demanded.

Brewer nodded to a pile of ration packs and bottles of water on a countertop. "Over there."

Grant searched briefly and found them. "What'd you do with your casualty?"

Hadley coughed nervously. "Arnam. He's in the

Sandcat. Figured he'd keep better out there in the cold until we got him back.''

"What's your schedule of comm checks?'' Kane asked. "Hourly, three times a day, what?''

The men exchanged fearful, surreptitious glances.

"Answer me,'' ordered Kane.

"No set schedule,'' muttered Hadley. "Our orders are to remain here until further notice.''

Grant rasped, "Bullshit. That's not procedure.''

Brewer nodded. "We know. But that was Barch's order. It's almost like he wants to keep us out of the ville for a while.''

Kane said, "Tell us what you know about Baron Ragnar's death.''

Brewer's lips compressed in a tight line. "You tell us. You did it.''

Grant said softly, menacingly, "Tell us.''

Brewer tried to shrug. "All we know is that a woman chilled him in his bed. She escaped somehow.''

"Chilled him how?''

Brewer stared hard at Grant. "Why don't you ask that gaudy slut who was with you how she did it?''

Neither Kane nor Grant wasted time or effort on voicing a denial. The Ragnarville Mags wouldn't believe anything they said, no matter how convincing.

Kane uttered a soft, thoughtful grunt. "All right, here's how we'll play it. We don't want to chill you, but we will if you give us reason. Any reason at all. We'll lock you in here. You've got food and water.

If you behave, we'll let you loose when we get back.''

Hadley shifted his feet. "When will that be?"

Grant showed the edges of his teeth in a cold grin. "That all depends. Look for us when you see us coming."

Brewer lifted his head. Defiance and hostility glinted in his eyes. "We could starve before then."

"Not if you ration your food," Grant argued. "Standard survival techniques as per your training. That is, if you haven't gotten so soft and flabby you've forgotten it."

Brewer muttered, "Fuck you, traitor."

Hadley stiffened in fear. Kane gazed at Brewer dispassionately for a moment, then reached down for the handle of his combat knife in its boot scabbard. He drew it with the slow rasp of steel against leather. He took a measured step toward Brewer.

The man leaned back, cringing away, eyes fixed on the razored, double-edged point. He cried, "I'm sorry! Forget I said anything. I apologize!"

Kane bent over him, pressing his knee against the man's stomach. He brought the knife up. Flatly, he said, "Don't move."

Inserting the point of the blade between the edge of the badge and the pectoral, he worked it around and up and down. He pried the disk of metal from the armor and stepped away from Brewer, who was too relieved to voice his confusion.

Turning his attention to Hadley, Kane repeated the

process, removing the man's duty badge. He handed it to Grant and picked up Brewer's helmet from the floor. He looked silently from Hadley to Brewer and then asked, "Is Klaw still the boss of the Ragnarville Pits?"

Both men looked startled. Hadley faltered, "I guess so. Haven't heard otherwise."

Kane and Grant picked up the weapons and backed out of the bunk room.

"Remember what we said," Grant declared. "Behave and you'll live to lie about this episode."

Before they stepped out into the corridor, Kane punched in the close and locking codes on the keypad next to the frame. As the door slid shut and the solenoids clicked into position, Grant commented morosely, "If they're determined enough, they could figure out how to get the door open with their noses or tongues."

Kane shrugged. "And do what and go where? They have no comms and no wheels. And I don't think they have the balls to try the gateway."

As they walked along the passageway toward the stairwell, Kane pulled off his badge and affixed Hadley's in its place by its flexible metal tabs.

"Knew this fake piece of shit wouldn't pass muster," he stated, putting it in a compartment of his belt.

Grant said nothing. A short while ago, Kane had lost his badge, and though Grant had offered to retrieve it for him, his partner had refused, viewing the loss as symbolic of his permanent break with his old life.

That impulsive decision had dangerous consequences, since a man in a Mag's armor without a badge drew instant suspicion. Wegmann and Farrell had crafted a duplicate using Grant's emblem as a template, but without the proper tools, they had produced only a very clumsy imitation.

Aside from their appearance, active-duty badges were keyed to photoelectric field sensors, which permitted Magistrates access to all levels of the Administrative Monolith. Although neither man envisioned entering Ragnarville's monolith, they would still be forced to pass through several checkpoints to enter the ville itself. The frequency of Grant's badge, even if it was still active, was attuned to Cobaltville sensors. He swapped out his badge with Hadley's as they climbed the stairs to the upper floor.

At the entrance, Kane manipulated the lever to lift the sec door. As it rose, a shaft of milky sunlight slanted in over the threshold. The midmorning sunlight was veiled by cirrocumulus clouds, and it sparkled only dully on the sweep of snow.

Two parallel grooves cut through the white-blanketed landscape, twisting around a copse of trees and disappearing into the distance. Kane gestured toward them. "Guess we can just follow the trail all the way to Ragnarville. Don't need a map."

They went out to inspect the Sandcat, Grant pausing long enough to close the sec door. A pair of flat, retractable tracks supported the Sandcat's low-slung, blunt-lined chassis. An armored topside gun turret concealed a pair of USMG-73 heavy machine guns. The wag's armor was composed of a ceramic-armaglass bond, shielded against both intense and ambient radiation. The interior comfortably held four people, but it held only one now.

Kane reached into the rear cargo compartment and tugged out the body bag. Rigor mortis had settled in Arnam's limbs, and his weight was unwieldy and cumbersome.

"Least you can do is give me a hand," he called to Grant. "You chilled the bastard."

Grant came around and helped him lift out the corpse and place it on the ground. They gazed at it silently for a few moments.

"Do we bury him?" Kane asked. "I mean, he was a Mag."

Grant coughed self-consciously. "Ground is frozen solid. Even with the tools in the Cat, it'll take more time than we should spare. I expect that's why his partners just bagged him. Temperature's low enough so he'll keep till they got back to the ville."

Kane said, "We leave him lying here, he'll be all torn to pieces by the time we come back." He intentionally refrained from saying *if.* "God only knows the kinds of animals roaming around here."

Grant glanced around, then nodded in the direction of a fairly deep snowbank near the tree line. "We can plant him there and cover him up. Might hide his scent from predators.''

They dragged the body bag over to the trees, kicked and dug out a hollow within the snowbank and collapsed it atop the corpse. With hands and feet, they smoothed and packed down the snow.

"Not much of a final resting place," Grant commented.

"Better than some Mags we knew," replied Kane grimly. "Maybe better than ours will be. The op is still young."

Grant gusted out a heavy, weary sigh. "It's such a pleasure to go out into the field with you, Kane. You always know just the right words to keep up morale."

He wheeled around and stalked back to the Sandcat, wrenching open the gull-wing door and sliding into the pilot's chair. By the time Kane climbed into the seat beside him, he had already keyed the 750-horsepower engine to roaring life. He let it idle for a minute to warm up.

"It seems to me," said Kane, "that Hadley and Brewer were stuck out here to keep them from asking questions about Baron Ragnar's assassination."

"Seems that way to me, too. By the time they get back, the cover story will be too strong to tear apart."

Kane asked, "You really think this Boss Klaw will know anything important about the baron's death?"

"Old Guana Teague back in Cobaltville knew just

about everything that went down,'' retorted Grant. ''That's the way of Pit bosses. Besides, I'd rather stay out of the monolith if I can help it.''

''Yeah,'' Kane agreed gloomily, thinking of their penetration into Cobaltville's Administrative Monolith only a short time before to rescue Lakesh. ''Easy to get in, hard as hell to leave.''

Grant snorted and put the Sandcat in gear.

Chapter 14

Lakesh frowned at the black blob, murmuring, "I don't believe I've ever seen anything like that before."

Brigid scooted her chair closer to the VGA screen, squinting through the lenses of her eyeglasses. The big monitor displayed dark, irregular humps, some of them shot through with variegated streaks of unearthly color. Taken over Alaska a couple of weeks before, the images had been relayed by the Vela reconnaissance satellite. The computer system's thermal line-scan filters turned the aerial photos into smears of colors and shapes.

"What do you think it is?" she asked.

"Weather systems," replied Lakesh. "Different types, different intensities, all occurring over a period of a few days."

She assumed the phenomenon was unusual or Lakesh wouldn't have commented on it. They were fortunate to view any imagery at all, since the Vela's flyovers couldn't be controlled from Cerberus. The pictures of whatever part of Earth the satellite transmitted were on a strictly random basis. Though it continuously sent images to the uplink, to find any of one particular region required a time-consuming process of trial and error.

Sometimes the images were fairly recent, as these were; more often than not, they could be months, even years old. It frustrated Lakesh that Cerberus couldn't establish direct telemetric control of the satellite, because the codes had long since been lost. Still, since the few satellites still in Earth orbit were husks of dead circuitry, Cerberus was lucky to have even a limited interface with the Vela.

Lakesh tapped the screen with a gnarled forefinger. "I'm not a meteorologist, but I estimate we're seeing thunderstorms, blizzards and tornadoes, all coming on the heels of one another, crowding one front out and another taking its place."

"Like skydark," remarked Brigid.

Lakesh acknowledged her observation with a short nod. "This is a pocket of skydark, confined to a few hundred square miles. Hell weather with a vengeance."

He leaned back in his chair. "This confirms my fear—someone reactivated the HAARP operational systems in Redoubt Zulu. What we see here is evidence of their experimentation."

"If that's true," Brigid said, "it doesn't necessarily follow there's a connection to Baron Ragnar's death just because the redoubt is within his ville's jurisdiction."

"True," admitted Lakesh reluctantly. "But one

doesn't necessarily have to be linked with the other to imply a very dangerous situation.''

She cocked her head at him quizzically. ''You mean the mind-control uses to which HAARP could be put?''

''That—and something else.''

Brigid waited for the old man to clarify his cryptic statement. His eyes acquired a vague, faraway sheen, as if he were trying to pierce the clouds of time into the distant past. She was familiar with that look, so she waited patiently. Given his age and experience, Lakesh had a substantial set of memories to riffle through.

Finally, his lips formed one word, and it came out as a whisper. *''Doomstar.''*

A chill of fear touched her spine and she straightened up in her chair. ''Explain.''

He rubbed his deeply seamed forehead as if trying to stimulate his brain into bringing long-buried memories to the fore. ''Did you ever wonder why so many of the Totality Concept redoubts remained intact after the nukecaust?''

The question startled her into silence for a moment. She thought about it, then ventured, ''I presumed because they were so protected, so difficult to enter.''

Lakesh nodded. ''True, as far as it goes. But a contingency plan was drafted, in the off chance Russian troops were landed to occupy the installations.''

Brigid knew that for a time in the late twentieth

century some aspects of Totality Concept researches and technology had been shared with the Soviet Union. It was part of an international deep-cover cooperative effort, even though the Russians had their own version, called Szvezda.

She had only recently learned that the final break in cordial relations came when the U.S. and the Russians entered a covert competition to colonize Mars, in the late 1980s.

"I take it that occupation never happened," she said wryly.

Lakesh's lips quirked in a sour smile. "I doubt more than three thousand combat-ready Russian troops remained in the immediate aftermath of the conflagration. And they had their own problems to contend with."

He lifted a shoulder in a shrug. "Still and all, certain kinds of Totality Concept technology falling into enemy hands was a very real fear. So a fail-safe plan code-named Doomstar was crafted to be programmed into the computer systems of a select few redoubts. It was designed as the ultimate insurance, a self-destruct device."

"Even here?" Brigid asked. "In Cerberus?"

"I circumvented the installation of the program here. I found it to be a difficult undertaking and more than a little inhuman."

"How so?"

"It had to do with recent advances made in the field of self-changing AI."

"AI?" echoed Brigid. "You mean Artificial Intelligence?"

Lakesh sighed deeply. "Exactly. Intelligent software agents, interfaced with the human brain, existing in an electronic web matrix. In the vernacular of the time, it was called 'wet-wiring.' That was the core idea of the Doomstar program."

Brigid struggled to comprehend the concept. "Why would a human brain be linked with a self-destruct device?"

"Because pure machine intelligences are not at all intelligent. They merely calculate at maddeningly high speeds. They don't generalize, they don't understand eye contact, vocal timbre or body language. That's the primary reason experiments in constructing security droids were discontinued."

Brigid recalled Lakesh mentioning those experiments. After a few prototypes were built, the researches were abandoned because the man-shaped machines couldn't make general distinctions between friend and foe.

Lakesh went on, "The drive to produce computer intelligences to perfectly imitate that of humans went only so far before the scientists involved decided it was simpler to create biointerfaces between organic and inorganic synaptic structures. From what I recall, that is the basic mechanism of the Doomstar program."

Not able to keep an edge of impatience out of her voice, she asked, "What is it, exactly?"

Lakesh gave her an abashed, slightly embarrassed smile. "To be frank, I'm not certain. I was so busy with building the Cerberus mat-trans network, I confess I paid little attention beyond the superficial aspects of it. All I know is that Doomstar was both a program and a device to safeguard Totality Concept technology, by either destroying it or those who had no business tampering with it. Or both."

"Nukes?" she inquired a little fearfully.

"Possibly. Perhaps even worse."

She tried to picture what could be worse, but Lakesh continued, "I remember something else, too. I overheard part of a briefing. The Doomstar program could, due to its biointerface, be represented and interact with the 'real world.'"

Lakesh gestured with his fingers, putting invisible quotation marks around the last two words.

Brigid frowned. "What is that supposed to mean?"

Lakesh laughed. "I haven't the faintest idea. I'm doing my damnedest to dredge up two-hundred-year-old memories, but so far I'm coming up with more silt than nuggets of truth."

"Is there anything in the database relating to it?"

"Possible, but not very likely. Doomstar was created at the tail end of the twentieth century, during the chaos of preparations for the nukecaust. To be honest, I'm not even certain if it progressed beyond the planning stages."

Brigid wheeled her chair over to a computer console. "I'll take a look. What subdivision of the Totality Concept did AI researches fall under?"

"Eurydice, I imagine, but hold off on that task for a bit."

She glanced over at him quizzically. The old man suddenly looked grave, even sad. "There's something else I want to discuss with you."

Brigid tried to ignore the sinking sensation in the pit of her stomach. During her years as an archivist, she had perfected a poker face and managed to keep her sudden apprehension from showing. "What is it?"

Lakesh cleared his throat and shifted in his chair in a distinctly discomfited manner. She half expected what he said next. "Beth-Li spoke with me earlier today."

"Beth-Li?" she inquired coolly. "You mean Rouch."

Lakesh nodded.

"Was she providing a report on her and Kane's efforts to turn Cerberus into a colony?" Though she strove for a flat, disinterested tone, she knew Lakesh detected the tinge of bitterness in her voice.

Only recently she had learned she was infertile, due to exposure to an unknown wavelength of radiation in the Black Gobi. She had suffered chromosomal damage but the extent and degree of permanency was still undetermined. DeFore was hesitant to offer an extended prognosis. She had yet to speak of it to Kane.

"Indeed," Lakesh answered, "that was what she was doing."

"And did Kane perform according to her—and your—projections?"

Lakesh's lips firmed. "As a point of fact, no. He threw her out. She said he even threatened her."

Brigid couldn't help it. A smile tugged at the corners of her mouth. One could never tell what Kane would say or do.

"I don't find this particularly amusing, Brigid," said Lakesh severely. "Beth-Li opines that you are the sole obstacle standing in the way of fulfilling her mission here. It saddens me to say that I'm inclined to agree with her."

"Me?" Brigid demanded, despising the strident note of anger in her voice. "Kane goes his own way, like always."

Lakesh made a spitting sound of derision. "I may wear glasses, but I'm not blind. The bond between you two is admirable, but it has its price."

Brigid did not want to be baited, forced into denying or trying to explain the bond between her and Kane. Logically, there was no explanation. On a mat-trans jump to Russia, the gateway had malfunctioned. Both she and Kane had suffered a bout of jump-sickness, but added to the nausea and nightmares were visions that seemed to be of past lives.

They had shared the same visions, the same delirious realization that Kane and she were bound by spiritual chains, linked to each other and the same destiny.

More than once, he had displayed a reckless disregard for his own life when hers was threatened. For that matter, during the mission in the Black Gobi, she had risked her own life to save his; acting on purely instinctive, almost primal impulses. She had been tortured, incapacitated, in a state of shock. Yet when she saw the Tushe Gun's saber at the helpless Kane's throat, only one emotion motivated her—she would not watch him die again. In the vision she had experienced during the mat-trans jump to Russia, then again in the subterranean chamber beneath Kharo-Khoto, an image floated through her mind, but it was more than a vision. She knew on a deep, visceral level it was a memory.

She was lashed to the stirrup of a saddle, lying in the muddy track of a road. Men in chain-mail armor laughed and jeered above her, and long black tongues of whips licked out with hisses and cracks. Callused hands fondled her breasts, forced themselves between her legs.

Then she saw a man rushing from a hedgerow lining the road. He was thin and hollow cheeked, perhaps nineteen or twenty years old. His gray-blue eyes burned with rage. She knew him, she called out to him, shouting for him to go back, go back....

She knew the young man was Kane.

As the former overseer of Project Cerberus, Lakesh presumably was familiar with all the side effects of mat-trans jumping. Brigid had never told him about her vision of a past life, just as she had never discussed it with Kane.

Hesitantly, she said, "I don't know what you mean about me and Kane. Half the time, I don't even like him."

Lakesh waved a dismissive hand. "Friend Grant has made the same statement on more than one occasion, too. But that is not what I'm asking."

"Then get to the point," she snapped.

"I need to know the depth and level of your involvement with him. I know this is a frightfully personal thing to ask, but you've left me no other choice."

Brigid tried to fix him with a haughty stare, hoping he'd avert his eyes, but Lakesh only blinked at her in owlish interest. In a low voice, she intoned, "Kane has never touched me—at least not in the way you mean."

That wasn't technically true, since he had kissed her during the mission to the twentieth century. Of course, it had been New Year's Eve.

"We do not have a sexual relationship. Satisfied?"

Lakesh fingered his chin contemplatively. "By no means. Whether you and he engage in sexual activities is far less important to my question than the emotional hold you apparently have over him."

Brigid ran her hands through her hair in weary frustration. "I never examined it, if there is such a thing."

"Perhaps it's past time you did so." Lakesh softened his voice, trying to sound sympathetic. "Dearest Brigid, Kane threw his entire life away, his future as one of the ville elite. Without a second thought, he sacrificed all of that for you. And he barely knew you."

A bit defensively, she reminded him, "Grant was in jeopardy, too. That was just as important a factor in his decision." Even to her own ears, her objection sounded lame.

"Regardless, if the plan to expand our numbers is to move toward fruition, Kane must modify his feelings toward you."

"I don't know what his feelings are—haven't you been listening?" she said in a ragged burst. "I don't know what *mine* are."

Lakesh regarded her speculatively over the rims of his glasses. "It's Beth-Li's strong impression—and mine, as well—that Kane's reluctance to engage in the project is caused by his loyalty to you."

"How can I be held responsible for that?"

"Perhaps it's your comportment, your attitude toward the plan and Beth-Li herself. Kane isn't a fool."

Coldly, Brigid said, "This is *your* plan. You didn't consult any of us about it, except for Rouch."

"You refuse to refer to her by her first name, I notice."

Brigid ignored the observation. "Kane isn't a stud animal, despite the quality of the genes you bred into him. Whatever prevents him from participating in your procreation program are his reasons alone.''

''But,'' Lakesh said with a sly half smile, ''his reasons, whatever they are, don't exactly disappoint you.''

Leaning back in her chair, Brigid folded her arms over her chest. ''What is it you want me to do?''

''For one thing, curtail your personal contact with him.''

She lifted an eyebrow. ''We work together, remember? You're the one who always partners us up.''

''For which I hold myself accountable. You do work well together—that I cannot deny. I doubt either one of you would have returned from your previous missions if you'd been dispatched separately.''

''Is that why you sent Rouch with Kane to Louisiana instead of me?''

''Partly,'' he admitted. ''Beth-Li volunteered, and I didn't oppose her. I had hoped that with the two of them alone, without the mitigating influence of you and Grant, nature might take its course.''

''It didn't, and so Rouch blames me? I think it was more in the nature of the way Kane smelled.''

Lakesh asked icily, ''You're simply determined to sidestep this issue, aren't you?''

Brigid stood up so suddenly her chair rolled backward on squeaking casters. Her voice trembled with barely suppressed fury. ''I don't see an issue that involves me except in the most marginal way. You look at Kane as something of your creation because you successfully tinkered with his genes—the only success out of God knows how much tinkering with God knows how many people.

"To you, he's your masterpiece, but he's also needed in the field. You're afraid if he's chilled without passing along those superior qualities you bred into him, then your work of art, your claim of immortality-by-proxy, will never be appreciated by future generations."

Lakesh sat calmly listening, not interrupting or interjecting.

"You have no right to ascribe that kind of value to Kane or anyone else here," she snapped. "I used to defend your actions to him when he accused you of arrogance. I'm starting to wonder now why I ever bothered."

Lakesh nodded in resignation, in acceptance. Quietly, he stated, "I do what I do for the greater good, dearest Brigid. The common good of us all and those who follow us. I hoped you could see that."

She drew in a long breath through her nostrils. "I'm withholding judgment, at least for a little while. If you'd rather Kane and I spent less time together, I'll abide by your wishes. But whatever he does or doesn't do with Rouch—Beth-Li—is up to him."

Lakesh smiled slightly. "Agreed, on both counts. In which case, there is no reason to wait for him and Grant to return from Minnesota before engaging in our own line of investigation."

"Into what?"

"Redoubt Zulu." Lakesh gestured to the Mercator map. "No mat-trans activity has registered in nearly eighteen hours, but that could change. I'd prefer to have some of our own people in place, waiting for whoever comes through the door next."

He angled an eyebrow at her. "Would you be interested?"

"What about the search for Doomstar data?"

"I'll take care of it. Hopefully, the memory banks will yield some results before you're ready to make the jump." He paused and added, "You may choose whoever you like to accompany you."

"If this is a recce," Brigid replied, "just an Intel-gathering probe, it calls for a minimum of personnel. I'll ask Domi."

Lakesh's face creased in a doubtful frown. "She's still not a hundred percent, you know."

"I know. But I'll take her ninety percent over just about everyone else's 110."

Lakesh chuckled, but it sounded forced and uneasy. "As you wish. Can you depart in...say, two hours?"

Brigid walked toward the door. "That should be enough time."

She found Domi in the dispensary, completing a session of physical therapy under DeFore's clinical eye and clipped instructions. Teeth sunk into her lower lip, hair damp with sweat, Domi hauled a weighted pulley arrangement up and down with her right arm. She wore a sleeveless undershirt, and the new scar tissue radiating out from her shoulder showed stark and inflamed against the whiteness of her skin.

"A few more reps," DeFore said to her. "You're making excellent progress."

Domi didn't respond, and Brigid guessed it wasn't just because she was concentrating on lifting the weights. According to Grant, Domi cared very little for the "fat-assed doctor lady" as she called her. She harbored suspicions that DeFore had designs on Grant.

"How is she doing?" Brigid asked.

"Far better than my initial prognosis," DeFore answered. "She's recovered muscle control since there wasn't an advanced degree of atrophy. The artificial ball-and-socket joint seems to be working smoothly."

Domi, still pulling and lowering the pulley, grunted, "Hurts."

DeFore smiled patronizingly. "I imagine it's exceedingly painful. Good thing you have a high tolerance for it, or your recovery time would have been extended by at least a month."

"How soon will she reach maximum medical improvement?"

DeFore glanced toward her, seemingly a bit irritated by her casual use of medical jargon. "Why all the questions, Baptiste?"

"I'm going on a recce to a redoubt in Alaska. I'd like Domi to go with me, if she's up to it."

Domi released the pulley, and the weights clanged loudly on the floor. "Ask me."

"Are you up to it?"

She pretended to ponder the query. "Depends. Do I get to carry my blaster this time?"

Brigid grinned. "You get to carry your blaster."

Domi returned the grin. "Then I'm up to it. We leave when Grant and Kane get back?"

"No, this is an all-girl revue. Just you and me this time."

DeFore eyed both of them dourly. "Just you two?"

"Just us," Brigid replied, "unless you're interested in volunteering."

DeFore grimaced, shaking her head. As one of the first of the Cerberus exiles, she had left the mountain plateau only once in the past three years, and that was as member of Lakesh's rescue team.

"I'll sit this one out. I need to be here in case a bullet has to be dug out of *your* anatomy this time."

She didn't smile when she said it, and Brigid knew why. Before she, Kane, Domi and Grant arrived at Cerberus, her doctoring duties consisted of little more than treating scratches and scrapes or dispensing medication. Over the past six months, she had sewn up knife wounds, set broken bones and performed major reconstructive surgery.

To Domi, Brigid said, "Grab your gear and meet me in the ready room in two hours."

Domi bobbed her head, working the stiffness out of her shoulder. "Gotcha."

Brigid walked toward the corridor. "I have just enough time for a swim."

DeFore called after her, "Have you seen Auerbach?"

"No. Why?"

"He was supposed to be on duty ten minutes ago. If you see him, tell him his shift started without him and the doctor isn't happy about it."

Brigid walked along the passageway to the elevator and took it to the second level. The small swimming pool had only recently been made functional again, and she used it whenever she had the opportunity.

She passed through an open area filled with weights, stationary exercise cycles and workout mats. The pool and exercise rooms had been built to provide the original inhabitants of Cerberus with a means of sweating off the stress of being confined for twenty-four hours a day in the installation. After the nukecaust, just staying alive was probably more exercise than they actually needed.

She reached the set of double doors leading to the pool room. As she put her hand on one of them, her ears caught the unmistakable sounds of lovemaking. She was glad her hearing was so acute and so saved her from barging right in, but she felt a flash of annoyance, too. The pool was a community area, and everyone in the redoubt had private quarters.

Brigid began to step back when she heard a female's voice, high with passion, giving instructions. Since she had just left the other two women of the redoubt, only Rouch was unaccounted for. And so was Auerbach.

Feeling like six different varieties of voyeur, Brigid inched the door open and peered into the dimly lit, bowl-shaped room. Auerbach lay on his back at poolside. Rouch sat astraddle him, riding him roughly, face a mask of determination. Grunting, Auerbach writhed beneath her.

Brigid backed away, letting the door close quietly. In that brief half second, Rouch looked up and stared directly into her face. Her dark eyes glittered not with lust, but defiance, and the smile crossing her sensual mouth was one of pure malice.

Chapter 15

As in all the fortress cities, a narrow roadbed of crushed gravel led up to Ragnarville's main gate. The first checkpoint station was a small concrete-block cupola, manned only by a single guard in the pearl gray duty uniform of the Magistrates, but without a badge. He was young, perhaps fourteen, which both Grant and Kane knew he would be.

Traditionally, the guards posted at the outer perimeter were the most recent, unbadged recruits. It was scut work, delegated to the greenest of the green. Grant didn't brake the Sandcat as it rumbled toward the striped wooden barrier; he only let up his foot's pressure on the gas pedal, slowing it just enough to give the guard time to get out of the cupola.

He peered through the wag's fore ob port, saw the pair of armored, helmeted men and hastily raised the barricade before the nose of the Cat rammed it. Kane gave the young man a cold nod as they passed by him, and the guard returned it with a deferential nod of his own.

Kane wasn't comforted by the ease of their passage. Neither was Grant. He tightened his hands on the horseshoe-shaped steering wheel and said darkly, "The next one won't be as easy, I hope you know."

Kane knew and so didn't respond. They had been waved through three frontier checkpoints without being questioned, but that wouldn't happen at the main gate a quarter of a mile up the road.

Massive, pyramid-shaped "dragon's teeth" obstacles made of reinforced concrete lined both sides of the path. Five feet high, each one weighed in the vicinity of a thousand pounds and was designed to break the tracks or wheels of any assault vehicle trying to gain access.

A dozen yards before the gate, stone blockhouses bracketed either side of the road. Within them were electrically controlled GEC Miniguns, capable of firing 6000 rounds of 5.56 mm shredders per minute. If the blasters opened up, the Sandcat would be caught in the middle of a cross fire, with no way to turn. Grant would have to throw the wag into reverse and back up blind.

Beyond the blockhouses, stretching the width of the road, rose a triple row of steel girders deeply sunk in a concrete pad.

Lifting his gaze, Kane eyed the Vulcan-Phalanx gun emplacement on the wall overlooking the checkpoint. Beyond it and above loomed the edifice of the Administrative Monolith. His eyes narrowed.

"Look at that," he said.

"Look at what?" Grant said tensely, not wanting the distraction.

"Damage to the monolith."

Grant glanced up, but he gave only a cursory inspection of the structure's white facade. He could just make out the black-edged holes and shallow cavities marring its smooth surface between B and A Levels.

"Looks like it's been shelled," he noted absently.

Kane took a second, closer look. "Yeah," he agreed. "But by who and what?"

"Something else for us to find out," Grant retorted. "If we live long enough."

As the Sandcat approached the checkpoint, a guard stepped out of the right-hand blockhouse and stood in the middle of the road. He was a badged Mag, in full armor. In his right hand, he held a remote sensor pad. He watched their approach, his body stance not communicating any emotion in particular. Kane only hoped he wasn't one of the guards on duty when Brewer, Hadley and Arnam had departed two days before.

The badges Grant and Kane had appropriated would get them through the sensitive sensors at the checkpoint, would identify them as Ragnarville Magistrates, but the guard might insist on a visual confirmation of their identities in lieu of an electronic one.

The Cat rumbled through the invisible photoelectric field between the blockhouses. The guard didn't move from his position, but he raised a languid left arm, gesturing for them to stop. Grant applied the brake but kept the engine running as the guard moved to the passenger's side, peering through the ob port at Kane. He consulted the information transmitted from the sensors to the remote unit in his hand.

"Hadley, Brewer," he said in a monotone. "Supposed to be three of you. Where's Arnam?"

"Left him to stand watch," replied Kane, matching the monotone. "Barch called us back. Some sort of emergency."

The Mag nodded in grim accord. His voice took on an animated inflection. "That's the fuckin' understatement of the century. You two heard?"

Kane said simply, "We heard."

"More than I have, I bet." The guard paused, obviously hoping Kane would respond to the overture and say more. Evidently, though the news of the baron's death was common knowledge in the Magistrate Division, actual details had been soft-pedaled. Kane said nothing more.

The guard waited, then asked, "You two get caught in that bastard storm?"

Kane hesitated before answering noncommittally, "It was a bastard one, all right."

"No shit, no shit!" The Mag seemed eager to talk about the weather since he had been rebuffed in his attempt to get more information about the murder of Baron Ragnar. "Lightning, burnin' hail—if it hadn't been so wet, half of Tartarus would have gone up in smoke. Never saw anything like it. Hell, never even *heard* of anything like it."

Although he would have liked to know more, Kane said matter-of-factly, "Pass us through. We're overdue as it is."

The Magistrate's mouth twisted in disappointment, and he stepped away from the Cat, gesturing to the blockhouse behind him.

The concrete pad holding the barrier of steel girders began sinking into the roadbed, lowered by hydraulics controlled from the bunker. As it sank beneath the surface, a thick slab of rust-streaked metal slid from a slot and spanned the aperture.

Grant took his foot off the brake and steered the Cat over it with a loud clanking of the metal tracks. Neither man spoke as they headed for the gate.

Fifteen feet high by twenty wide, with a two foot thickness of rockcrete sheathed by cross-braced iron, the portal groaned aside, pulled by huge gears and cables the thickness of Grant's wrists.

The Sandcat entered a walled compound topped by coils of razor wire. Parked beneath an overhang were a number of vehicles, Land Rovers, personnel-carrying AMACs, and two other Sandcats. Grant pulled the wag into an open space between the other Cats and keyed off the engine.

An attendant hurried up, his leather belt weighted down by various hand tools. Despite the grease and grime smearing his face, both Grant and Kane saw his expression of surprise when he looked through the ob ports. They were not the Mags he expected to return the Cat to the vehicle depot, but he was intelligent enough not to bring it to their attention.

Grant left the keys in the ignition as he opened the gull-wing door. Tersely, he said to the attendant, "Fuel her up and give her a once-over, but leave the keys inside. We may need her again in a hurry and I don't want to have to hunt your oily ass down."

The man nodded. "Yes, sir."

They crossed the compound to the door on the far side. Kane tapped in the control numbers on the keypad and pulled up on the control lever. The door squeaked to one side, and he stepped out into the outskirts of Ragnarville's Tartarus Pits. Grant joined him and stood silently for a moment, trying not to recoil from the overpowering stench.

The air was redolent with the mixed odors of cookfires, rotting meat, open cesspits, unwashed bodies, urine, human and animal droppings. Both of them experienced a momentary pang of nostalgia, but when a dank breeze wafted a singularly repulsive stink over them, they struggled to hold their gorges down.

"Did the Pits in Cobaltville smell like this?" Grant asked.

"They all smell the same," replied Kane. "Remember the old saying."

"Yeah," Grant muttered. "Leopards can't change their spots, and the Pits can't change their *phew*."

They headed for the inner sanctums of the ville, assuming that the procedures for Magistrates returning from the field would be the same in all the villes. A narrow footpath, more like a channel, wended its way around the outer limits of Tartarus proper, leading to the impregnable base of the monolith. The pathway was strictly forbidden to anyone but Magistrates. Vid spy-eyes affixed to posts made sure no Pit denizen planted a muddy foot on it.

Nothing could be done to avoid the surveillance, so they ignored it. When the walkway jogged to the left, near the broad shadow cast by a warehouse, Kane and Grant slipped smoothly into it.

They marched through the muddy, squalid alleys between ramshackle buildings and hovels, following them into the deepest parts of the Pits, where they weren't spy-wired. Only the main avenues were under video surveillance. Although the population of the Pits of any ville was ruthlessly controlled, they usually roared with lusty life, but these streets seemed less crowded than they expected. A pall of gloom hung over the shacks and squats.

The planned ghettos of the villes were named after Tartarus, a lower section of Hades where Zeus had confined his enemies. Kane always thought they were well named.

The Pits were melting-pots, swarming with slaggers and cheap labor. Movement between the Enclaves and Pits was tightly controlled—only a Magistrate on official business could enter the Pits, and only a Pit dweller with a legitimate work order could even approach the cellar of an Enclave tower.

The barons had decreed that the villes could support no more than five thousand residents, and the number of Pit dwellers wasn't allowed to exceed one thousand. Both Grant and Kane retained vivid memories of making Pit sweeps, seeking out outlanders, infants and even pregnant women. They didn't relish those memories.

Despite the ruthless treatment of the Pit dwellers, the one constant, in any version of any ville, was a Pit boss. By no means an official title or position, Pit bosses nevertheless served a purpose of varying degrees of importance, depending on the ville.

Part crime lords, part information conduits and part procurers of luxuries, the Pit bosses were tolerated in most villes as long as they knew and kept their place. If the bosses maintained a certain order among the seething masses, Magistrates were inclined to look the other way if they engaged in limited black-marketing or the elimination of troublesome elements.

According to the Intel they remembered from their Mag days, Boss Klaw had been the overlord of the Ragnarville pits longer than anyone else, but that was all they knew. Presumably, Klaw had proved useful to the ville elite on more than one occasion or he wouldn't have enjoyed such a lengthy reign.

As they walked the slushy back alleys, they encountered only a few people, most of them rooting through heaps of garbage. When they caught sight of the black-armored figures, they froze, hunkering down like rabbits, trying not to draw any notice. Kane and Grant paid no attention to them, though inwardly they were alert to every nuance of their surroundings. It was tactically unwise to become too relaxed in the Pits, regardless of how cowed the citizenry appeared to be. Both kept a wary eye out for other Mags.

Magistrates in full battle armor weren't commonplace sights in Tartarus, and their presence portended any number of awful events. As both men strode along, they unconsciously reverted to their Mag personas, swaggering in step, heads held at prideful angles, mouths drawn in grim, slightly superior smiles as the lesser breeds scrambled out of their path.

Old habits and customs died hard with Magistrates, particularly because of the rigorous discipline to which they had submitted themselves. Casting aside their identities as Mags and accepting new roles as outlanders and exiles hadn't been easy for either Kane or Grant. Although they never admitted it to each other, sometimes they yearned to return to their former lives. If nothing else, the world had made more sense back then.

Some of the more flimsy buildings showed recent signs of fire damage, the smell of charred, scorched wood still fairly strong. Remembering the checkpoint guard's words, Kane said, "Burning hail. Think that's what did it?"

Grant shrugged. "Who the hell knows. All Pits are tinderboxes."

At rustling sounds from a pile of maggot-infested meat scraps behind a butcher's shop, Kane and Grant stopped. The scavenger was a middle-aged man with a milky cataract over his left eye. Leathery warts sprouted around his bewhiskered chin and cheeks. Because their approach had been on his blind side, the man hadn't noticed them, the sound of his pawing through the bones and strips of reeking fat masking their footfalls.

"You! Slagger!" Kane barked, employing the command voice.

The scavenger's head came up and around so swiftly, it was a wonder he didn't dislocate his neck vertebrae. When he glimpsed the pair of black, red-visored figures looming not more than six feet away, he uttered a strained squeal of pure, undiluted terror. Staggering half-erect, toothless mouth gaping open, he fell against the wall. A stream of urine gushed down his right leg.

"Puh*leeese*," he croaked. "It's garbage, they threw it out, I'm hungry, my family's starving, puh-*leeese!*"

Kane glanced down at the stinking meat crawling with flies and squirming white larvae and went frosty with disgust. "I only want to ask you one question. Answer it and you can go on your way, back to your starving family."

The man said nothing. He seemed paralyzed, oblivious to anything other than the Magistrates.

"Where can we find Boss Klaw today?"

The scavenger blinked as if he hadn't understood the question, or if it held a hidden meaning he was expected to ferret out.

"Are you half-deaf as well as half-blind?" demanded Grant. "Answer the officer's question. If you don't know, say so."

The man tried several times to speak, lips working, Adam's apple bobbing. Finally, he half gasped, half snuffled, "Grifter's Gristle."

Kane cocked his head at him. His "What?" sounded very impatient.

The scavenger gestured feebly. "Tavern, next alley over."

"You sure he's there?" pressed Grant.

The man nodded desperately. "Saw Lejacque, his strong-arm, outside. He's there, I swear, puh*leese*."

Kane and Grant walked past him. They glanced back once to see the man slap-footing it away in the opposite direction, arms full of meat scraps. A cloud of flies followed him.

"Poor stupe bastard," Grant muttered. "Thought we were going to chill him because he was stealing garbage."

Kane didn't bother to remind him that in the past they had chilled Pit dwellers for less serious offenses. He figured if Grant didn't recall it, he wasn't going to jog his memory.

From the open door of a clapboard building floated the murmur of voices and the squalling of a poorly played concertina. The flat-roofed structure had the shreds of paper windows flapping in the splintery frames.

It also had a strong-arm standing in front of the door, a black man slightly taller and a good deal heavier than Grant. A shirt of bilious green was stretched tight over his huge biceps and bulging pectorals. His thighs looked ponderous.

Lejacque didn't appear to be armed, but then, he probably didn't need to be. None of his weight looked like fat, and if he meddled with Grant and Kane, the outcome would have to be decided by a bullet.

But he wasn't inclined to tussle with a pair of armored Magistrates. Although he looked as if he had an IQ well into the double digits, he stepped respectfully aside at their approach.

The Grifter's Gristle tavern was half-filled with around twenty or thirty people, mostly men standing at the bar or seated around the tables. The reek of home-brewed liquor cut sharply into their nostrils.

The tavern was longer than it was wide, and both men noted there were no rear or side doors. At the end of the room, half a dozen shabby men sat hunched around a table.

The murmur of the conversation and the cacophony made by the concertina died away instantly, as if a giant bell jar had been dropped over the building. Kane and Grant stood just inside the doorway, grimly surveying the faces, looking for one that would meet their gaze. None did.

Kane announced flatly, "Klaw, Boss Klaw."

The people at the far table shifted their feet, and chair legs scraped against the floorboards.

"I'm Klaw," spoke a clear, melodic and altogether cultured voice.

Grant and Kane stalked toward the table. Both men had difficulty keeping the astonishment from showing on their faces. The woman staring up at them was short, not more than four feet five, but her hands, resting on the table, were huge and blunt.

Metal thimbles capped four fingers of her right hand, and light glinted from the cruelly curved steel spurs tipping them. A massive head, the size and shape of a pumpkin and matted with fiery red hair, squatted between her broad shoulders. The skin of her cheeks bore a maplike pattern of broken blood vessels.

Her large, yellow eyes rested on them as they walked forward. In a remarkably modulated and undeniably feminine voice, Boss Klaw said, "I've been waiting for you."

Chapter 16

Before going to the control center, Brigid stopped by the armory to select a new handblaster. Grant's admonitions about her Mauser, as much as she resented them, had foundation.

For a while she had carried an H&K VP-70, then a Beretta, but she found the weight and recoil of both guns a little uncomfortable. On the mission to *Parallax Red,* she had opted for an Uzi, but never had the chance to use it, though she had test-fired it on the range Grant had set up on the plateau.

Removing one of the lightweight Uzi autoblasters from the glass-fronted case, she inspected it briefly, going through the motions of acting as if she knew what she was doing. Grant had explained to her its semiauto blow-back and floating firing pin. It weighed less than three and a half pounds, even with its 20-round magazine of 9 mm parabellum ammo.

In principle, Brigid detested guns, but she wasn't so blinkered that she couldn't accept their necessity, especially if an adversary didn't share those qualms. So far, none she had encountered did.

From a foam-cushioned crate, she selected four grens, a high-ex, an incend and a pair of Alsatex stunners. After attaching the grens to the metal rings of a combat harness, she slipped it on, then donned her long coat over it. She slung the Uzi over a shoulder by a leather strap, slipped two extra magazines into her pocket and left the armory.

Domi was already in the control center, obviously eager to be off. She wore similar garb of dark whipcord and high-laced combat boots. Brigid saw the .45-caliber Detonics Combat Master snuggled in shoulder leather beneath her coat. She chattered gaily to Lakesh, who nodded and smiled at her absently.

The smile left his lips when he caught sight of Brigid. Despite the thick lenses of his glasses, she saw the worry in his rheumy blue eyes.

"You found something about the Doomstar program," Brigid declared flatly.

Domi fell silent as Lakesh said, "Not nearly enough, but what I did find out is sufficient cause to make me incontinent for a week."

Though Lakesh was prone to melodrama, Brigid heard the genuine edge of anxiety in his tone.

"What was it?" she asked.

Lakesh gestured to the wall concealing the mainframe computers. "What little data the memory banks have indicates that the energy principle of Doomstar is antimatter."

Brigid's eyes narrowed as she reviewed her mental index file. "Antimatter is opposite of ordinary matter. It has positively charged electrons and nuclei with a negative charge."

Lakesh nodded. "Simplistic, but close enough. Experiments were conducted with antimatter, and it was manufactured, albeit slowly and in microscopic amounts, in laboratory settings. It was put to limited use. For example, when Cerberus was built, a force screen, energized by particles of antimatter, surrounded the plateau."

He snapped his fingers. "As matter touches antimatter, they annihilate each other."

Brigid recalled him speaking of the force field and how it had been deactivated sometime over the past century.

"The old term for antimatter," Lakesh continued, "was CT, meaning 'contraterrene.' That term figured prominently in the very incomplete data I found pertaining to Doomstar."

"Are we talking a bomb or what?" asked Brigid.

Lakesh shrugged. "I wish I knew. If Doomstar is a bomb, it is well named. The destructive energy would be ghastly beyond imagination. For example, the output of a conventional nuclear warhead is about one percent of its total radioactive payload. The figure for an antimatter bomb could approach one hundred percent. One kilogram of antimatter would explode with the force of up to forty-three million *tons* of TNT—as though several thousand bombs of the kind which obliterated Washington were detonated at once and the same time."

Brigid couldn't help but wince. "That sounds like overkill to an infinite factor."

"Infinity plus one," Lakesh said unsmilingly. "However, I doubt the Doomstar program was designed to be a bomb. But contraterrene, antimatter, is most definitely involved."

"You said you remembered that Doomstar could be represented in an interface with the real world. You found nothing that expanded on that?"

Lakesh shook his head dolefully. "Not even the most oblique reference. Regardless, whatever the dynamics at work here, the implications are terrifying."

Domi, though she comprehended little of the discussion, said uneasily, "Mebbe should wait for Grant and Kane to come back."

Brigid felt a flash of annoyance. "That could be days from now. They've been gone for nearly eight hours, the Comsat is tracking their transponders and they're definitely on the move. They obviously found transportation to Ragnarville."

Lakesh nodded in reluctant agreement. "I concur. Whoever is tampering with Redoubt Zulu must be identified as soon as possible. Though this latest information adds an element of danger I hadn't foreseen, it also indicates urgency."

Brigid moved swiftly toward the jump chamber's ready room, walking down the aisle between the rows of computer consoles. "Let's get to it, then."

A flat equipment case lay on the table filled with self-heat ration packs, bottles of water and first-aid items. A Mnemosyne rested within it, part of their standard field equipment. The Syne, as it was commonly called, was a small electronic lock decrypter. Two trans-comm units and a pair of Nighthawk microlights had been placed atop the case, as well as the motion detector. A copy of the redoubt's layout, acquired from the database, was also there.

Lakesh followed them in. "It's very cold up there, sub zero temperatures almost the whole year. I recommend you don't go outside the installation for more than a few minutes. You could easily freeze to death."

Brigid frowned at him. "I thought you wanted us to get a look at the HAARP array."

"It's some distance from the redoubt proper," he replied. "If it's functioning, you should be able to confirm it with the instruments inside the complex."

Domi slung the equipment case over a shoulder. Pocketing the map of the layout, Brigid made sure the frequencies of the trans-comms were in synch and that the pair of microlights worked. She slipped the motion sensor around her left wrist.

"Primed," she announced, unconsciously imitating Kane's way of saying he was ready for an op to commence.

Lakesh smiled at her choice of her words. "Be exceptionally careful, dearest and darlingest ones. Don't hesitate to use the LD option if the situation warrants."

The Last Destination setting was a standard feature of all gateway units in the Cerberus network. If activated within thirty minutes of a materialization, it transported the jumpers back to their origin point.

Brigid and Domi stepped into the mat-trans chamber. As Lakesh closed the armaglass door behind them, they exchanged jittery, reassuring smiles. Brigid couldn't deny it felt strange to make a jump without Kane or Grant. Actually, it felt more than strange. It felt decidedly wrong.

The fresh memory of Rouch's malicious smile popped unbidden into her mind, and she wondered if she shouldn't have mentioned the incident to Lakesh. The circuitry on the door engaged, automatically initiating the jump process. She deliberately divorced her thoughts from her emotions.

Silvery light, like a distant heat shimmer, sprang up from the hexagonal floor plates. The droning hum climbed in scale to a howl, and the plasma wave forms, which resembled vapor, floated from above and below.

Domi grinned and intoned softly, "I hate these fucking things."

Her impression of Grant's prejump mantra was so dead-on, Brigid couldn't help but laugh. Her apprehension faded away, and then so did she as she was plunged into a black nanosecond of nonexistence.

BRIGID BLINKED and the glowing patterned metal in the ceiling swam fuzzily back into focus. The whining of the interphase-transition coils beneath the platform wound down into inaudibility. The last tendrils of vapor, a phenomenon associated with the mat-trans quincunx effect, vanished.

Carefully, she pushed herself into a sitting position, waiting for the familiar touch of vertigo and nausea to abate. The translucent armaglass walls were pale blue streaked with gray.

Domi stirred on the floor plates, murmuring something inaudible.

"Are you all right?" Brigid asked.

Domi levered herself up, fiercely staring around, lips peeled back from her teeth in a silent snarl. When she saw Brigid, she forced the snarl into a grin.

"Had dream," she said simply. "Back with Guana. Got to chill him all over again."

Brigid didn't reply. Even the cleanest jumps sometimes resulted in terrifyingly vivid dreams and deliriums. Climbing unsteadily to her feet, she consulted the motion detector. The LCD showed clear.

Domi stood up, wincing a little as she worked her right shoulder. Brigid noticed, but didn't comment on it. "Ready?" she asked.

Domi nodded, drawing her Combat Master and expertly cycling a round into the chamber. Brigid lifted the wedge-shaped handle, and the armaglass door swung outward. She stepped out into the adjoining room, seeing pretty much what she expected to see. Rectangular and roughly ten feet long, the anteroom was slightly smaller than those she'd seen in other redoubts.

The far door was open, and beyond it lay the main

mat-trans control site. Consoles and instrument panels flashed with green, blue and red lights. Computer banks whirred and chittered softly in machine language.

Brigid led the way, glancing at the electronics, seeing nothing unusual. The instruments in Cerberus were more advanced, the control center twice as large, but that was to be expected in an installation that had served as the seat of the gateway project.

Domi said suddenly, "Look."

Brigid turned quickly. The white wraith of a girl pointed to the floor tiles. "Tracks."

Brigid followed her finger and could barely discern several faint markings, made by thickly treaded boot soles.

"Had wet feet," Domi stated. Bending, she touched a track with forefinger. "Couple of days old. Big man. Walked back and forth, like he was pacing, waiting for somebody."

Brigid envied Domi's keen eyesight, honed to near preternatural acuity in the Outlands.

Domi gestured in the direction of the jump chamber. "Then went to gateway. Not come back."

Brigid glanced over an electronics console, trying to locate the molecular-imaging scanners. Every record of every gateway transit was stored in the scanners' memory banks. They could be downloaded and reviewed, but they had to be physically removed, which took time and tools they didn't have.

She made another motion-detector sweep, but

nothing registered. The control room's sec door was open, revealing a blank, cream-colored corridor running to the left and the right, curving gently out of sight in either direction.

Domi sniffed the air, wet a forefinger and waved it back and forth. "Nothing."

Brigid removed the map of the redoubt from her coat pocket. As she unfolded it, Domi remarked, "Not cold."

Brigid, trying to fix their position in relation to the gateway unit, didn't understand what she meant for a moment. Then she realized what the girl remarked upon. Lakesh's warning to the contrary, the temperature was very comfortable; in fact, the room felt a little too warm for the clothes they were wearing.

Of course, that could be only a tribute to the original engineers of Redoubt Zulu that the heating system still functioned at peak efficiency, but Brigid found that explanation unsatisfactory.

When the redoubts and stockpiles were secured during unification, nonessential systems were shut down. Nuke generators still powered the gateways because the tie-in was direct, but keeping an installation the size of Zulu toasty warm required an enormous and wasteful output of energy.

Brigid found an exit marked on the layout and she turned to the left. Their boots scraped noisily on the concrete floor. They passed no rooms opening off the corridor. It was just a long, wide passage with a high, half-domed ceiling. Glowing light fixtures were recessed into it, covered by panes of smoked glass. Thin stalks of flexible metal tipped by tiny glass beads protruded from the ceiling at regular intervals. She recognized the vid spy-eyes and didn't like the way they swiveled on their stems to follow their movements.

She wasn't sure if they were actually transmitting their images somewhere, or if she and Domi were only activating their motion detectors. She only knew the electronic ears and eyes made her uneasy.

The farther they progressed down the passageway, the warmer it seemed to become. Brigid seriously considered shedding her topcoat. She decided to keep it on when they reached the T junction. The transverse arms stretched in both directions, and according to the map, the right-hand path led to an exit.

Domi drew her attention to a narrow slot running the width of the ceiling at the junction. Glancing up, Brigid saw the double frame and the retractable sec bulkhead within it. Though she looked for them, she saw no controls on the walls. The sealing-off procedure had to be controlled from elsewhere in the redoubt.

She and Domi strode swiftly along the right-hand corridor. The outlander girl gazed up and down and around alertly, but she didn't seem apprehensive. Brigid wasn't sure if she should be comforted or disconcerted by that.

Tension coiled like a length of heavy rope in the pit of her stomach. She had the overwhelming sensation their every move was watched by dispassionate eyes.

They had walked, by Domi's calculation, nearly a mile since leaving the gateway. Even the map couldn't accurately convey the immense size of the redoubt.

Finally, they reached a circular foyer area, with three passages branching off from the central axis. One stretch of corridor was barely ten yards long and blocked by a vanadium-steel barrier. Brigid searched for and saw the keypad controls and green lever on the wall and breathed a silent sigh of relief.

Domi held her blaster in a two-fisted grip, barrel pointing to the ceiling as Brigid stepped to the keypad. Before she punched in the code, she said, "Get ready. No telling what the weather is like out there, but it's bound to be bastard cold."

Nodding in acknowledgment, Domi lowered her head between her shoulders, lifting the padded collar of her coat. Brigid tapped in 3-5-2 and threw up the lever. With a hissing, squeaking rumble, the massive door began to rise. She stepped back, slitting her eyes to protect them from a roaring blast of Arctic wind.

When the door reached the halfway point, she squinted even more, but not against a wintry gust. Brilliant sunshine flooded over the threshold like a stream of molten gold. A warm breeze caressed her face.

Stunned into immobility, into silence, Brigid could only stand and stare at the valley spread out below her. New green growth pushed its way up out of the ground, and sunlight gleamed wetly on the smooth surfaces of rocks. Lazy white clouds hung in a sky of deepest, purest azure.

Alaska was as warm as a summer's dream.

The soft feminine voice spoke from everywhere and nowhere. "Quite breathtaking, isn't it?"

Chapter 17

Royce pivoted on his heel, spinning to face Hoffman. "*Who* did you say is back?"

Hoffman gazed at his superior officer in momentary confusion, wondering if he might have made an error. He glanced again at the hourly Intel report. "Hadley and Brewer, sir. They arrived around noon."

"Bullshit!" Royce crossed his office in one stride and savagely snatched the sheet of paper from his subordinate's hand. He ran his index finger across the columns of closely set type until he came to the routine log-in. He read Hadley's and Brewer's names and the serial number of the Sandcat.

Eyes boring into Hoffman's, Royce demanded, "Did they report to the watch commander?"

Hoffman groped for a reply, nonplussed by Royce's extreme reaction to an offhand remark. "I don't know, sir. I mean, I'm sure they did. It's SOP, right?"

Royce stomped over to his desk and pressed a key on his trans-comm. "Fitz!"

A moment later, a bored voice filtered out of the speaker. "Fitz here."

"Did Hadley and Brewer report back to you today?"

"No, sir," came the response. "I thought they were out in the field, on an away assignment."

"Try raising them on their comm-links," Royce snapped.

Fitz coughed to cover his bewilderment. "I'll have to patch into the long-range transmitter, since they're out of the ville. That'll take a couple of minutes."

"I'll give you one. Try the local channels, too." Royce released the key and glared at Hoffman as if he held him responsible for some offense too heinous to be named. Stabbing a finger at him, he snarled, "I want you to get to Intel. Pull all the exterior vid tapes made around noon. Have them ready for me to review."

Hoffman backed out of the office and into the corridor without a word, relieved to be out of the range of his superior's furious eyes, if even for a few minutes.

Royce looked again at the log, noting the name of the guard who had checked Hadley and Brewer in. Peeling back the cuff of his sleeve, he looked at his wrist chron. The time was close to 1330 hours. That meant Hadley and Brewer had been back in Ragnarville for nearly an hour and half.

The trans-comm warbled. Royce slapped at the key. "Royce here."

Uneasily, Fitz said, "Sir, I tried it both ways. Several times. No response on either long-range or local."

"Something wrong with the equipment?"

"Absolutely not, sir. The signal carries fine. They're just not answering."

Royce released the key and stood at his desk, trying to control the cold flip-flops his stomach was performing. He wasn't sure why he felt so afraid. All he knew was that his lord would be monstrously displeased by this mystery. As the new division administrator, even if his promotion had yet to be formally or officially announced, Barch would still hold him responsible for inefficiently dealing with this situation. Also, the very notion of disappointing Barch upset him deeply.

Barch was in private conference with the new personnel he had requested. Royce didn't want to divert his lord's attention from far greater matters with something as superficially minor as two Mags disobeying orders. Still, Barch himself had specifically stated he wanted Brewer and Hadley to remain isolated in the redoubt, away from Ragnarville.

Since the emotionally draining ceremony of Royce's induction into the Trust, Barch had talked at length about the future, about how important it was to prepare themselves for the new world to come.

Unity Through Action had been a serviceable rallying cry nearly a century ago, he explained, but its usefulness had come to an end. It was now a constraint to progress, an empty slogan synonymous with stagnation.

Barch had told Royce all about the Archon Directorate and the hybrid barons, but also pointed out that he didn't necessarily subscribe to the dogma as the unvarnished truth. If entities such as the Archons had ever existed and interacted with humanity, it was so long ago it no longer mattered. It was past time for humanity to seize its own destiny and determine the future for itself.

They shouldn't expend any more time or energy on mourning Baron Ragnar. In the long run, everyone in the ville could benefit from his death.

Royce found Barch's words disquieting, confusing and thrilling all at the same time. Despite his bewilderment, his reservations, he knew he wanted to be part of the new world Barch intended to build.

Swiftly, Royce strode out of his office down the corridor, then turned to the big room housing the Intel section. The room was spacious, with vaulted walls—more than a dozen people sat before banks of computers with flashing readouts and indicators. Vid monitor screens displayed black-and-white images, from residential Enclaves, the promenades, the Pits. The cool semidarkness of the whole place hummed with the subdued beeping of machines and the quiet murmur of techs communicating with other villes and Magistrates.

He joined Hoffman at a vid console, leaning over him. "What have you found?"

"A couple of things, sir," answered Hoffman, a nervous catch in his voice. On the screen flickered an image of the vehicle depot. Even though the resolution was grainy and the view partially blocked by the rear of an AMAC, Royce knew the two armored Magistrates walking across the compound were not Hadley and Brewer.

Hoffman punched a button on the console. "Another one, sir."

The scene shifted, the perspective tightened, showing the pair of Mags striding along the walkway, the direct route to the monolith.

"After they left the range of this eye," Hoffman said, "they don't show up again. They left the path sometime after this."

"Freeze it," ordered Royce.

Obediently, Hoffman froze the frame so Royce could study the image of the two men. Half to himself he said, "Left the walk. Into the Pits."

"Evidently, sir. But there's no vid record of them there, either. They must have stuck to the side lanes and alleys where it's not wired."

Royce turned to an Intel officer. "Do you have any of those posters sent here from Cobaltville?"

The officer rummaged through the contents of a drawer and brought over a square of stiff paper. Royce took it, comparing the likenesses of the two men to that displayed on the vid screen. Though only a portion of their faces was visible, the jawlines matched and so did the complexion of one of them.

Royce felt a wild surge of an unidentifiable mixture of emotions. Fright, jubilation and satisfaction all warred for dominance within him. The hand holding the poster acquired a tremor.

"Sir?" Hoffman peered up at him curiously.

Royce said quietly, "Come with me. Get Gage and armor up."

Hoffman's eyebrows rose. "Sir?"

"We're hitting the Pits."

Hoffman swallowed very hard. Though it was hard to tell in the dim light, his face seemed to have turned a shade paler. Royce turned to leave, saying over his shoulder to the Intel officer, "We've got a situation. When Barch is free, tell him that the assassins of Baron Ragnar are in Tartarus."

"Hadley and Brewer?" Hoffman's voice hit a high, shaky note of incredulity.

"They're not Hadley and Brewer. They're Grant and Kane, the Cobaltville renegades. And I think I know just where we can corner them."

"EXPECTING US? WHY?" Kane asked, pretending not to notice the proffered chair.

Boss Klaw idly dragged her hook-tipped fingers over the surface of the table, shallowly scoring the wood. "Why else? Information. I'm surprised it took you so long to get here. I suppose you exhausted all your other avenues."

Grant eyed the plug-uglies at the table impassively. These men were her lieutenants, thugs she could rely on, but they steadfastly avoided making eye contact with the Magistrates.

Klaw was far more bold. Her eyes appraised both of them, one after the other. Pleasantly, she said, "I don't know either one of you. Usually it's just Dixon, sometimes Royce and they never gave me the pleasure of their company dressed up like you two. Poor Dixon."

She lifted a shoulder in a shrug. "Heard his nervous system was fried. A sweet fellow really, beneath his posturing. Hope he makes some kind of recovery."

Neither Kane nor Grant knew whom she referred to, but they didn't let on. Gruffly, Grant asked, "Just what do you know?"

Boss Klaw laughed, a lovely sound made grotesque because of the stunted creature who voiced it. "The terms first, big man. What do I get in return?"

"Information first," bit out Kane.

Klaw tsked-tsked in disapproval. "My, you are new, aren't you? Royce should have told you how it's played."

Kane's Sin Eater slapped into his hand. He didn't point it, but he growled, "Got no time to dicker with you, bitch. This isn't a street market."

Boss Klaw's finger spurs dug into the tabletop. Her eyes flared with sudden yellow anger, then dismay. She said softly, "Yes, I suppose the circumstances are abnormal, so I should be flexible in my approach. What do you want to know?"

"Everything you've heard about the baron's death," Grant said.

"Surely you have more details than I."

"Humor us," said Kane curtly. "Pretend we're strangers to the ville who just arrived."

She glanced at him sharply, even suspiciously, but Boss Klaw did as they asked. As they hoped, she knew far more than Brewer and Hadley. The depth of her information was disquietingly profound.

Traditionally, Pit bosses had intelligence pipelines into all levels of ville society. Klaw apparently operated a very efficient and widespread network of informants and spies. What she told them bordered on the unbelievable, but Kane and Grant refrained from saying so.

However, when she mentioned how Barch had assumed the role of grand ville administrator-in-residence, Grant couldn't suppress a grunt of disbelief. "What the hell is a grand administrator-in-residence?"

A slow smile spread over Boss Klaw's unlovely features. "Ah, a bit of the light of understanding begins to shine on my benighted brain. You weren't being facetious when you said you were strangers. You're not from Ragnarville at all. You're Mags from some other ville, sent to investigate the assassination. No wonder no one came to question me. Barch already has the answers he needs and wasn't interested in any I might supply."

Grant and Kane made no comment, not disputing

her assertion. Klaw accepted the old axiom of silence giving assent and nodded. "Then you aren't empowered to exchange anything in return for the information I just gave you. I should close this interview."

"We're still Mags," Kane warned, suggestively raising his Sin Eater.

Smoothly, Klaw said, "But I won't. All I wanted was a half-hour period of spy-eye blindness in the marketplace quadrant so one of my associates could take receipt of a shipment of jolt. It was a small thing, anyway. Since you're not from the Ragnarville division, I'd like to speak more freely with you. However, as you reminded me, you're still Mags."

In an undertone Grant said, "But we're not Barch's Mags."

"How do I know you won't repeat to him what I tell you?"

"You don't," said Kane. "And you wouldn't believe us if we promised otherwise, would you?"

"No, I wouldn't." She sighed. "I've been useful to the Mags here over the years and I've acquired a certain degree of immunity. I'd hate to forfeit that, since my life would probably be forfeit at the same time."

Grant and Kane said nothing. They stared down at Boss Klaw. She met their visored gazes unflinchingly. A slagger she was, but she possessed a dignity and courage that they found impressive. The usual intimidation ploys would have little effect on her.

Kane made a deliberate show of holstering his Sin Eater. "We have our own mission, which Barch knows nothing about. What we learn from you is not for his ears."

Boss Klaw drummed her spurred fingers on the table. "Do you know why I wear these?"

"A Ragnarville fashion statement?" Grant asked flatly.

She smiled appreciatively. "You're right, to an extent. They *are* fashion statements, symbols of my name and power. To get where I am, I've blinded, scarred and flayed my enemies."

Pushing back her chair, Boss Klaw touched the belt girding her waist. Kane and Grant looked at the intertwined strips of dried and cured human skin without expression.

She lifted her right hand and waggled the hooked thimbles. "You wear armor and badges as symbols. These are my emblems of power, here in the Pits. Poor things, I know, but all someone like me is permitted to have. I take them very seriously."

She dropped her hand back onto the tabletop, the talons clinking. "Lately, I've had the sense, call it a premonition, that my position is threatened. Therefore, I need allies."

"We can't protect you," Kane said.

"I'm not asking for that. I'm asking if your mission includes unseating Barch."

Her eyes darted back and forth between them. "A nod will suffice."

Kane inclined his head a fraction of an inch. Boss Klaw grinned, exposing a set of perfect teeth. "Then I will regard us as allies united in a common cause. Temporarily, of course."

"Of course," echoed Grant.

Klaw affected not to have heard him. "Take this morsel back to whatever ville you came from—I recognize the thirst for power, and Barch's is unquenchable. He will not stop with usurping the baron's power over Ragnarville. He will extend his grasp to all the others."

Grant snorted in derision. "How? All the villes are evenly matched in arms and manpower. A balance of power. It's always been that way."

Earnestly, Klaw explained, "Barch has upset the balance. He has access to a weapon no one else has or even dreamt existed. He demonstrated it here, two days ago."

Kane looked at her blankly. "Do you mean the storm?"

She nodded. "The elements themselves, the furies of skydark returned and are under his command."

Kane didn't smile at her melodrama. "How do you know this?"

Boss Klaw did not answer for a long time. She dropped her lids over her yellow eyes. When she spoke, it was in such a low tone they had to strain to hear her.

"Would it shock you to learn that I have family among the Enclaves? A grand-niece who works in the Historical Division. She has, on occasion, offered me her help in small ways. Her name is Roberta. The foolish child fell in love with Barch and did his bidding. She learned of a predark weapon, lying forgotten in the north country. Now she has disappeared, while Barch lords it over the ville."

Opening her eyes, she inhaled a slow, sad breath. "Roberta went to great pains to disguise her familial connections with me, but they can find out whatever they want to find out. You know this to be true."

Grant and Kane saw no reason to dispute it.

"Barch may have reason to suspect Roberta spoke to me before her disappearance. And though I could pose no threat to him, he is very thorough."

"You've given us that impression," Kane said dryly. "But damn little else. Did Roberta tell you where in the north country they found this weapon?"

Klaw absently combed her talons through her mat of red hair. "No, but she said something about it that made no sense to me. She joked it was a musical instrument that should not be played."

"A harp?" ventured Grant.

The woman opened her mouth to answer, then her eyes flickered in sudden alarm, looking past Kane and Grant. At the same instant, they heard a thudding of feet against wood, a scuffle, a short outcry. They whirled, Sin Eaters flashing into their hands, just as a gunshot boomed.

Lejacque catapulted through the open doorway of the tavern, arms flailing, legs kicking. They caught only a glimpse of the raw, fist-sized exit wound in the rear of his skull before he crashed heavily to the floor. Dust squirted up between the boards.

Within a heartbeat, Lejacque was followed into the Grifter's Gristle by three armored Mags, hands full of Sin Eaters. They halted right inside the door. The man standing in the center trained his blaster on Kane. A tiny tendril of smoke curled up from the muzzle.

In a flat, dead voice, he announced. "My name is Royce. Your names are Kane and Grant. Maybe you can guess what's going to happen to you now."

Chapter 18

The voice, so finely projected and filtered it could have spoken right at her ear, caused Brigid to skip around, slapping at her Uzi, trying to bring it to bear.

A wild, searching gaze showed her nothing but empty corridor and a startled Domi swinging the barrel of her Combat Master in short arcs. Brigid spared a half second to glance at the motion detector, but the LCD showed clear.

The voice spoke again, feminine but with an odd quality to it, as of steel striking steel. "A beautiful landscape, reclaimed from the frozen tundra, is an accomplishment in which one may take pride."

Domi glanced sideways at Brigid, raising her eyebrows in a silent question. The woman's voice didn't sound crazy or hostile, but it didn't alter the fact she could see them while she remained invisible and presumably untouchable by bullets or anything else.

"Where are you?" Domi demanded.

"Non sequitur. You were preparing to admire the valley. We would like to hear your opinion of our work."

"'We'?" Brigid questioned.

"The pronoun was employed correctly."

"Who is we?"

"We are," came the prompt reply.

If adrenaline hadn't been racing through her bloodstream and her heart trip-hammering, Brigid might have been inclined to smile. Domi edged close to her, whispering from the side of her mouth, "Make run for it back to gateway."

The pneumatic hissing of compressed air, the squeak of gears and a sequence of heavy thuds resounded through the corridor. Brigid knew instantly what had happened and didn't need the woman's voice to state, "Those sections are now sealed off from egress. We are still waiting for your opinion."

Brigid exchanged a glance with Domi and whispered, "I want to try something."

In a normal tone, she said, "We are still waiting for you to say 'please.'"

The voice responded immediately. "We are still waiting for your opinion, please."

Domi's eyes widened in surprise. She and Brigid walked over the open threshold and onto a stone ledge. A deeply rutted, crumbling blacktop road stretched to the mouth of the shallow valley. They stared out at the rolling, sun-drenched terrain, shading their eyes. While much of it was barren and rocky, in many places it was covered by a carpet of green grass and the colorful blooms of wildflowers. Brigid estimated the temperature to be in the high seventies.

Far in the distance, a pattern of dark, spindly

shapes arose, too symmetrical in formation and configuration to be natural. She could just make out the skeletal towers connected by crisscrossing rods and bulky disks. They were over a mile away, so their size had to be truly gargantuan to be seen at all. Faintly, at the very edges of her hearing, she detected pulsing crackles, hisses and pops.

Lowly, she said to Domi, "The HAARP array. That explains the climate here."

Domi seemed less interested in the weather than the abilities of the invisible woman. "Think she can hear us out here?"

"Yes," said the voice, but it sounded different, slightly tinny and thin.

At the flicker of movement behind them, Domi and Brigid turned quickly. They gaped at the tiny bead of glowing light hovering at head level. Brigid immediately thought of a firefly, then of a radioactive bee. She squinted her eyes, reducing the glare from the halo of light dancing around it, and discerned a gleam of metal beneath the shimmer.

She remembered the mechanical, bug-shaped surveillance drone that attacked her in the Manhattan installation when she and Kane had traveled the temporal stream back to New Year's Eve, 2000. When she reported the encounter to Lakesh, he told her about the servo mechanisms used in certain redoubts, colloquially called beetles. The tiny device floating before them reminded her more of a bee than a beetle.

Domi stared at it fearfully, raising her blaster. Recalling the high-voltage kick delivered by the device in Manhattan, Brigid reached over and pushed down the barrel of her Combat Master. "Pretty small target."

Domi made a wordless scoffing noise. "Hit smaller."

The woman's voice emanated from the bee. "Your opinion. Please."

"Beautiful," Brigid told it. "A lot of hard work. The HAARP system came in handy, I imagine."

"A tool is only as precise as its wielder," the bee retorted.

Choosing her words carefully, Brigid said, "You must be very proud of yourself."

The bee darted upward a few feet. "I—" The voice was interrupted by a harsh buzz. "We— Non sequitur."

The momentary hesitation confirmed Brigid's suspicions. They weren't communicating with a human being operating a remote-controlled surveillance drone. A machine intelligence spoke to them. She recalled in detail everything Lakesh had said about AI and its connection to the Doomstar program.

"What are your designations?"

The question was unexpected. After a moment's hesitation, Brigid answered, "I am Baptiste. This is Domi." She paused, then asked bluntly, "Are you Doomstar?"

Another faint buzz came from the bee. "We must

have your security-authorization codes before that interrogative may be definitively answered.''

Brigid's lips pursed in impatience, but she detected a developing pattern. The woman's voice would change in both tonal quality and response time depending upon the nature of the question.

"Do you have a designation?'' she asked.

"We are the Thermonic Autogenic Robotic Assistance data network out-feed. You may call us Tara.''

Always in the plural, Brigid thought. "What are your intentions toward us?''

"We have no intentions. We have priorities.''

"Which are?''

Once again sounded the electronic buzz. "They have been amended from the original.''

"What were the original priorities?''

"To assist.''

"What are the amendments to those priorities?''

"We must have your security-authorization codes before that interrogative may be definitively answered.''

Domi groaned in frustrated anger. "Show yourself.''

"We have done so. We are represented by—and you may interface with—the remote sensor unit before you.''

Brigid's eyes narrowed at the choice of words, so close to what Lakesh had recollected about the AI aspects of the Doomstar program.

"You a bug?" Domi challenged, a hint of mockery in her voice.

"Non sequitur."

"She means," said Brigid smoothly, "is the remote-sensor unit your true form?"

"Do you require more assistance and deeper interaction than this unit can provide?"

"Yes," Brigid replied.

"Stand by."

A blaze of dazzling light fanned up and out from the hovering bee. Pixels danced around it, joined with each other and shaped themselves into the form of a woman. She was nude, totally hairless except for the suggestion of delicately arched eyebrows and sweeping eyelashes. Her naked flesh had a translucent quality to it, seeming to exude a shimmer like quicksilver.

Brigid stared in stunned fascination. Domi only appeared gratified to have a target for her blaster other than a glowing bee. She assumed a combat stance, aligning the woman's bald head with the sights of the automatic. The woman seemed serenely unaware of the purpose of the pistol.

"She's not flesh and blood," Brigid said to Domi. "She's a hologram, a three-dimensional image of some kind."

Tara's full lips parted, and she said calmly, "Inaccurate assessment. This form is composed of cohesive energy patterns secured within an active omnidirectional visual matrix and powered by medium-duty electroplasma taps.''

Brigid eyed Tara's lissome body closely, feeling something akin to envy. ''You're basically a human-shaped force field, aren't you?''

Tara's eyes shifted toward her. ''We would accept that as an oversimplified description worded in nontechnical terms.''

Brigid nodded wryly. ''Thank you. I have a question about your energy patterns.''

''You may proceed.''

''Are particles of contraterrene mixed within them?''

Though her lips weren't parted, a distinct buzz issued from them nevertheless. ''We must have your security-authorization codes before that interrogative may be definitively answered.''

Brigid stopped short of rolling her eyes. ''Another question, then.''

''You may proceed.''

''Did you kill Baron Ragnar?''

''We ended his life functions,'' Tara responded crisply.

''May I ask why?''

''The action was part of our amended assistance priorities.''

An indefinable expression crossed Tara's face, but it could have been a trick of the light. She gracefully and soundlessly stepped backward over the threshold. ''Follow us. Please.''

Although they heard no overtone of threat or menace in her voice, Domi and Brigid did as Tara requested. As soon as they entered the corridor, the sec door rumbled down, joining with the floor with a crunch.

Brigid ignored the cold fingers of fear tapping her spine and inquired, "Do you have complete control over the redoubt?"

"We are interfaced with its primary operational systems, those that are not on automatic settings."

"'We.'" Domi spat angrily. "Only one of you!"

Tara tilted her head on her slender neck, the first truly human gesture she had made. "We were singular before the amendment."

She turned and half glided, half walked down the corridor. Though neither Brigid nor Domi wanted to, they fell into step behind her.

Domi whispered, "She like a doll, or a puppet."

Brigid didn't agree or disagree. If Tara was a puppet, not only was she amazingly lifelike, but she also displayed levels of independence. Brigid couldn't help but wonder about the limitations.

They entered the circular foyer area. Only one of the security bulkheads was up, and Tara ghost-walked toward it. Brigid came to a halt in the center of the chamber and restrained Domi with a hand. "Where are you taking us?"

Tara did not look back. "Follow us, please."

Flatly, Brigid declared, "No."

Tara came to an abrupt halt, then pivoted on the

ball of her left foot. She regarded them expression-lessly. "Why do you respond with a negative to our request?"

"Because you did not answer my question."

"We are not obligated to answer interrogatives that may adversely impact on the parameters of our priorities."

"Do your refer to your original or amended pri-orities?"

There came the split second of hesitation and the buzzing noise. "Irrelevant. Our priorities are what they are."

Brigid took a breath to cover her mounting ten-sion. "Who amended your priorities?"

"Is your interrogative a request for assistance?"

Brigid nodded. "Yes, I need assistance so that I may understand."

Tara's perfectly sculpted features suddenly rippled like water disturbed by a breeze. They swirled, shim-mered and molded themselves into the broad, bearded face of a man with a patch covering his right eye socket.

Domi barely managed to bite back an outcry at the sight.

The man's heavy lips stirred, speaking one word in a deep, masculine voice. "Barch."

The man's head atop the beautiful, nude female body evoked a sense of horror within Brigid, but she sublimated it in a swift analysis. Tara could easily manipulate her energy patterns, drawing on imagery from a database somewhere. Conceivably, she could metamorphose into anything.

A shudder shook Domi's slight frame. Hoarsely, she said, "That is *so* sick."

Brigid asked, "Is Barch one of the 'we' to which you refer?"

"Negative," replied the man's voice. "Barch's amendment altered our matrix from singular to binary."

"Will you show me the two components of your matrix?"

Tara's slender body shifted, her entire left side wavering, stretching out like melting wax. It broke up into a pattern of jagged pixels, then rebuilt itself.

A woman stood beside Tara, shorter and smaller of frame, with close-cropped, feathery hair. Her eyes held a clinical, impersonal expression. She wore a pale green bodysuit with a rainbow-hued insignia Brigid had no difficulty recognizing.

"Berrier," the woman stated, in a clipped, no-nonsense tone. "Roberta, J. Age twenty-nine, genotype Gamma Minus C. Quatro-rated archivist, Ragnarville Historical Division."

Brigid could only stare, trying to grasp the implications of Tara's demonstration. The image of Roberta J. Berrier flickered and wavered, seeming to be absorbed into Tara's body. The face of Barch disappeared.

"I have granted your request for assistance and

answered your interrogatives." She turned. "Follow me, please."

Numbly, Brigid did so. Domi walked beside her, shaking her head in disbelief and frustration. "Don't get any of this. Not a bit. Do you?"

Although Brigid's mind grappled with a theory, she had no clear frame of reference or hard experience to draw on to attempt even a partial explanation. She replayed Lakesh's words, searching for a hidden clue. *The Doomstar program could, due to its bio-interface, be represented and interact with the "real world."*

She kept replaying the words as they followed the shining figure of Tara deeper into the redoubt. She always maintained the same distance from them, no matter how fast or slowly they walked. She led them, like a will-o'-the-wisp, down what seemed like miles of corridor. The vast installation was such a labyrinth Brigid doubted even Domi's superior tracking abilities could get them back to the mat-trans unit.

They reached a junction, turning to the right. They walked another few minutes, then passed beneath a broad, square arch and into a great, open mall of vast proportions. The floor was patterned in mosaic tiles, soft and resilient beneath their feet. At the center of the mall stood a multileveled fountain made of curving sweeps of polished metal. No water bubbled or splashed within it, nor had it for a very long time.

All around were glass-paneled storefronts, but they showed dark and empty. Brigid guessed they were in the community center for Redoubt Zulu, an enclosed town square with shops and places of entertainment.

"Why did you bring us here?" she asked.

Tara turned to face her. "To wait."

"For what?"

"For what will happen."

"Why here?"

"It was once a place where personnel gathered. You will be comfortable."

Abruptly, Tara's body compressed as if it were no more substantial than paper being crushed within a gigantic fist. The tiny glowing bee hovered where she had stood, and it darted so swiftly toward the archway Brigid's eyes could scarcely follow it.

As soon as it flitted beneath the arch, a slab of vanadium steel dropped, striking the floor with a booming thud that sent hollow echoes chasing each other throughout the mall.

Snarling in anger, Domi stormed over to the door, glared at it, fetched it a kick, then spun toward Brigid. Between clenched bared teeth, she snarled, "Trapped."

Brigid walked to the rim of the waterless fountain and eased herself down on it. "Yeah," she said with a bitter weariness. "You think I'd be used to it by now."

Chapter 19

What little cover the interior of the Grifter's Gristle offered was inadequate, and the trio of Mags blocked the single exit. The only tactic that occurred to Kane and Grant was to stand their ground and blast it out. The AP rounds in their Sin Eaters provided a slight edge, but even if they managed to shoot their way out of the tavern, they would be trapped and pursued through the Tartarus Pits.

The patrons of the Grifter's Gristle stood motionless, as if their feet were glued to the floorboards. They didn't dare make any movement that would draw attention and fire their way. Even Boss Klaw and her lieutenants were as silent and still as statues.

Royce said, "You've got termination-on-sight warrants hanging over you. I mean to serve them."

Kane smiled thinly. "That much we were able to guess."

"You want it here or outside?"

Grant shifted his right foot a couple of inches to avoid the ribbon of scarlet streaming from the back of Lejacque's bullet-broken skull. "You're giving us a choice? That's class. If it's all the same to you, inside is fine."

As he spoke, his visored eyes studied the mags on either side of Royce. They had fanned out in order to catch him and Kane in a crossfire. But they were also nervous, nonplussed by the fearlessness showed by the traitors. They had expected cowardly ferrets, not men who smirked in the face of certain death.

"Why did you come back here?" demanded Royce.

"This is our first visit," Kane replied pleasantly. "Nice enough burg, seems like."

Royce's lips writhed as if he meant to spit at him. "Why did you chill Baron Ragnar? Are you working with the Preservationists?"

"I thought you were going to serve our termination warrants," said Grant brusquely. "It's the least you can do, since you made us guess and all."

Royce suddenly stiffened, mouth opening slightly in surprise. Reflexively, he lifted a hand toward the side of his helmet. Though he kept his Sin Eater trained on Kane, he said uncertainly, "Yes, my lord. No question. It's them. We're preparing to serve the warrant."

Kane and Grant gazed at Royce as he listened to someone over his helmet comm-link. His form of address startled them both. Even the Mags cast him quick, questioning glances.

Royce listened without speaking for a handful of seconds. Then he said, "Stand by."

He licked his lips, cleared his throat and, in a low, quavering voice said, "Ragnarville is prepared to offer you amnesty, at least for a time. You are requested to holster your side arms and come with me. You will not be harmed.''

Kane and Grant were too shocked to respond for a moment. Kane recovered first. Suspiciously, he demanded, ''By whose authority do you make that offer?''

''Barch, Ragnarville's grand administrator-in-residence.''

''What the hell kind of post is grand administrator-in-residence?'' Grant challenged.

Royce's lips stretched tight. ''The offer is extended to you in good faith, out of respect for your accomplishments, both as Magistrates and after. Will you accept it?''

Grant and Kane's minds raced with speculations, fears, calculations and options. Conceivably, they could blast their way out of the Grifter's Gristle, but not out of the walls of the ville. It was a dead certainty they would not be able to reach the vehicle depot and retrieve the Sandcat.

Even if they got through a firefight with the three Mags unscathed, they would only be buying themselves time. The outcome was inevitable. Kane in particular found the notion of running through and seeking hiding places in the Pits revolting.

Glancing over at Grant, he said, ''Your call.''

''For once you leave a decision up to me,'' he replied in exasperation, ''and it has to be this one.''

He hesitated before saying bleakly, "Seems the better part of valor."

Turning to Royce, Kane declared, "We accept your terms."

Although no one visibly relaxed, the atmosphere of tension lost some its charged edge. Into his helmet's microphone, Royce said, "They've agreed, sir."

He listened for a moment, then protested stridently, "But, sir—"

He stopped talking, closing his jaws with a click. He canted his head slightly to one side. At length, he said in a cowed voice, "As you wish. We'll be there directly."

Lowering his Sin Eater, Royce pushed it back into its forearm holster. To his officers, he commanded, "Leather your side arms."

Both men appeared reluctant to obey the terse order. They didn't say anything, but they didn't move, either.

Raising his voice, Royce shouted, "Do it or I'll have both your asses up before a disciplinary tribunal!"

The Magistrates holstered their weapons, but kept a steady eye fastened on Kane and Grant. Kane felt almost as astonished, but he slid his Sin Eater into the holster. Grant did the same.

Royce gestured to them, stepping back toward the door. Looking past Grant and Kane, he said, "Klaw."

Kane cast her an over the shoulder glance. She still sat calmly at the table, unperturbed and smiling politely. "Yes, Royce?"

"Barch has a message for you. You've got until sundown to get your slagging ass out of Ragnarville. If you decide to stay or if you come back, he'll chill you personally."

Boss Klaw nodded in acknowledgment of the ultimatum, her expression as mild as if Royce had just delivered a bit of news about the price of eggs.

Kane suspected the only reason Royce hadn't chilled her as swiftly as her strong-arm was strictly diplomatic. A tenuous truce had been struck with him and Grant, and another brutal execution would shatter it. As it was, Kane wouldn't be surprised to learn that Boss Klaw didn't live to make the sundown deadline.

Flanked by the Mags, Grant and Kane marched along the lanes of the Pits. Though the Magistrates had put up their arms, they arranged themselves to catch them in a crosssfire if the situation changed.

They reached the walled compound surrounding the base of the Administrative Monolith. The rockcrete walls were six feet thick and twenty feet high. The sharp points of razor wire glinted atop them.

An armored guard cradling a Copperhead in his arms stood beside the massive sec door. When he saw them approach, he keyed in the code numbers and pulled up the control lever. The gate rumbled and squeaked as it opened to one side like an accordion.

The five men walked into the compound and crossed it to the elevator cage. Royce set the toggle switch for a fast ascent, and the elevator shot upward. Grant and Kane expected the car to halt at C Level, the Magistrate Division. It continued on, past C and B. It didn't slow until it approached A Level, where the work of the ville administrators was conducted.

The elevator sighed to a halt, and the doors opened. A black man with a shaved head stood in the carpeted hallway, big fists planted on his hips. A short, square goatee covered his upper lip and chin, and a leather patch covered his right eye. Despite the standard gray duty uniform he wore, he didn't exude much in the way of a magisterial personality.

"My name is Barch," he proclaimed. "I've so wanted to meet you both."

In the few seconds of appraisal time he had, Kane pegged him as a poser. Ville manufacturing facilities had long ago reached the stage of producing simple prosthetics, from false teeth to glass eyes. He figured Barch wore the eye patch strictly for effect, to give him a ruthless, piratical air.

Kane and Grant opted to say nothing as they stepped out of the elevator, followed by Royce. As the other two Magistrates began to exit, Barch waved at them imperiously and dismissively. "Return to the division. Don't make a report of this to Fitz."

They nodded, obviously relieved to shut the door

of the elevator and return to a familiar setting where slaggers and traitors were chilled, not politely greeted by ville administrative officials.

Barch inspected Kane and Grant closely. "You may remove your helmets."

They unsnapped the under-jaw lock guards and pulled the helmets up and off their heads. Barch's single black eye looked keenly into their faces, as if committing them both to memory.

"Yes, it's you two, all right. The pix Cobaltville forwarded didn't do you justice."

"Well," Kane said with a studied nonchalance, "they were taken a few years ago."

"Before you found your new calling." With that, Barch turned smartly on his heel and strode purposefully down the hallway. "Come with me. Things want us to talk about them."

Grant and Kane exchanged mystified glances and followed the man. Royce brought up the rear. They passed several offices before Barch entered an open door. One wall of the room was nothing but a big plate-glass window, overlooking the smooth promenades linking the residential Enclaves with the monolith.

Barch stepped behind a low, curving desk, though it looked like an elongated lap-level computer console, studded with buttons, keys and toggle switches. An egg-shaped object with a copper-colored shell stood on a tripod at the center of the desk. Barch touched its broad base, and a horizontal crack appeared about its middle. The cupped upper half of the object rose, rotating on pivots and pointed at Grant and Kane. Neither man had ever seen anything like it, but it looked innocuous. Grant figured it was a recording device of some kind.

There were no chairs other than the one behind the desk, so Kane, Grant and Royce stood as Barch seated himself.

"I've heard a lot about you," he said conversationally. "Kane, you were a member of the Cobaltville Trust, right?"

Kane nodded. "For a few hours, anyway."

"Then you and Grant rescued an archivist from execution, escaped from the ville, shot down a couple of Deathbirds and disappeared for several months. Recently, you returned to Cobaltville and kidnapped one its high councillors. Since then, you two have been popping up all over hell and gone. Kane, you reportedly critically wounded Baron Sharpe less than a month ago."

Tightly, Royce said, "And they murdered Baron Ragnar. If they didn't do the deed themselves, they were in on it."

Barch ignored him. "How much of what I've just told you is the truth?"

"Pretty much all of it," Grant replied. "As far as it goes."

"I've got the Intel reports on your activities, if you want to read them over and fill in some of the blanks."

Kane shook his head. "No, thanks. We've lived it."

A grin split Barch's face. "Insurrectionists, terrorists, agents of the Preservationists. You're called that and far worse. Criminality on the scale you've been practicing hasn't been seen since the days of the baron blasters."

Grant clenched his fists, his jaw muscles bunching. Barch's words stung him. Between him and Kane, he had the most difficult time coping with his new status as an outlaw.

"Yet only termination warrants have been issued against you," Barch continued. "Seems to me if you were all the things I just said you were, you'd be exceptionally valuable fonts of information."

"About what?" asked Kane.

Barch shrugged. "This and that. Off the top of my head, your apparent knowledge of the mat-trans gateways and how you've been using them to lay false trails. Why haven't you put Baron Cobalt's adviser up for ransom yet?"

He leaned forward in a fast surge. "And more importantly, what the fuck are you doing nosing around in my ville?"

Striving for a light tone, Kane said, "What do you think terrorists are doing in your ville? Use your head, Barch."

Royce growled angrily, sharply. "My lord, you shouldn't subject yourself to insolence from the likes of these slaggers."

"Slaggers?" Barch said with a flinty chuckle. "No wonder your career has advanced so little, Royce. You can't recognize opportunities. These are great men, they've done great things, even if they are against the law."

His eye scanned them unblinkingly. "But your energies are unfocused. I know why you're doing what you're doing, gentlemen. You are opposing an adversary who does not exist."

"And who," inquired Grant disinterestedly, "might that be?"

"The Archon Directorate." Barch's tone was flat, bland.

Kane cursed himself for not being able to prevent the surprise from showing on his face. Even Grant jerked slightly in reaction to Barch's words.

"You know about the Archons," he went on, "Don't waste my time denying it."

Kane exhaled a slow breath. "I won't. Why are you so sure they don't exist?"

Barch spread his arms to encompass the office, the Administrative Monolith, the entirety of the ville. "Baron Ragnar was murdered in his own bed. Where are the Archons? Why haven't they arrived to avenge or even inquire about his death? Why haven't they sent an emissary?"

Kane wasn't about to speak of Balam or the creatures he had seen at Dulce, so he commented noncommittally. "You tell me."

"No, you tell *me,* Kane. What are you doing in Ragnarville?"

"You said it was your ville," Grant reminded him. "What's a grand administrator-in-residence, anyway?"

Barch barked out a laugh. "A euphemism right at the moment. It's a bit too premature to proclaim myself baron, but that will change very soon."

"You?" Kane asked skeptically. "The baron of Ragnarville?"

"Why not? Whatever the barons are, half human, half Archon or something else, they have no right to rule us. Why should humans be subordinate to these hybrid or mutie bastards?"

"For one thing, they've got all the power."

"You mean the Totality Concept technology."

Kane nodded. "And other things."

Barch smiled slightly. "If the Archons did indeed provide the basics of the Totality Concept, then its choice of names was not an accident."

"What do you mean?"

Barch's voice acquired a fierce fervor. "Think about it—the so-called Archon Directorate set for itself the goal of unification of what was left of humanity, with the rebuilding of the world into the image it foresaw, with all antiproductive and nonproductive people eliminated and the productive ones producing under their control. A *totality* of effort."

"They pretty much accomplished that, didn't they?" Kane suggested.

"They did indeed. They laid a sound foundation upon which to build a new order. One determined by humanity."

Grant made a thoughtful grunt. "So you want to exchange nonhuman tyranny for pure-blooded human tyranny, is that where you're coming from?"

"*Tyranny* is just a word, with many differing interpretations. A human hand should guide human destiny. Sometimes that hand must be closed in a fist."

Kane smiled coldly. "And most of the time, that hand never opens. No one ever seizes power with the intention of relinquishing it. If nothing else, you should have learned that from Baron Ragnar."

"All I learned from Baron Ragnar is that he's mortal. The oligarchy can die. They can be chilled. But I'm not telling you anything new, am I, Kane?"

Kane didn't respond to the query. His pointman's sense rang an alarm, but he wasn't sure if Barch was the trigger.

"But we're not discussing what we may or may not have learned from the barons," the one-eyed man said. "We're discussing what I can learn from you. Why are you in Ragnarville? I won't ask again."

Kane considered it, then with a mental shrug decided there was little point in further evasion. "We heard about his assassination. We came to find out more."

"Bullshit," Royce snapped. "You Preservationist bastards came back here to gloat, to find out if the ville was falling apart. You didn't know we had a man like Barch here—"

Barch glared him into silence. Royce cast his eyes down to the floor. Returning his attention to Kane, he asked, "And did you find out more? What did Boss Klaw tell you?"

"Damn little," Grant answered frankly.

Barch chuckled again. "You're lying. I'm sure she told you she suspects me of orchestrating his death."

Royce made a spitting noise of outrage.

Barch said musingly, "She's very perceptive for a slagger. But then, so is her niece."

He smiled then, not one of humor, but of malignant self-satisfaction. "Gentlemen, I don't really blame you for lying. I understand. But believe me, I'm not interested in holding you up as the baron's assassins. We're of like minds, and I have no intention of sacrificing you to make a few fools like Royce happy."

Grant and Kane met his gaze stolidly, waiting for him to say more.

He did. "The undertaking I have in mind is so great, with such mind-boggling rewards, I need men like you involved. You're my own kind, and I need my own kind in on this. I don't trust anyone else."

Kane found himself in grudging agreement with Barch. What the man wanted dovetailed with his own dreams. He tried to find holes in the man's reasoning, and with a faraway shock found that he couldn't.

"We aspire toward the same goal," Barch continued. "I see no reason for a duplication of effort."

Barch went on talking, dropping his voice in pitch. Kane found his attention wandering, drifting from the man's actual words, but he fancied he could feel the vibrations of his voice caressing his inner ears. The words *trust, we're the same, identical goals* seemed to echo endlessly.

Suddenly, Grant uttered a muffled grunt. Frowning slightly, he rubbed his forehead. Barch asked sympathetically, "Are you all right?"

Grant smiled self-deprecatingly. "A little headache. I get them when I'm subjected to a blizzard of bullshit. It'll pass."

Barch nodded. "That it will. Royce can attest to that."

Grant shifted his gaze toward Royce. "What do you mean?"

Barch's smile widened. He checked his wrist chron. "I think sufficient time has passed. Let's try a little experiment. Are you two gentlemen game?"

Grant and Kane looked at him in baffled silence.

"I want you," Barch stated confidently, "to draw your weapons and point them at me with the intention of shooting me."

Their brows knitted, their eyes slitted.

"My lord—" Royce began.

Barch cut him off with a sharp gesture. "Do it, gentlemen."

Kane and Grant stiffened their wrist tendons. The Sin Eaters slapped into their palms simultaneously. Though the bores of both weapons were trained on Barch, their index fingers didn't press the triggers. They trembled, and they felt the joints locking in place, seeming to freeze.

Kane swore in agitated surprise. Clenching his teeth, he focused all of his concentration and will-power on his hand, commanding his finger to do his bidding. Out of the corner of his eye, he noted Grant undergoing a similar struggle, his entire right hand starting to shake.

Barch's voice purred with amusement. "Very well done. Now, aim at Royce and let's see what happens."

Before they consciously realized it, they shifted the Sin Eaters away from Barch in Royce's direction. He bleated in terror. The barrels spit flame and roared with thunder.

They managed to jerk the blasters aside and down at the last millisecond, and the rounds screamed past Royce, missing him by a fractional margin, plowing into the wall and digging into the carpeted floor.

Kane spun around toward Barch, distantly aware of sweat beading at his hairline. When he tried to squeeze the trigger, his hand froze, the metacarpal bones and tendons seizing in a painful cramp.

Barch grinned in genuine pleasure. "You may put up your side arms. I believe I've made my point."

Kane didn't want to holster the Sin Eater, but he found himself doing so before he was consciously aware of it.

Voice rich with amused triumph, Barch declared. "For the past few minutes, you've been subjected to a stream of microwaves. Exposure in the 0.5-kilohertz to 30-megahertz range causes deviations in brain patterns. Even at low intensity, microwaves can seriously alter the rhythm of brain waves, causing drastic perceptual distortions."

He reached over and affectionately patted the odd egg-shaped object on the desk. "This is a miniature HAARP oscillator, a prototype with a very limited range. It's still effective, if utilized properly. Took me a while to figure it out."

Kane's tongue felt as clumsy and thick as an old sock. He managed to force out the words, "Mind control."

"On a modest scale, nothing like the magnifying transformers of the main array. I impressed upon your subconscious a predilection toward trust in me, and a phobia against harming me."

Seeing the fearful expressions crossing Kane's and Grant's faces, Barch added reassuringly, "Don't worry, you're not zombies, I haven't turned you into droids or anything like that. You're just slightly impaired. You'll recover."

"Why not just make us your slaves?" Grant asked

hoarsely. He nodded toward Royce. "Like you did this stupe bastard?"

"Royce was already predisposed to follow the orders of a superior. He's a grunt, and he needs commands to obey, procedures to stick to, lines to toe, marks to hit. I just supplanted the baron in his perceptions as his lord and master. Simplicity itself, really."

"You don't want the same thing of us?" Kane asked.

Barch shook his head. "Not at all. Every commander in chief needs generals to implement his strategies. You two are the likeliest candidates I'll ever find."

Barch stood up from the console. "And every general needs to know the strategies and capabilities of the weapons to be employed in the campaign. You'll come with me."

"Come with you where?" Grant demanded.

Smiling, Barch answered, "To a paradise on Earth. A new Eden. North to Alaska."

Chapter 20

Despite its size, Brigid and Domi explored the mall in less than an hour. The place had served as Redoubt Zulu's primary stockpile area, with back passageways interconnecting the shop fronts and storerooms. All of it had been cleaned out of anything useful a very long time ago.

They found several side corridors, but they didn't walk them, assuming they were all sealed by the sec bulkheads, so they returned to the fountain. Brigid studied the map of the complex, overwhelmed by the seventy miles of corridors distributed among eight levels. The mall, gateway unit and secondary exit were all on the fourth level. The main entrance appeared to be on level two.

While Brigid pored over the layout, Domi prowled around the perimeter of the mall, her impatience reminiscent of a snow leopardess frustrated in her search for prey. She spent some little time shooting out spy-eye lenses until the ringing echoes of the gunshots and the reek of cordite began to give Brigid a headache and she asked her to stop.

"Save your ammo for real targets," Brigid told her sternly. "Tara will let us go when she's good and ready. You won't make her mad enough to come back in here. You can't make a machine mad."

Domi stalked back to the fountain and sat down on the rim. Her eyes snapped red sparks of anger. "How we going to escape, then?"

Under emotional stress, Domi's clipped, almost abbreviated outlander mode of speech was even more apparent.

Brigid shook her head, tossing back her mane of hair. "I don't know. I don't know if it's possible."

"You got grens," Domi argued. "Use 'em on door."

Brigid glanced bleakly at the ponderous slab of vanadium steel. "It'd take more than grens to knock that monster down."

"Put Syne on lock, then."

"I already thought of that. It doesn't have a lock. Tara controls it."

"Should have put it on her, then."

Domi glowered around, drumming her heels against the fountain's enclosure. "This really pisses me off. Grant will laugh at us."

Brigid smiled at her wanly. "Is that why you're so worked up? You're embarrassed?"

Lips compressed, Domi jerked her head in a nod. "We fuck up big-time."

"Grant and Kane wouldn't have done anything differently than we did," Brigid told her soothingly.

"Puppet trapped us. Puppet working for a machine."

"Not exactly. Tara is a manifestation of a program."

Domi considered that for a few silent seconds, nipping her full underlip. "Part real woman, too, right? Roberta J. Berrier. Mebbe another real woman part of Tara, too."

Brigid began to voice a dismissive reply, then realized Domi had made a salient point. By her own admission, Tara had once been a singular entity and if she had indeed originated from a wet-wired biointerface, then another human brain, a woman's, was part of the matrix.

But more than likely, so much time had passed that the entirety of the woman's personality and identity had been submerged by the program. The thought made Brigid shudder inwardly.

The hybrid of organic and inorganic substances calling himself Colonel Thrush had described himself not as an individual, but as a program. Something similar was in operation here, but with far uglier and more destructive implications. She had prevented Domi from shooting at Tara for two reasons. The primary one was exactly what Brigid had told Domi, that Tara was not flesh and blood or even a droid.

The secondary reason was a fear that Tara's energy pattern possessed antimatter particles swimming around in the flux. Conceivably, Tara could direct a backlash that could obliterate Domi in an eye blink.

Brigid stretched out the map to its full length and

laid it on the floor tiles, eyes scanning it level by level, section by section.

"What you looking for?" Domi inquired.

"I'll know it when I see it," Brigid replied absently.

Domi opened the equipment and took out a ration pack. She opened it and ate it, washing it down with swallows of water. She chewed and gulped noisily, and though irritated, Brigid didn't reprimand her. The girl had a hair-trigger temper in the most relaxed of circumstances. Though she probably wouldn't stage a tantrum, she was prone to extended bouts of the sulks. Brigid needed her full cooperation, untainted by resentment or anger.

After she had finished her snack and unsuccessfully suppressed a belch, Domi asked suddenly, "What are you going to do about Rouch?"

The abruptness of the question startled Brigid, took her so aback that she snatched her attention away from the map. Straightening up, she glared at Domi.

"What's that supposed to mean?"

Domi shrugged her shoulders negligently, as if she were only vaguely interested in the topic she herself had raised. "Don't know. She want Kane. You want Kane." Bringing both her fists together, she puffed out her cheeks and imitated the sound of two vehicles colliding. "Big-time fight. Mebbe a chillin'."

"What?" Brigid demanded in scandalized anger.

"I have no intention of fighting her, let alone chilling her over Kane...or anyone else."

"Not talking about you. Talking about her."

"Whatever business Rouch and Kane have, it's their own, not mine. Not yours, either."

Domi favored her with a slightly mocking smile, unoffended by the rebuke. "Whatever. But you better watch your back. Rouch hates you big-time."

Trying to keep what was left of her patience from unraveling completely, Brigid asked, "She told you that?"

Domi laughed scornfully. "Tell me? Bitch never talk to me, think I'm outlander trash. No, I can tell what she wants. She wants you gone. She like black widow, doing mating dance. You stand in way of her dance."

Brigid didn't know if she should be angrier with Domi for raising the subject at such an inappropriate time or herself for even bothering to discuss it.

With great effort, she returned her gaze to the layout. As soon as she did, she noticed an element about it that had eluded her before. Actually, it was a lack of an element. Domi launched into a sneering diatribe about Rouch's haughty manner, and Brigid rudely hushed her into silence. Domi stopped talking, but she looked at her reproachfully.

Brigid's finger traced a double line representing a corridor. She tapped a point on it. "See that? There's a sealed-off section with no ID number or reference key. It's on a sublevel, between levels two and one."

Domi asked, "How we get there?"

Brigid folded over a section of the map and found the mall. Lifting her head, she stared around the dark shop fronts, murmuring, "Service lifts. Freight elevators. There are a couple here, but they're probably unpowered."

Domi stood up swiftly, shouldering the equipment case. "Let's take a look-see."

They searched the rear of several stores and the interconnecting service passages. The little beams of their microlights danced over the floor and walls and came to rest on a pair of wide doors, framed by corrugated metal. They were closed horizontally rather than vertically. The words Freight Only were stenciled on them. Long ago, some jokester had used a felt-tipped pen to cross out the *e* so the sign read Fright Only.

Domi slapped at both buttons on the wall, and as they had expected, nothing happened. Reaching under her coat, Domi drew a ten-inch knife with a serrated blade and inserted the point into the crack where the two doors joined.

"How long have you carried that?" Brigid asked.

"Long time," the girl answered as she worked at the blade. "Since I cut Guana's throat with it. My lucky charm."

Domi's expert probing found a catch lever, and she snapped it open. The lower door slid into its frame, and Brigid heaved the other one up. No car hung inside the shaft, but thick metal cables dangled down into impenetrable darkness.

She directed her microlight down, and though it emitted a powerful beam, it didn't pierce the blackness more than ten feet below. Domi kneeled, staring into the yawning opening, hawked up from deep in her throat and spit a glob of saliva into the shaft. She cocked her head, listening. After a few seconds, she said, "Heard it. Long way down. A hundred feet at least."

Brigid eyed the hanging cables critically, stretched out her arm and snagged one. It was rust streaked and dry, free of grease. She experimentally tugged at it, then strained backward using all her weight and strength. It seemed securely anchored.

Domi watched her doubtfully. "We climb down?"

"Is your shoulder up to it?"

"Not me I'm worried about. You."

Grant had extolled Domi's climbing virtues, claiming she was remarkably agile with a surprising tensile strength. "Let me do it," the girl said. "I can mebbe fix elevator, send it back up to you."

Brigid smiled wryly. "Are you saying I'm not in condition?"

Domi shook her head gravely. "Takes skill and experience."

Brigid appreciated the concern, but after thoughtfully considering her words, she said, "Thanks for the offer, but we'd better stick together. You could be stuck down there and have to climb back up to me, if you could.''

Domi shrugged. ''Suit self. Just watch me. Do what I do.''

She pulled a pair of gloves from her jacket, tugged them on and, without a word, sprang into the shaft. She slapped both hands around a cable, hooking her left leg around it, resting the ball of her foot on the arch of her right. ''Like this.''

Brigid transferred the cable from hand to hand while she put on her own leather gloves and edged out to the rim of the shaft. She pushed herself off into empty space, swinging for a moment pendulum fashion.

Although she wasn't particularly afraid of heights, dangling over a pit of utter blackness sent a sudden jolt of irrational terror jumping through her. She copied Domi's placement of arms and legs.

Slowly, Domi began sliding down the cable, hand over hand, squeezing it between her thighs to control the speed of her descent. Brigid imitated her motions, tentatively at first, then with growing confidence.

Her confidence ebbed after a few minutes when a gnawing ache settled in her hands, wrists, forearms and crept into her shoulder blades. Clambering hand over hand down the cable was harder work than she had envisioned. Twice she had to stop, legs tight around the cable, to relax some of the tension in her muscles. She blessed her gloves twice over. Without them, the coarse steel splinters and threads sprouting from the heavy metal hawser would have abraded her hands.

She knew there was no way she could ever climb back up. Even going down, her coat felt like it was spun from lead and the Uzi weighed as much as a child. Judging from her speed, Domi didn't seem in distress, even with the equipment case bouncing and bumping against her hip and the backs of her thighs.

With what seemed like maddeningly, infinite slowness, they continued to descend into the deep dark. When Brigid's toes finally touched a solid object, she almost had no strength left to lower herself the last couple of inches. She and Domi stood there, inhaling deep breaths and gingerly straightening out their legs. They flexed their fingers, working and kneading the stiffness out of them.

Turning on her microlight, Brigid saw they stood on the roof of a big elevator car. The emergency hatch was almost wide enough to accommodate them both at the same time. Domi lifted the square of sheet metal and dropped down, landing lightly on bent knees. Brigid followed her, clinging to the raised lip for a moment.

Once inside the car, Domi got to work on the double doors, prying up the rusty catch. The doors opened onto a stretch of corridor identical to those they had already traversed.

They moved out cautiously, Domi's blaster tight in her fist. "Really hate this nuke-shitting place," she whispered. "Feels like it's haunted."

Brigid silently agreed with her. Many of the redoubts she had visited exuded an atmosphere of despair, intolerable fear and inconsolable grief. Redoubt Zulu was no exception, or perhaps it was little worse, because it did have a ghost of sorts.

Half to herself, she murmured, "The ghost in the machine."

Domi glanced at her quizzically, but didn't question her about the meaning of the comment. She understood.

Brigid had no idea if they were on the sublevel, since any identifying numbers or maps had long ago been removed from all the walls. The corridor continued to curve gently, then arched around the base of a wide spiral staircase, stretching onward into the gloom. A few yards beyond it they saw a double set of heavy steel doors with a square lock mechanism set in the center.

They increased their pace, Domi reaching the portals first. She ran her fingers over the panel and jerked them back. "Cold," she announced in surprise. "Like a freezer."

Brigid looked at the lock and said, "Sonically controlled, I'll bet."

"That way out?" Domi demanded.

"No, there's an exit farther down. Let me have the Syne."

Domi obligingly unslung the case from her shoulder and opened it, saying, "Let's find way out first."

"And then what? We'll be stuck outside."

"Better than in here. Weather's decent."

"I have a feeling that could change on a whim."

Brigid plucked the Mnemosyne from the case and ran it over the lock. When a tiny light lit up on its metal skin, she placed it flat against the lock and initialized the decryption sensors. The device transmitted an electronic signal that overrode the lock's microprocessors.

Two *queeps* sounded, solenoids snapped and, with a prolonged hiss of compressed air, the double doors slowly swung inward. A surge of painfully frigid air belled out between the doors, forming a cloud of mist as it entered the corridor.

Through the mist, they saw glowing lights as overhead light tubes flickered and shed a yellow luminescence.

Domi and Brigid stepped through the vapor and into a long hexagonal shaft, its sharply angled walls gray and glassy. A low hum seemed to fill the passageway, a subsonic tone that vibrated rhythmically against their eardrums.

Behind inlaid-glass panels in the sharply angled walls they saw patterns of circuitry, with thousands of tiny lights flashing in perfect sync. Brigid and Domi walked past them, shivering and wondering at the bone-deep intense cold.

After twenty yards, they reached the edge of a circular area, enclosed by a continuous lap-level console, studded with regular rows of alternating red and white buttons and small, flickering readout screens.

In the center of the circle, inset in the floor, rose a low dais of gleaming chrome. The square dais supported a couch with curved sides. On the couch, wrapped tightly in a muslinlike fabric, lay a woman. She lay unmoving on her back, eyes closed.

Nausea roiled in Brigid's belly, bile threatening to leap up her throat. Domi hissed in revulsion, averting her eyes.

The woman looked like a botched autopsy or the subject of a brain surgeon who learned his technique by eavesdropping on real doctors.

A large portion of the left side of the woman's head was missing, the scalp peeled and cut away like an ear of partially shucked corn. The blue-white cranial bone beneath was nakedly exposed. Red scraps of tissue still clung to it. Socketed electrodes sprouted from crudely bored holes in her skull, fiber-optic threads curling to sleeve attachments on the console directly behind her head. She wore a metal band around her brow, which helped to keep her detached scalp from sagging over her face. In its center gleamed a small round lens crafted of convex dark crystal. Crusts of dried, frozen blood showed starkly against the pallor of her skin.

"What the fuck is this?" Domi demanded in a strangulated gasp. "Dead woman wired up…why?"

Though horror threatened to consume her, Brigid noted the almost imperceptible rise and fall of the woman's chest beneath the muslin. "I don't think she's dead. If she knew what happened to her, I'm sure she'd wish she was.''

She forced herself to stare at the woman's face, noticing that the left hemisphere of the brain bore most of the electrodes. She knew that the left side of the brain controlled speech, language comprehension and mathematical ability, while the right focused on abstract thinking, music, concepts, spatial ability and higher math.

She looked for any sign of consciousness. Despite the faint respiration, she found none. Then, with a new surge of loathing, she recognized the woman's face. Tara had shown them her in her image. The face belonged to Berrier, Roberta J., one half of Tara's binary matrix.

"Yes," said a deep voice from behind her. "She doesn't look her best, but she's so much more tractable this way. And useful, too."

Domi had already spun around on her heel, leading with her Combat Master before the man's words fully penetrated Brigid's horror-clouded mind.

A man strode through the scraps of mist, followed closely by black armored figures. Both Domi and Brigid recognized his dark, one-eyed face. His voice was familiar, too.

"Barch," Domi said flatly.

A half-dozen Magistrates spread out in a double row behind him, blaster barrels bristling. Domi knew better than to fire, but she kept her blaster aimed at the big man wearing the eye patch.

"You know my name," he said with ingenuous curiosity. "You have the advantage of me, and I'm unaccustomed to that."

A Mag stepped forward to stand beside Barch. Kane's unemotional voice stated, "Their names are Baptiste and Domi."

Chapter 21

Barch fixed his unblinking, cyclopean stare on the two women. He inquired, "Baptiste, the renegade archivist?"

Kane nodded, not speaking.

"And the little outlander slut?"

"Like I said, her name is Domi."

"One of yours?"

Grant stepped up, rumbling, "More or less."

Barch laughed, but the humor didn't reach his eye. "My congratulations. While you two diverted my attention in Ragnarville, you put your own partners in place to find out what I was up to. My already high estimation of your abilities has just risen several notches. I had no idea the Preservationists were this thorough."

He said it as if the words *the Preservationists* explained everything.

Grant and Kane didn't respond. They were just as surprised, but more dismayed than Barch. Kane gambled that inasmuch as Barch sought them as allies, he wouldn't act on his first impulse to order the women imprisoned or chilled.

Gesturing to the armored men behind him, Barch

said, "Lower your weapons. You, too, ladies. No harm will come to you. We're all in this together now."

Brigid and Domi said nothing, nor did they move. Kane noted approvingly that Brigid had her poker face on, but Domi's ruby eyes shone with suspicion.

"Domi," Grant barked. "Do as the man says."

Slowly, reluctantly, Domi returned her pistol to the shoulder holster. To the assembled Magistrates, Barch said, "Stand down."

As the barrels of the Sin Eaters dropped, he ordered, "Wait for me outside. Grant and Kane—stay. Royce, you might as well be here for the orientation, too. Not that you'll understand any of it."

Three of the black-armored men filed out into the corridor. Barch approached the women a little warily, but with a self-confident swagger. "How did you know about Zulu?" He addressed his question to no one in particular.

"Like you said," answered Kane, "the Preservationists are thorough."

Barch seemed satisfied with the explanation, at least temporarily. In Ragnarville, Barch and Royce had escorted them up to the baron's penthouse and to a hidden mat-trans unit. There they had been joined by three hard-contact Mags. All of them crowded into the jump chamber and made the transit to Zulu.

Barch had spoken very little during the long walk from the gateway, except to express annoyance at the lowered sec bulkheads and to mutter peevishly about someone named Tara. He used a small sonic key to raise the barriers.

Both Kane and Grant considered testing the recently imposed aversion to causing Barch harm, but they opted to wait until they were absolutely certain the mental block had faded.

Trailed by Royce, they followed Barch as he strode directly to Brigid and Domi. When he stopped and cast his gaze down, they followed suit. Grant and Kane struggled to tamp down their reactions of revulsion when they saw the mutilated woman lying on the couch.

Quietly, addressing the two women, Barch said, "I see you've met Roberta. Have you met the animated version of her?"

"Tara, you mean?" Brigid's tone was as icy as the air around them.

"Who's Tara?" Grant inquired.

"For one thing," Brigid answered, "Baron Ragnar's assassin."

Royce stiffened, drawing in a sharp breath.

Barch regarded her respectfully. "So you've reasoned it out."

"Not really. She told us about it herself."

Royce exclaimed, "My lord, if the baron's murderer is here, why haven't we—"

Barch didn't even bother turning his head. "Shut up, Royce."

Kane forced himself to look at the supine woman. "This isn't Tara?"

Barch chuckled, a hard, flinty sound. "In a manner of speaking, yes. In another manner of speaking, this entire complex is Tara."

Grant and Kane regarded him blankly, but he seemed disinclined to expand on his statements.

"What you're really interested in is HAARP," the one-eyed man went on. "I brought you here to establish my bona fides. Let's get on with it."

He walked deeper into the hexagonal shaft, assuming the four people would follow him. Brigid caught Kane's eye, and he surreptitiously lifted a finger to his lips, slightly shaking his head.

What appeared to be a featureless back wall split apart as Barch pointed the sonic key at it. The hum at the edges of their hearing became an almost deafening whine, cutting into their eardrums like white-hot wire. The very air seemed to shiver with the sound. Protected by their helmets, Kane, Grant and Royce only winced, but Domi and Brigid put their hands over their ears. Regular pulsing pops and the harsh crackle of static overlaid the whining noise.

Barch led them out onto a railed catwalk overlooking a vast mezzanine that seemed to be lit by a hundred halogen lamps. Their eyes pierced the glare enough to see that a center area sloped symmetrically upward from all directions like an amphitheater molded from metal. The convex sides steepened at the top, branching into forked pylons. Skeins of electricity sizzled between them.

Projecting from the slightly sunken concave area in the dead center of the amphitheater was a column of metal. Though it took him a few moments to make the connection, Kane realized he was looking at an enormous parabolic transmission dish. It was at least fifty feet in diameter.

Barch shouted, "The heart of Redoubt Zulu—the terrestrial stationary wave transmitter."

He pointed to the left and strode off along the catwalk in that direction. The walk jogged into a small, glass-enclosed booth. Once the heavy door was shut behind them, the whine instantly became bearable, if not comfortable.

A row of vid monitor screens lined the far wall, all displaying different uninteresting images. Scattered on a desk were bits and pieces of various electronic components.

Barch stepped to the last screen on the row and tapped it. It held a low-angle view of a skeletal forest of metal, with dark trunks and spindly branches. "The HAARP array."

He spoke loudly, as if his eardrums were still numbed by the electronic cacophony outside the booth. He cast a sly look toward them. "But I have a feeling you know all about it."

"You're giving us more credit than we deserve," Brigid replied. "You're the one who had the knowledge to reactivate the system."

Kane repressed a smile. Brigid had assessed the man's monstrous ego and played to it. If he had possessed feathers, he would have preened. Smugly, he said, "I must confess I didn't have that knowledge when I first arrived here, about a month ago. But I did see and seize an unparalleled opportunity."

He planted his hands on his hips, tilting his head back at an arrogant angle. "HAARP was the key to geophysical warfare, to use the environment as a weapons system. Weather manipulation, climate modification, earthquake engineering, ocean-wave control and brain-wave influence—all using the planet's natural energy fields."

Barch waved to the scattering of odds and ends on the desk. "I found prototypes of miniaturized stationary wave carriers here. You were subjected to a demonstration of how they work."

He spoke tersely, as if he were reciting a lesson he had learned by rote, or heard from someone else. "All in all, weapons provided by HAARP would be virtually undetectable by their victims."

"And those victims would be the barons," Grant stated.

Barch nodded. "I'm still in the experimental stages, testing HAARP's limits and full capabilities. I've managed to alter the climate here, in a hundred-mile radius. I affected the weather patterns in the vicinity of Ragnarville to create a storm of such destructive magnitude that even I was surprised. But gratified, nevertheless."

Royce gaped at him, jaw creaking open in shocked disbelief. "*You* did that, my lord?"

Barch's lips twisted contemptuously. "I thought you would have figured that out by now. Should have known. Once a grunt, always a grunt."

He returned his attention to the others. "But you're different. We're of like minds and spines. We can lay waste to the baronies from here, reclaim the Earth, chart the course of human destiny."

"With you at the helm?" Kane inquired.

"Who is better qualified? I found HAARP, I put it back on-line." He gestured to the throbbing transformer outside the booth. "Do you think I'd just cover it back up, forget about it and continue to piss my life away in service to Baron Ragnar, bending my knee before that twisted little scut, tugging my forelock?"

Genuine anger and hatred seethed in his words. He swept his arm toward the outlanders. "All of you hate the barons, so don't deny it."

Brigid said quietly, "We hate them because they've made hate necessary in order for us to survive. We don't hate them because they stand in the way of our own baronial ambitions."

Barch didn't respond to the observation. "I can make all of you very powerful. I'm not asking you to sell your souls to the devil. There is no catch to my offer."

Kane was nearly overwhelmed by temptation. Why not agree to help further Barch's ambitions, then when the goal was achieved, the baronies destroyed, turn on him and gain control of HAARP for themselves? They could reshape the Earth for the good of all.

Sindri's plans to visit catastrophes on Earth to make it useless to the Directorate had been stupendously unworkable. Even if it had worked, the extreme overkill would have made the cure far worse than the disease.

As egomaniacal as he was, Barch was not a madman like Sindri, and seemed to know precisely what he was doing. Kane wasn't sure if his willingness to join Barch was due to a residual of the mind-altering device or his fierce desire to release humankind from the heavy harness of servitude. Sourly, he reflected he could not trust his own judgment at the moment.

Barch stretched out his arms to them, as if inviting a group hug. "Please, don't argue with me anymore. I need people like you, resourceful and daring."

"And Roberta Berrier," ventured Brigid, "was she daring enough to volunteer to have herself wet-wired into a database?"

Barch heaved a sigh that sounded like an expression of genuine regret. He passed a hand over his bald pate. "To gain mastery of this installation, of HAARP, certain problems had to be overcome, certain sacrifices made."

"The main one being," Brigid said with no particular emotion in her voice, "the compromising of

Tara's programmed priorities. To achieve control of HAARP, you had to first get control of Tara.''

Impatiently, Kane demanded, ''Will somebody tell me who Tara is supposed to be?''

''Not a who,'' Domi said. ''She's a what.''

''She's both,'' Barch declared. ''An artificial intelligence operating on human engrams instead of circuits and microchips. Organic brain cells fused with electrodes was the only way of interfacing with the computers governing the HAARP array.''

''She's more than a communication interface,'' said Brigid. ''She's the Doomstar program.''

Barch's eye narrowed, then widened. ''The what?''

Brigid's eyes glinted emerald hard. ''You mean you don't know?''

Dismissively, Barch answered, ''I know all I need to know about this place and Tara.''

Domi glowered at him, at his pompous tone. ''Why is that woman out there with her head all hacked up?''

Before Barch could respond, Brigid stated, ''Roberta was the only way to insinuate your control of Tara. You used her brain as a way to integrate with the operational systems.''

Barch pursed his lips. ''It wasn't entirely my idea.''

He stepped to the bank of monitors, turned a knob and pressed a switch. A woman's high-planed face filled the center screen. She was fairly young, with long dark hair brushed back behind her ears.

"Anne Malloy," he said, "director of the Special Cybernetics Op Unit, attached to Project Eurydice. I found her video log. Her brain, her essential personality and devotion to HAARP served as the template for Tara."

Brigid noted absently that Tara's face was an idealized version of Anne Malloy's.

"When Zulu was abandoned," continued Barch, "a couple of years into skydark, she stayed behind as its guardian angel, so to speak. Her living body was preserved, in artificial hibernation, by a form of cryonics. Her conscious mind slept, while her unconscious animated Tara and watched over the redoubt, making sure it was not occupied by the enemy.

"According to video records I found, this place *was* occupied a time or two over the past century, but not by enemy troops. Squatters and scavengers, in the main, but they didn't tamper with HAARP or try to get in here. Tara did not react to their presence. She left them alone."

Barch paused for a moment, closely eyeing the image of Anne Malloy. "I'm not sure when it happened, not even Tara can provide a specific date, but Malloy's organic life functions ceased. She died. But the basics of her mind, her synaptic structure, her neural pathways lived on."

In a very unsteady, very low tone, Brigid asked, "Where is her body?"

Barch made a scoffing noise, as though he found the question unbelievably stupid. "We got rid of it, we disposed of it, what do you think? This place has a very efficient incinerator."

Grant said, "And so you tried to substitute Roberta for Malloy as the biointerface?"

Barch snorted. "I didn't try, I succeeded. Of course, Tara oversaw the actual surgery. She had all the information on the techniques, since her human self had designed it. Roberta's interface is not as aesthetically pleasing as Malloy's, but I went for results, not beauty. It all paid off. Tara is under my complete control."

"But," Brigid interjected, "she's never told you about Doomstar."

Barch surveyed her coldly. "Perhaps you will enlighten me."

"A very apt choice of words, considering that Doomstar could light up this whole part of the planet."

"Explain."

"Have you ever heard of contraterrene?"

Barch shook his head. "No."

"Antimatter, then?"

Recognition flickered dimly in his eye. "I think so. The opposite of matter, right? Something predark whitecoats fooled around with. Strictly theoretical."

Brigid chuckled mirthlessly. "You wish. Antimatter and matter were created and used in limited degrees. When two particles of it meet, their mass is converted to high-energy radiation in mutual annihilation.''

Barch gazed at her in irritated impatience. "I don't need a science lesson, Baptiste."

"You do about this," she responded curtly. "It's quite possible—actually, probable—that Tara is composed of particles of antimatter, held by a magnetic field which is part of her energy form."

Fingering his beard, Barch said musingly, "You may have something there. Tara emits some kind of energy that has exceptionally destructive effects on matter. That's how she chilled Baron Ragnar, you know."

Royce's shoulders stiffened, then slumped.

Brigid asked, "How did you manage to get her out of the redoubt?"

"After I integrated Roberta, I convinced her that in order to assist me, she must assassinate the baron. Since she's just energy, just a hologram, she can alter her mass and shape at will. She stored her pattern in a tiny remote drone, and I sent it to Ragnarville by mat-trans. Once she'd done the deed, she came back."

Brigid shook her head pityingly. "You're like a baby, playing with the detonator of a nuke warhead. You may have Tara under a certain amount of control due to interfacing her with Berrier, but you haven't come close to penetrating her prime directive and priority."

Defensively, Barch said, "She never said anything about a Doomstar program."

"Because you didn't know about it to ask her," Brigid retorted.

"And you did?"

"Yes, but my questions met a lockout. She said she needed my security-authorization codes before she could say yes or no."

"I amended all those old codes," Barch explained matter-of-factly.

"How could you have amended the Doomstar codes since you knew nothing about them?"

Skeptically, Barch asked, "How did you know about it?"

Brigid jerked her head toward Kane. "Like he said *you* said, the Preservationists are thorough."

If Barch detected the edge of sarcasm in her voice, he gave no sign of it. "I have a real problem believing this."

Brigid shrugged. "Well, let's go to the source. Ask Tara. Summon her or invoke her, or bring her on-line or whatever you do."

Barch glared at her for a long silent moment, assessing the challenge Brigid had tossed his way. With a sharp, peremptory wave of his right hand, he directed them toward the door of the booth. They returned to the catwalk, breasting the invisible surf of sound rolling from the transformer.

Back inside the hexagonal chamber, Barch closed the rear wall, cutting off the near painful whine. He marched over to the body of Berrier and announced, "Accessing the Thermonic Autogenic Robotic Assistance data network out-feed. I request assistance."

A chime suddenly bonged softly, and the electronic hum dropped in pitch. Console readouts flashed brightly. Circuitry clicked. From the lens on Berrier's brow, a pinpoint of light sprang up and out. Domi and Brigid recognized it as the little sensor bee.

Barch said, "Put the holographic interactive program on-line."

Dazzling light erupted from the bee and shimmered into the figure of a naked, hairless woman. Kane, Grant and Royce gaped in astonishment—in more than astonishment—at her lissome form and shining skin.

The woman said, "I am the holographic interactive program of the Thermonic Autogenic Robotic Assistance data network out-feed. Please be specific in the manner in which I may assist you. I am here to serve."

Smiling, his fists on his hips, Barch said, "Assist me by explaining the Doomstar program."

When the buzz issued from Tara, the smile fled Barch's face. It twisted into a mask of incomprehension when she said, "We must have your security-authorization codes before that interrogative may be definitively answered."

All of them saw Barch struggling to maintain his

composure, to keep from losing his temper. "What is the classification?"

The reply was immediate. "SCOU B-18 and above."

"You will grant me that classification immediately."

Tara seemed puzzled. "We cannot meet such a request. It is outside the parameters of our programmed priorities."

Barch looked stunned, as if a cowed servant had suddenly and for no apparent reason become rebellious. He gaped at Tara, speechless, unable even to move.

Brigid asked, "What is your prime, unamended priority?"

"To observe, maintain and protect the integrity of this station."

"From whom?" she pressed.

"From those who mean it harm or intend to alter it from its original specifications."

Brigid turned toward Barch, smiling a small but very triumphant smile. "That loophole is all that saved you from ending up like Baron Ragnar. You and the squatters in here before you didn't intend to harm or alter the installation. Therefore, Tara didn't defend it. She's probably programmed to respond to certain kinds of uniforms, maybe even to the Russian language."

"So the fuck what?" Barch rasped angrily. "She's

still under my control, this Doomstar shit of yours notwithstanding.''

Brigid's triumphant smile became cold and taunting. "Let's test that, why don't we?"

To Tara, she declared, "I require your assistance. I need to access Malloy, Anne, SCOU, Project Eurydice. I need to access Berrier, Roberta J., genotype Gamma Minus C. Quatro-rated archivist, Ragnarville Historical Division.''

Barch whirled on her. "What are you doing?" He heeled back toward Tara. "I countermand that request.''

Tara cocked her head, lips moving. "Whadoyuwanwithme?''

The voice came out as a garble, unpracticed, like a defective sound tape.

"Berrier, Roberta J.," Brigid repeated firmly, "Malloy, Anne. I wish to access those components of your binary memory matrix.''

Neither Kane, Domi nor Grant could imagine what Brigid had in mind, so they stayed quiet, watching. Kane poised himself to leap on Barch if he made a violent move toward Brigid. Royce seemed too transfixed by the hologram of the nude woman to notice anything else.

Tara's curvaceous body twisted, wavering like water in a violently shaken glass container. Grant uttered a muffled curse and took a half step backward as both sides of Tara's torso stretched out in sparkling light patterns and dancing pixels. Though they had seen the phenomena before, Domi and Brigid stared in fascination.

Apparently it was new to Barch, because he grunted in astonishment, fists dropping limply to his sides. The light swirls formed into a pair of figures, one standing on either side of Tara.

Anne Malloy, wearing a drab olive jumpsuit with insignia patches on the sleeves, stood on Tara's left. Roberta Berrier, in the green bodysuit of an archivist, stood on her right. The images of both women spoke at that same time.

"What do you want with me?"

The tonal qualities and inflections differed greatly, though each word was in perfect synchronization.

"One at a time," said Brigid. "Malloy, Anne. You served as the neural and synaptic template for the Thermonic Autogenic Robotic Assistance data network out-feed."

"Affirmative," said Anne Malloy's image.

"Did you volunteer for the biointerface process?"

"As its major software designer and as a soldier in the service of my country at wartime, it was my duty."

Brigid nodded and turned toward Berrier. "Berrier, Roberta J. You were the amendment to the template."

"Affirmative."

"Did you volunteer for the biointerface process?"

Berrier stared at Brigid for a long moment, then slowly swiveled her face in Barch's direction. The hologram seemed to stare at him with only a faint flicker of recognition, then with a dawning comprehension.

"Volunteer..." The word passed her lips in the most distant of sighs.

Leaning down, Kane whispered into Brigid's ear, "What are you doing?"

"This is the only way to learn the extent of Tara's memory patterns. I'm betting Berrier's neural pathways haven't been fully integrated yet."

Kane murmured doubtfully, "I hope the odds of this bet paying off are greater than the usual one percent."

The hologram of Berrier continued to gaze steadily at Barch, who seemed discomfited by it. He gestured savagely, "Enough. Access closed. Data out-feed off-line."

The image of Anne Malloy blurred, shivered, broke apart and flowed into Tara. Berrier's figure wavered, horizontal streaks running through it, but it remained standing.

Barch half shouted in frustration, "Access closed! Out-feed off-line! *Now!*"

Brigid said, "Berrier, Roberta J. Respond to the interrogative. Did you volunteer for the biointerface process?"

Whirling on Royce, he snarled, "Shut this bitch up!"

Royce made a reflexive move toward Brigid, looked briefly at the others, then stepped back.

"No, sir," he said firmly. "I want to hear what she has to say."

Grant and Kane pricked up their ears, noting how Royce hadn't addressed him as *my lord*, substituting a rather sardonic *sir*.

Barch roared, "There's nothing to hear! The whore didn't volunteer, all right? I wired her up myself. What the fuck difference does it make?"

He jabbed an arm toward Berrier's maimed, supine body and then at her whole, standing image. "I already explained why I did it. Berrier was an expendable nobody. She serves a far greater purpose now than punching keys and rewriting history in the ville."

Slowly, as if he were feeling his way around the words, Royce said, "Kind of like me. An expendable nobody. A grunt. A tool."

This time, he couldn't even summon up the effort for a *sir*.

The hologram of Berrier shifted forward, gliding to the head of the couch, staring down at the upturned waxy face. Like someone clawing her way out of a nightmare-haunted slumber, she murmured. "Barch did that to me...I didn't volunteer. He studied how it had been done with Malloy. He used a machine he found to control my mind, force me to cooperate."

Berrier's head lifted, and her stricken face showed grief, fury and the comprehension of a betrayal so deep that a living human being would have dropped dead on the spot. "Barch...I loved you. I gave you my heart. *I gave you my heart!*"

Barch opened and closed his mouth several times, like a landed fish gasping for air. "Roberta, you know why I did this. We talked about it often enough, about taking control of the redoubt, of the array."

He forced a persuasive, wheedling note into his voice. "Remember what I told you?"

Suddenly Tara spoke, though not in her alto tones, but in Barch's voice. "'I trust you as I hope you trust me. I'm looking for something to help both of us. So we can always be together. A Mag and an archivist can't be legally matched, you know. To be together, we need to find a place for ourselves, far from the power of the baron.'"

Barch's face registered shock, then anger, as if he suspected the hologram of the nude woman was mocking him.

The image of Berrier froze, her outline rippling. Tara stood motionless, serenely detached, like a statue.

"What's going on?" Grant demanded in a husky whisper. "What's wrong with her?"

"I think she's processing," answered Brigid, "trying to reconcile her programmed memories with what she's feeling now."

Barch overheard and spit derisively. "She can't feel, you stupe bitch. She's a fucking machine."

"Is that right, Roberta?" Brigid asked in a challenging tone. "Is that all you are now? A flesh-and-blood woman who only wanted love, transformed into circuit boards and digital data streams?"

The hologram of Berrier suddenly, swiftly moved. There was no misinterpretation of the emotions crossing her face now. It was twisted with a wild, deranged fury. She lunged for Barch, hands outstretched for his throat, fingers hooked to claw out his eyes.

She passed completely through the couch, and her body and her hands floated harmlessly through his face. After a stunned second, the realization that she couldn't touch him sank in and brought a baretoothed, snarling grin to his lips.

"Incompetent to the last, Roberta," he said in a gloating croon. "It's all over now. You've had your moment of freedom, but it's finished. You can't do a goddamn thing to change the way things are. You'll do what I tell you to do."

Brigid started to mention that Berrier was only a projection from Tara. As the primary manifestation, she possessed solidity, as artificial as it was. She bit her comment back, to watch what would happen next.

Barch strode through Berrier as he would a plume of smoke, stepping to the head of the couch. He rested his fingers lightly on the electrodes and sockets studding the exposed, trephinated skull.

"Get back into the out-feed, Roberta, or I'll end what little life you have."

In sudden alarm, Brigid blurted, "Barch, don't make threats—"

Barch ignored her, lips twisting as if he intended to spit at the hologram. "I'll pull your fucking plug, Roberta. I'll shut you down. You'll spend all of eternity in the big dark. You know I'll do it."

Between clenched teeth, Brigid hissed, "Oh, *shit*."

Kane and the others weren't certain of the cause of Brigid's sudden agitation, but she telegraphed it to them by her tense posture.

Berrier's image dissolved into a glittering swarm of pixels that leaped across the room and into Tara. In a clear voice, she announced, "Implementing maximum defense measure *Z* for Zulu, *D* for Doomstar. Activation code zero-zero-doomstar-zero."

Tara extended her arms outward from her body, keeping her palms flat and parallel to the floor, forming a T. As she arched her back, thrusting out her firm breasts, a diamond-shaped slit opened between them. A swirling splash of multicolored light fanned out.

Calmly, she said, "Doomstar program on-line."

Chapter 22

Barch staggered back, hands raised to shield his eye from the radiance washing from the aperture in Tara's chest cavity. "Off-line!" he bellowed. "This is a verbal override of all systems! Off-line!"

Squinting away from the blaze, Brigid shouted, "You stupe bastard, that's why it's called Doomstar! It's irreversible. Once the program is activated, you can't shut it down!"

Royce smoothly and deftly raised his Sin Eater, training it on the diamond-shaped opening. "No!" Brigid cried. "You don't know what will—"

A thread-thin line of light whiplashed out and touched the barrel of his Sin Eater. It instantly enveloped him and exploded in a blinding, man-size fireball. The concussion was so overwhelmingly loud their ears couldn't completely register it, but everyone certainly felt it.

A wrecking ball seemed to smash against their bodies and slam them violently down the hexagonal shaft. Glass-covered panels and gauges shattered in shards. Compressed air crowded them toward the open door.

They caught only glimpses of Royce's body hurtling in fragments in all directions. Arms and legs, a substantial portion of his torso and chunks of polycarbonate thudded down all around. Scarlet sprinkled the ceiling, the walls and the floor.

Kane staggered erect, pulling Brigid with him. Domi hauled on Grant's arm as Barch scrabbled on hands and knees toward the corridor. Kane narrowed his eyes against the almost intolerable glare even through his visor and panted into Brigid's ear, "Any ideas?"

His eardrums were stunned, so he almost didn't hear her one word answer: "Run."

They all did, stampeding pell-mell for the exit. Barch regained his feet and tried to elbow Domi aside, but received a backhand to the nose for his efforts. When they reached the corridor, he activated the sonic key. As the doors began to close, Brigid said angrily, "That's not going to stop antimatter."

Barch didn't reply; he simply raced for the spiral staircase and the three Magistrates milling around its base. They had been taking their ease on the risers until they heard the explosion. They shouted questions as Barch pushed past them without a word.

They stood in slack-jawed surprise as Domi, Brigid and Grant reached the staircase and began clattering up. As he dashed after them, Kane barked, "Start running, assholes."

His foot had just landed on the third step in a running leap when he heard the rumbling screech from behind him. He looked back long enough to see the doors burst outward violently, the heavy metal spewing sparks and showing great bulges.

"Move!" he yelled, pushing Grant forward.

The Magistrates cried out in fear and heaved into action as one body, jostling each other as they fought to reach the upper level. The stairs continued to wind up and around, and Kane began to feel a little dizzy before he reached solid flooring. Barch was already sprinting madly down the corridor, and they all took after him. Brigid, who was very fleet of foot, dropped back to say breathlessly, "I don't think she'll let us reach the gateway."

"Any way to talk her out of this?" Kane panted as he ran.

"She's a computer program, running to completion. She won't stop until all the perceived threats are neutralized."

Kane gasped out a groan. "Hell of a woman for Barch to scorn."

"Look who's talking," Brigid retorted.

Sec bulkheads began dropping in front of them, and they were forced to crouch and dodge under them, and once executed shoulder rolls to get through them all. Amazingly, none of the Magistrates was trapped or crushed, though one of the portals came within a fractional margin of amputating Grant's left foot.

They continued to sprint, but Kane felt his muscles tightening, his lungs burning. He knew he couldn't keep up the pace in the armor for much longer, nor could Grant, even with Domi to pull him along.

"One chance," Brigid said. "There's an exit up ahead, if Tara hasn't locked out the controls."

"So we hide from her outside?"

"She may have a limit on the distance she can travel from the redoubt in her human form."

As they rounded another bend, they saw that Barch evidently had the same idea. Frantically, he punched in the code on the green liquid crystal display pad. With a hissing, squeaking rumble of buried hydraulics, the multiton door slid up. Before it had risen more than three feet, Barch had scuttled beneath it in a crablike shuffle.

None of them, including the Magistrates, waited for the door to reach full ascension before they ran out onto the blacktop road. The sky wasn't the clean blue Domi and Brigid expected. Thick black clouds had massed, boiling and building above the HAARP array a mile distant. The pulsing crackling they had heard earlier was now much louder.

The temperature had dropped considerably and felt as if it was plunging even lower. A stiff, chill wind gusted up from the valley, flattening the new plant growth.

They raced down the sloping road, heedless of the treacherous footing. Large chunks of the asphalt were broken and cracked, and once Kane nearly pitched headfirst down the incline. As he recovered, he heard a Magistrate shouting orders and glanced behind him.

The Mags quickly arranged themselves in a standard deployment of personnel and firepower, training their blasters on the doorway. He slowed down, not simply because of the stitch in his side, but because he felt the urge to join them.

"Don't even think it!" Brigid snapped over her shoulder, snatching a windblown strand of hair from her face. "Bullets won't stop an energy field!"

Grunting with the exertion and pain, Kane forced more speed into his pumping legs. Though he and Brigid quarreled frequently, he had the utmost faith in Brigid's assessments of situations, especially when they were bizarre.

He ran only a few more yards when he heard the triple-jackhammer roar of Sin Eaters on full auto. Though he risked another misstep, he couldn't help but turn to watch.

Her body almost completely obscured behind the blazing funnel of light washing from her chest, Tara strode out of the redoubt, directly into the Mag's fusillade.

What little breath he had left in his lungs seized up when he saw her continue to walk down the road, her gait not faltering or reacting to the simultaneous multiple impacts. A flesh-and-blood woman would have died almost immediately, all her bones shattered, internal organs ruptured, brain shot away. But Tara's purposeful stride was completely unaffected.

Delicate white threads sprang from the shimmer enveloping her. Each one touched a Magistrate, and with each touch a sharp report shook the mountainside. There were brief bursts of blinding flame, and when the flashes faded, only heaps of split-open polycarbonate and charred, broken bones remained of the Mags.

Kane almost panicked then, but he managed to restrain his mounting terror. All of them were doomed to be obliterated by a relic of predark scientific hubris and paranoia.

As the roadbed met the valley floor, Kane's fear gave way to fatalism. He saw no point in making a stand, but Brigid's hope that Tara had a prescribed distance limit outside of Redoubt Zulu was definitely a futile wish.

Tara kept coming, maintaining a steady, graceful stride. Kane watched her in something close to admiration and awe. He wasn't much of a scholar, but he had skimmed a few texts about myths and religion he found in Cerberus. As Tara descended from the mountainside, he was reminded of stories he had read. She was like an avenging goddess, an Athena in battle, or a Valkyrie or a Lilith. She was a scorned woman whose hell-spawned fury could destroy far, far more than a faithless lover.

Kane turned and began to run after the others again. Barch seemed to sense he was the true target of Tara's wrath, programming notwithstanding. He sprinted in a raw panic, a gibbering explosion of mindless terror erupting from his mouth. He emitted wild cries and yelps with every footfall.

Though the rest of them were winded, especially Grant, Barch gave no hint of fatigue. Not that it mattered; he, all of them, could run all the way across Alaska, over the Bering Strait and into Russia, and Tara's inexorable pursuit wouldn't let up. But they would have to stop eventually, no matter how much distance they might put between her and them.

At the thought, Kane rocked to a halt and summoned enough oxygen in his aching, straining lungs to yell, "Stop! Everybody stop!"

The two women and Grant cast him incredulous looks over their shoulders, but they complied, stumbling as they slowed.

The Sin Eater slipped into Kane's hand, and he sighted down its length, bracing the barrel on his left forearm. He brought Barch into target acquisition and lightly touched the trigger. His finger didn't cramp or waver, but he didn't vent a sigh of relief. He whispered, "We aspire to the same goal," and squeezed the trigger.

The gun jumped in his hand as he fired a single shot.

Barch's babbles dissolved into a scream of pain as the 9 mm round plowed into the back of his right leg, between knee and thigh, shearing away a fistful of fabric, flesh and muscle as it exited. He performed a limb-flailing somersault, his head violently reversing position with his feet.

Kane lowered his blaster and glanced behind him. Tara was less than twenty paces away so he walked swiftly forward. Grant, breath coming in harsh, ragged gasps, demanded, "Why'd you do that?"

"An idea," Kane answered. "The only thing I can think of that has any chance of working."

"Let me guess the odds," Grant muttered, falling into step beside him. "One percent."

"This time," said Kane grimly, "it's probably half that."

Barch lay on the grass-carpeted valley floor, his thigh bone shattered. Blood pulsed from between his clutching fingers. His eye was already glazing over as he succumbed to shock.

A rattling gasp bubbled past his lips as he looked up and saw the Sin Eater in Kane's hand. "Why?"

"You started this shit with a woman," Kane told him very quietly. "Let's see if you can finish it the same way."

The thickening cloud cover spread out in a whorling canopy from the HAARP antenna array, racing across the sky toward them, blotting out the sun. Strong, cold gusts of wind slapped at their clothes, and tiny particles of hail stung their exposed flesh.

Tara continued to advance as the weather worsened, as if the building storm was only a reflection of her intent.

"This won't accomplish anything," Brigid said, her green eyes dulled by exhaustion and fear. "She's a program, not a victim seeking redress for a wrong."

"I'm gambling that she's more victim than program. You reached Berrier once. Maybe you can do it again before she flash-fries us all."

As Tara grew closer, a crimson-hued conoid cloud stretched down toward her, spinning above her head, whirling a miniature, compressed tornado. A muted rumbling roar filled the valley.

Grant glanced toward the distant antennae and muttered darkly, "She's controlling HAARP now, too."

Brigid swallowed hard. "Makes sense she would be interfaced with it. She said as much to Domi and me."

Barch groped wildly for Grant's boot with scarlet-coated fingers. He sobbed, "Don't let her—" But Grant stepped away from him, not bothering to disguise the disgust on his face.

Tara reached a point less than five paces away. They narrowed their eyes against the light glare, and she once more spread her arms wide and arched her back. Though it was almost impossible to tell, Tara appeared to pay Barch no particular attention.

Brigid shouted, "Berrier, Roberta J.! Access that component of your binary matrix! Berrier, Roberta J.!"

They saw no outward change in Tara's stance or the intensity of the light. But after a few moments, when Brigid realized they were still standing and not vaporized, she said in a warm, urgent tone, "Roberta. I request Roberta's assistance."

Tara spoke, but her voice sounded like an odd

blend of her own flat alto and Berrier's clipped, precise diction. "What is it you request?"

"Your understanding. Only Barch meant harm to the redoubt. Barch, who used and betrayed your love. Barch, who amended the priorities and used you to do it. He is the only transgressor here."

"The program must be completed."

The blended feminine tones were difficult to judge, but Kane was certain he detected a hesitation in them.

"You may complete the program with Barch." Brigid gestured to him. "Here he is. We are assisting you to complete the program."

She paused, then said in an emotionally charged, impulsive burst, "We're helping you heal. We—all of us—know what it's like to believe in something, in someone, and then find out it was a sham to benefit another."

To Kane's discomfort and dismay, he saw tears suddenly well up in Brigid's eyes. In a low, quavering voice, she said, "I'm so sorry for what he did to you, Roberta."

Tara stood motionless for a long, tense tick of time. Then, slowly, she lowered her arms. As she did so, the blaze of radiance lessened in intensity, but the diamond-shaped aperture didn't close up. Her face was blank, as devoid of expression as a mask as she gazed one by one into their faces.

Snow sifted down in light flurries. Flakes touched her gleaming skin, and they disappeared with little hissing sounds. Her gaze finally traveled to Barch, lying on the ground, grasping his bullet-punctured leg. His one eye blinked rapidly.

He gasped out his apology and plea, "I'm sorry, too, Roberta. Believe me, I am. Can you find it in your heart to forgive me?"

It was such a stupid, desperate ploy, Kane nearly gagged.

Tara's lips curved in a dreamy half smile. From them came Berrier's voice, with no trace of Tara's modulating it. "Of course I can find it in my heart to forgive you. If you swear to pledge your heart to me, forever and always."

Barch nodded wildly. "I swear, Roberta, oh, I swear. I belong to you."

She dropped to one knee beside him as if to offer him comfort, cradling the back of his neck with her left hand and laying her right flat on his chest.

Delicate sizzling lightnings suddenly sprang up between Tara's fingertips and the front of his bodysuit. Barch flung back his head and howled, spittle flying from his lips. He convulsed, arms and legs spasming. With a mushy tearing sound and a splintering of bones, Tara plunged her hand into his breast. Blood pumped up around her wrist.

Tara yanked her hand out and up, holding his quivering heart, squeezing it between her fingers. Smoke wisped up as the bloody organ began to cook within her grasp. Softly she said, "I have your heart, forever and always."

She stood up in a lunging rush, standing over Barch's trembling body, his eye blank and staring, reflecting nothing but the storm clouds overhead. Blood streamed in crimson rivulets down Tara's slender wrist and forearm, drying and smoldering.

They did their best to maintain neutral expressions when Tara looked at them again. She pointed with the heart to the road leading to Redoubt Zulu.

Still speaking in Berrier's voice, she said, "This is the last time that I, Berrier, Roberta J., can assist you. Go. Do not return. The eternal winter will reclaim this land, burying it beneath the snow and ice. There is no reason to ever come back."

Kane wasn't inclined to offer a word of protest or thanks. He turned and began walking swiftly out of the valley. The snow fell heavier and the cold crept into his bones. He hoped the others were following him at a spritely pace, since he was a little afraid to look back.

They were, and they were just as anxious to obey Tara's command as he was. Brigid caught up to him as they reached the road. "Good thinking, Kane. Another one-percenter pays off. You know more about women than I gave you credit for."

He acknowledged the remark with a wry smile. "What were you and Domi doing here in the first place?"

"Lakesh thought it was a good idea if we worked separately for a while. He thinks you and I spend entirely too much quality time together."

Kane was too numb from exhaustion and the creeping cold to come up with a verbal response, so he opted for a laugh. Even in his own ears, it sounded nervous and forced.

The four of them trudged up the cracked and split slope to the redoubt's entrance in only a little more time than it had taken them to descend it. Grant removed his helmet, and despite the cold, perspiration glistened on his face. Once inside, he and Domi made for the gateway area straightaway.

Though Kane told himself he wasn't going to do it, he found himself stopping at the threshold to look back at the valley. He wasn't sure if he was disappointed when he saw little but a shifting curtain of snow. The HAARP array, Barch and the beautifully gleaming figure of Tara were lost within the swirling white veils.

Brigid paused to look too. Softly, she asked, "When will the reign of blood and mad ambition end?"

Bitterly, he answered, "As long as there are men like Barch, never."

He smiled then, but only a little sadly. Reaching up, he lightly brushed away the tears still wet on her cheeks.

He said, "As long as there are people like you, Baptiste, I can at least have hope that it will someday."

Coming in December 1998 is Iceblood,
the next way station in the Outlanders saga.

Iceblood

When the microlight illuminated Brigid's face, Kane almost wished they were in darkness again. Her face was smeared with dried blood from her scalp wound, her emerald eyes dulled with fatigue and pain and surrounded by dark rings. Even her curly mane of hair drooped listlessly.

She looked at him and said, "You look terrible."

"Thanks to you," Kane retorted angrily. He scowled at her, then forced a laugh. He stood up slowly, silently enduring the spasms of pain igniting in his back and legs.

"Well," he said after a moment, "Zakat and his crew are behind us, so we can't go back. Balam is somewhere ahead of us. So we have to go out."

"And down," Brigid added gloomily. Gingerly, she stepped toward the mouth of the tunnel and peered into the yawning blackness below.

She took a deep breath and inched out onto the ledge, flattening herself against the rock wall, digging the fingers of her hands into the fissures and crevices. After a moment of hard swallowing, Kane stepped out after her, strapping the microlight around his left wrist.

The ledge made a sharp turn to the right after a few steps, and its pitch descended at an increasingly steeper angle. Kane and Brigid were forced to edge their way along it with their hands gripping the wall tightly. Kane wondered how deep beneath the Earth they were. He couldn't hazard a guess, but he suspected the ledge beneath their feet wasn't natural. Its smoothness bespoke craftmanship, though whether it was carved by human hands, he had no way of knowing. Nor did he particularly want to know.

It was slow, laborious work and it was perilous, for ominous cracklings at the lip of the ledge warned that their combined weight might start a slide, sending them both plunging into the blackness.

Kane worried that the batteries of the Nighthawk were dangerously low, but he didn't turn off the microlight. The ledge gradually widened into a true path. Both of them breathed easier when they no longer had to inch sideways, but the dim glow of the microlight dampened their relief. The flashlight exuded little more than a firefly halo when the ledge met and joined with a rocky floor.

A faint rumble sounded to their right and they halted, halfway expecting another downpour of stones. A few seconds of hard listening told them the noise was made by an underground stream or river. Kane was suddenly, sharply aware of how thirsty he was.

They moved along the path, beneath ponderous masses of stone. The Nighthawk abruptly went out.

The echoes of Brigid's despairing groan chased each other through the impenetrable blackness.

They stopped walking, their hearts trip-hammering as they stood motionless in the stygian darkness. Kane's breath came in harsh, ragged bursts as he struggled to control his mounting terror. Finally, the mission priority was the spur that drove him forward, made him start walking again, taking Brigid by the arm and feeling his way along the rough walls. Then, far away, he saw a tiny blue-yellow flicker of light. He pointed it out, and they increased their pace. The crunch of their footfalls sent up ghostly reverberations.

The path suddenly debouched into a gloomy underground gallery with walls of black basalt. Like jagged teeth, stalactites and stalagmites projected in weird formations of rock from the roof and floor of the cavern. To their dismayed surprise, they saw that the source of the ectoplasmic light was a small square panel of a glassy substance inset in the gallery wall.

Walking over to it, Brigid eyed it curiously, reaching out a tentative hand to touch it. "I've never seen anything like this before."

"I have," declared Kane grimly.

She jerked her hand away and turned to face him. "Where?"

"In the Black Gobi, in the tent of the Tushe Gun. I guess there isn't any need to wonder where he got them...or where this one came from."

Brigid nodded and stepped away from the glowing panel. The self-styled Avenging Lama had made the ancient Mongolian city of Khara-Khoto his headquarters. Beneath the black city lay an even more ancient structure, a space vessel. The Tushe Gun had looted much Archon technology from it, without understanding what it was.

Softly, Brigid said, "And I guess there's no more need to wonder why Balam was drawn to this place."

They strode through the gallery, accompanied by the hollow echoes of their footsteps. Every few yards, they came across more of the light panels. The illumination provided was weak and unsatisfactory, but even so, they could only be grateful for it.

The gallery narrowed into a crevasse and they squeezed into it, clambering over fallen masses of stone. The splash of rushing water grew louder as the fissure veered to the left. After a few steps, they found themselves standing on a stone shelf a foot or so above the surface of a river. The opposite bank was about seventy feet away, butting up against a wall of basalt.

The water looked black, but Kane rushed to it anyway, lying flat and plunging his head into the icy current. Brigid kneeled beside him, taking off her gloves before cupping handfuls of water to her mouth.

The water had a peculiar tang to it, a sour limestone aftertaste, but they drank their fill, washing away the blood and grime on their faces. When Kane blunted the edge of his thirst, he became aware of a gnawing hunger and he wondered aloud if there were any fish in the stream.

Brigid didn't reply. She peered downstream. "There isn't a path. If the river leads to a way out, we'll have to swim. Or go back."

Kane raked the wet hair out of his eyes. "There's nothing to be gained by that. Zakat and his crew are better armed than we are."

Brigid nodded. "Yeah, but I'm not up to swimming. The river is cold, probably fed by meltwater. We'd both succumb to hypothermia inside of a couple of minutes."

Kane arose, looking past Brigid to the other side of the stream. Though the light was uncertain, he was sure he saw a long object bobbing on the surface, almost directly across from their position. Leaning against the rock wall, he tugged off his boots, shucked his coat and slid into the water.

"What are you doing?" Brigid demanded.

"Wait and see, Baptiste."

His feet touched the gravelly bottom. The water was shockingly, almost painfully cold, and it took all of his self-control not to curse. He started wading across, moving as quickly as he dared. After a few steps, the icy water lapped at his thighs, then up to his waist. He kept on, fighting the strong current. A time or two, loose stones turned beneath his feet, and he nearly fell.

When he reached the other side, he was gasping and out of breath. From the hips down, he was completely numb, but the bobbing shape was what he had hoped it would be. A six-foot-long boat made of bark and laced yak's hide was tethered to a boulder by a length of leather. A wooden pole about ten feet long lay on the bank.

Pulling himself ashore, Kane snatched the tether free and took the pole. Tentatively, he eased into the little boat. The craft sank a bit, the hide-and-bark hull giving a little, but it seemed river worthy.

Shoving off with the pole, he propelled the boat across the river. He had difficulty crossing because of the current, but the pole always touched bottom. When the prow bumped against the opposite bank, Brigid handed him his boots and coat. She hesitated only a moment before gingerly climbing into it.

Hastily, Kane put on his coat and boots. He shivered as he did so. Taking the pole again, he pushed off and the boat slid out into the river, rocking a bit. He poled the craft so it hugged the right-hand wall, close to the light panels, not voicing the host of new fears assailing him.

He was afraid the river might debouch in a dozen different directions, or lead to a waterfall or that the boat might spring a leak. But after twenty minutes of steady poling, with none of his fears materializing, he tried to relax. Because of his strained shoulder muscles, he turned the task of poling over to Brigid.

Kane sat down while she expertly directed the

craft. She said, "This used to be a form of recreation. It was called punting."

"Offhand I can think of a dozen recreational activities I'd rather be doing."

"All with Rouch, I'll bet," she replied with a studied nonchalance.

He glowered at her, but didn't respond. Linking his hands behind his aching neck, he inquired, "What do you think, Baptiste?"

"What do I think about what?"

"Is this Argharti, the Valley of the Eight Immortals that Zakat is so crazy to reach?"

Brigid pushed her shoulder against the pole. "If it is, it's a far cry from the way the city was described in legend. I haven't seen a speck of gold or a chip of diamond yet. If there ever were Aghartians, they came down here ages ago to die."

Brigid paused, started to say something else, then stopped talking and poling. Kane straightened up. The waterway opened into a huge, vault-walled cavern. It was immense, most of it wrapped in unrelieved darkness. Black masses of rock hung from its jagged roof.

The river narrowed down to a stream, and the current carried the boat beneath an arching formation. A constant sound of splashing beyond it indicated a waterfall.

She pushed the craft toward the nearest bank. She poled them aground on the pebble-strewed shore. They climbed out of the boat and looked around at the city of stalactites and stalagmites all around them. Illuminated by dozens of light panels were towers of multicolored limestone disappearing into the darkness overhead, flying buttresses and graceful arches of rock stretching into the shadows.

Kane and Brigid moved forward uncertainly, struggling not to be overwhelmed. Then Brigid stabbed out an arm, pointing ahead, and they stopped and stared, surrendering to awe.

The thing was a statue, standing in an erect position. At least fifteen feet tall, it represented a humanoid creature with a slender, gracile build draped in robes. The features were sharp, the domed head disproportionately large and hairless. The eyes were huge, slanted and fathomless.

The stone figure pointed with one long-fingered hand toward the farther, shadow-shrouded end of the cavern. There was something so strikingly meaningful about the pointing arm and the intent gaze of the big eyes that the statue seemed not crafted out of stone at all, but a living thing petrified by the hand of time.

"Somebody lived down here," Kane muttered.

Brigid nodded thoughtfully. "A long, long time ago."

They started in the direction of the statue's solemnly pointing arm. It led them across the cavern, to a crevasse that yawned at the far end. A warn path was still discernible, and they followed it toward the black opening.

Kane suddenly tugged Brigid to a stop. "Are you sure nobody's lived down here for a long, long time?"

Nettled by the touch of sarcasm in his tone, she followed his gaze downward.

In the fine rock dust on the cavern floor, they saw the clear, fresh print of a small foot with six delicate toes.

**It's blitzkreig time as new and
improved Nazis invade Europe!**

THE

Destroyer™

#113 The Empire Dreams
The Fatherland Files Book II

Created by
WARREN MURPHY
and RICHARD SAPIR

Vacationing in London, Dr. Harold Smith feels a strange déjà vu as
World War II planes bomb the city and skinheads roam the streets.

A rogue Nazi with a new blueprint for world domination becomes
Remo's target as the world gets stranger by the minute.

This is the second in The Fatherland Files, a miniseries based on a
secret fascist organization's attempts to regain the glory of the
Third Reich.

Available in November at your favorite retail outlet.

A preview from hell...

JAMES AXLER

DEATH LANDS ®

Dark Emblem

After a relatively easy mat-trans jump, Ryan and his companions find themselves in the company of Dr. Silas Jamaisvous, a seemingly pleasant host who appears to understand the mat-trans systems extremely well.

Seeing signs that local inhabitants have been used as guinea pigs for the scientist's ruthless experiments, the group realizes that they have to stop this line of research before it goes too far....